Praise for *Not*

"The world of work, li.., a..u iuve changed seismically in the early 2000s and Sean Murphy's narrator Byron, like everyone else, has been scrambling to keep up ever since…or wondering whether keeping up is even possible. In *Not to Mention a Nice Life*, Murphy's masterful storytelling takes us on an honest, searing, sardonic ride through the decade that wasn't."

—Jeremy Neuner, co-author of
The Rise of the Naked Economy

"It's early in that lamentable decade of the 2000s, and while the good times continue to roll in corporate America, they won't be rolling for much longer—and no one knows it better than Byron, the Everyman narrator of Sean Murphy's witty and wise firecracker of a debut. If you liked Joshua Ferris's *And Then We Came to the End*, you'll love *Not to Mention a Nice Life*. Byron might not have a future, but Sean Murphy certainly does."

—Greg Olear, author of
Totally Killer and *Fathermucker*

"Murphy has provided a wry sendup of the manners and mores of 21st century American culture, which inspects all the Prufrockian frailties and foibles we carry through life."

—Martha's Vineyard Times

"Sean Murphy has cleverly transformed Byron from Lord to dot-com schlub. Instead of chasing minotaurs through labyrinths, he hunts for meaning among the cubicles. *Not to Mention a Nice Life* is a wry, acerbic, and terrifying critique of the notion that there is really nothing left to critique. Modern Corporate America is less an enemy than a state of reality. They have won. We have lost. Byron, like the rest of the 99%, is left with layoffs, failed stock options, and the slight possibility of love. Read this very funny book. Like, right now. And then pour yourself an ice-cold laudanum."

—Sean Beaudoin, author of
Wise Young Fool and *Welcome Thieves*

"Sean Murphy's *Not to Mention a Nice Life* offers a voice rarely seen—that whisper of human suffering that comes from an insular heart. It's as if the photo negative suddenly spoke, and claimed to be the real image, the real person behind the living color and magnetism of what we find in our everyday moment-to-moment existence. As Byron moves into and through his "Terrible Thirties," and the dot-com boom of wild heights and terrifying drops, we move with him…but we also get to watch, and be that cautious eye which only has to watch, and doesn't have to be. Which is both blessing and curse in this romp of Americana, half *Fight Club*, half *Catcher in the Rye* for the middle-aged. Regardless, I'm hooked—and want to stay that way."

—Jesse Waters, author of *Human Resources*

Praise for *Please Talk About Me When I'm Gone*

"*Please Talk about Me When I'm Gone,* which pulled me
in from the first page and never let go, is a mosaic love
letter from a son to his lost mother, so everyone in the
bereavement club should read it. But this memoir is also
a thoughtful, compassionate meditation on being alive.
I nodded in recognition, dog-eared pages containing
lines I loved, felt my eyes well with tears. In the end you
should read it for the reason anyone reads good writing:
to feel less alone."

—Jenna Blum, NYT best-selling author of
Those Who Save Us and *The Stormchasers*

"As an oncologist treating a difficult and often fatal
group of cancers, I witness firsthand as patients and their
'villages' cope with the diagnosis. So many decisions, so
much emotion, and everyone does it a bit differently. No
one path will serve; instead it is a truly individual course
we choose. Sean Murphy's book is a great new resource
for patients and families, and frankly for us all."

—Dr. John Marshall, Chief, Oncology
at Georgetown Hospital

"As both the President of a colorectal cancer non profit, and more importantly a son who also lost his mother to this disease, I found this memoir emotional, educational, and edgy. I highly recommend this read for patients, survivors, caretakers, and physicians alike. Congratulations Sean, for this amazing story, your mother would be proud."

—Michael Sapienza, President and Founder, Chris4Life Colon Cancer Foundation

"Sean Murphy brings a poetic voice and insightful contemplations to the largely unexplored territory of dying and death. With deep compassion and philosophical curiosity, he processes his individual grief while confirming the universality of loss."

—Roy Remer, Director of Volunteer Programs, Zen Hospice Project

"In some moments of profound experience, we see and feel in extraordinary ways. That is what happened to Sean Murphy after his mother's death. He has had the courage to look honestly at death, and the talent to express his love and grief in a way that will comfort and sustain his readers."

—Steve Goodwin, author of *Breaking Her Fall*

"Sean Murphy writes of his loss in a way that is compelling and insightful. Anyone early in the process of grief should hear his message—that you never get over the death of a loved one, and that's as it should be."

—Elizabeth Rogers, Social Worker,
Advanced Illness Management Program

"An extremely moving, beautifully written, heart-felt and touching chronicling of the life and death of a parent."

—Charles Salzberg,
author of *Devil in the Hole*

"When I started Sean's book, I read a section and said to myself, 'I'm going to email Sean to tell him how amazing that sentence is.' Then as I read a little further I thought, 'No, I'm going to email Sean to tell him what an amazing depth of knowledge and perception he's giving us.' And then, yes, you got it, on the very next page he wrote something that made me think, 'His Mom is looking down on Sean with unending love for what he just wrote. This is one amazing book!"

—Donald R. Gallehr, Director Emeritus,
Northern Virginia Writing Project

not TO mention
A nice LIFE

not TO mention
A nice LIFE

SEAN MURPHY

BRIGHT
MOMENTS
BOOKS

BRIGHT
MOMENTS
BOOKS

Bright Moments Books
Reston, Virginia
Printed in the United States of America

Trade paperback ISBN: 978-0-989-88051-0
Ebook edition ISNB: 978-0-989-88052-7

Book design and typesetting by Damonza.com
Cover by Damonza.com

Visit the author's website at:
seanmurphy.net

For Jack Murphy,

an ally and advocate;
my friend, my father

All he had to do was solve the mystery of the universe, which may be difficult but is not as difficult as living an ordinary life.

—Walker Percy, *Lancelot*

Prologue

TAKE A GUY.

Let's say he's about my age: old enough to own his own condo and pay almost all his bills, who is young enough to be unmarried but old enough to understand he is not getting any younger. Add a fresh dose of alienation—not enough to be unhealthy, of course, but enough to enable him to function in a world full of a-holes, imbecility and indifference. Take this guy and provide just enough stability so that there are no excuses, but plenty of alibis. Maybe he's estranged from too many old friends, or aggrieved about an absent parent, or perhaps he is just emerging from the wreckage of a ruined relationship or, probably, he is utterly average in every regard, except for the uncomfortable fact that, unlike almost everyone else he knows, he is aware of it.

Listen:

I am just like everyone else (I think).

I work for a living. I like my job less than I probably should (it's not *my* fault). I drink too much coffee. I don't eat breakfast. I forget to eat lunch. I remember to eat dinner (oh I remember), I piss sitting down, I shit standing up, I have nightmares constantly, except when I'm asleep, I grind my teeth all day, admittedly in half-assed fashion because talking, swallowing and breathing interfere, but then at night I really get down to business: I grind and then dream about grinding, and above all, I have the ceaseless, scary taste of rust in my mouth. I suspect, in short, that I am dying.

I am, in other words, just like everyone else (I know).

I am not alone. I have a best friend, who happens to be a dog. He's really good for me, reminding me to eat, sleep, go to the bathroom and generally making sure that I get out a few times a day. He walks me whenever he gets the chance. Our favorite time is after work, when we reenter the building and the walls and halls come alive, warm with the savory smells of home-made meals (I can never smell fast food, although that scent lingers in the elevator, as if ashamed to be associated with the honesty, the effort and industry of these prepared productions).

No one sits down to dinner anymore, but all around me, people are sitting down, eating meat loaf, or some sort of roast that has simmered on low heat all afternoon. Maybe there is even a pie prepared for dessert. Maybe, inside someone's kitchen, it's still the 1950s.

I remind myself that someday, if my cards play me right, I will enjoy a real meal around a table, and experience all that I've been missing during these autonomous years of isolation. I will clear the table and clean the dishes, I will sit on the couch and take a crack at the crossword, or catch a made-for-TV movie, or go run errands or consult a book of baby names for the offspring on the way, and eventually I will work on improving my bad habits and attempt to overlook my wife's inadequacies (the quirks that were so endearing in those early days). I will, at last, learn to communicate openly and as an adult. Mostly, I will not be alone.

My dog is a trooper.

He's never called in sick a single day of his life: up at the ass-crack of dawn, including weekends, stretched, eager and anxious to take on the world. Or at least take a walk.

My dog takes his work very seriously, and has succeeded in making more friends than I have. He does not discriminate: men, women, cars, trees, and other dogs—especially other dogs. He wants to meet everyone, and he patrols the neighborhood like it's his job (which, of course, it is). I can't help but admire his dedication.

Thanks to him, I'm on a first-name basis with all the other dogs in my building, though I have a hard time remembering what to call their owners.

Take this guy: an older man (I don't want to call him an *old* man), whose name I've never gotten around to establishing. I sort of prefer it that way, as he provides me with a mystery I enjoy embellishing each time I encounter him. Whereas most of my neighbors are obviously what they are: mothers, fathers, bachelors, wives, working stiffs, senior citizens, anonymous law-abiding entities, *et cetera*, this man alone retains, for me and my imagination, an enigmatic air. He wears a wedding band, but I've never seen or met his spouse. He is friendly, so much so that it initially took me a while to warm up to him.

Maybe this is the way other people saw *my* old man. Yes, he is definitely someone's father: he has rolled up his sleeves to punish, praise, clean, counsel, inspire, admonish, argue, approve, second-guess, support and silence. In short, things I have never done. And I think (I can't help myself): he is a way I'll never be.

All of us, of course, are more or less the same: we live, we work, we sleep, we eat, we love, we fight, we forget, we try to remember, we think, we wear down and then we die. In this regard, all living creatures are more alike than not.

But humans are, ultimately, different.

We know who we are, so we wonder (we can't help ourselves) things like: What has that man done that I'll never do? What has he seen that I'll never see? What parts of the world he once lived in are now gone forever, replaced by newer things that younger people, not yet born, will wonder about, in time?

I think:

If I had lived in the 50s, that man might have been a spy; a professor, a pedophile (I would have called him a *pervert*), a recluse, a con artist—but above all, he most certainly would be a *Communist.*

If I had lived in the 50s, I would eat an egg for breakfast each morning with either bacon or sausage or sometimes both, I would also eat pastrami sandwiches, drink whole milk and smoke endless streams of cigarettes, I would be father to as many children as God (most certainly a *Capitalist* God) saw fit to provide, I would live closer to my parents, I would miss church service seldom on Sundays and never on Holy Days of Obligation, I would know how to fix my toilet and sink if they dripped, I would never have had a shirt professionally pressed, I would drive an American car and never wear a seat belt, I would have a job that I could actually describe in one or two words. I would be, quite conceivably, content.

My dog is content. One thing is for sure: if my dog lived in the 50s, he would be content, just as he would be content fifty years from now. After all, all dogs want is other dogs (I think my dog thinks I'm a dog). People aren't like that, which, I suppose is why people love dogs. The older man and I love our dogs, and for a few seconds we watch them sniff each other.

"Hot enough for ya?"

"Yeah well, it's the humidity!"

(To ourselves we say this).

Then we go our separate ways, exchanging pleasantries.

I say: "Have a nice day."

"Likewise," he replies, and then smiles. "Not to mention a nice life."

I smile, and then walk away, still smiling. Who the hell does this guy think he is, saying something like that? How *dare* he say something like that. Unless he means it. No one says something like that. Unless they are actually, inconceivably *content*.

I'm still smiling, but then a sobering thought sideswipes me (again): That man is a way I'll never be.

Part One:
AMERICAN DREAM ON

One

WELCOME TO THE OCCUPATION

L IKE A LOT of people, I had plans. Good plans, the type of plans that most young, ardent men like to make, and hopefully make good on. Then, as often happens, something (or, some things) got in the way. What got in the way? Life. Life got in the way.

I wasn't careful enough about what I asked for, and therefore, I got it.

A job, that is.

Everyone gets one, sooner or later. That fact is either comforting or distressing, depending upon how you look at things. Like jobs.

Where was I?

Something was wrong with me. I applied to the appropriate colleges and one of them accepted me. I applied to the appropriate graduate schools and one of them accepted me. I decided not to apply to any PhD programs (it didn't seem appropriate) and so none of them accepted me. The unreal world of academia still beckoned; the unreasonable world of reality awaited. Neither seemed particularly appealing so I was paralyzed: only a overfed American, like me, could understand that there were options aplenty, and still find none of them enticing. And so I decided it was time to go underground, back to the service industry, where at least what I did know couldn't hurt me (too much). I found myself serving the people who had the sorts of jobs I regarded with the ugly envy of the underclass. I made less money than I might have liked but I got more free drinks than I could ever have imagined. One way to see the glass being half-full is to ensure that it's always half-full. While I worked on emptying those glasses I came to the conclusion that money is wasted on the wealthy and retirement is wasted on the elderly.

Something was wrong with me. I drank myself insensate and couldn't commit to more serious indiscretions. I did the unthinkable: I thought about that unreasonable world again. I found myself skulking around the library, picking up magazines and thinking about that itch I could never quite scratch. I read an article about this world wide web. How ridiculous it all seemed. So *this* is what people do during the day, I thought. Unlimited possible futures unfurled in unreal time, right in front of my not so open mind, none of them remotely appealing. There it was, I thought: it's already over; I'm out of options. And then a funny thing happened. I got a new job.

Like most work, it's nice if you can get it. Like all work, it's nice when it doesn't involve physical labor, being outdoors, or doing much of anything that could, with any accuracy, be described as *work*. It already seems like a million years ago, but remember how radical the shift from old-school to online was? As we now know, or accept, or understand we'll be obliged to accept at some point soon, all these computers and the digitization of everything we used to do with our hands, or at least our brains, is going to replace many of us, giving everyone a whole new set of things to worry about (like finding work). But at the time, during that fin de siècle insurrection, it all happened online: no blood was shed and all of a sudden everyone had a job.

That was me. I was that guy. Actually I was the guy who knew a guy who had already figured out a thing or two. Like me he was almost thirty. Unlike me he had just bought his own townhouse, in cash. Like me he was successful at his job. Unlike me he was satisfied with his work, and unlike me he got paid very handsomely. "Hey," he said one night as I poured him another of whatever he was having, "if you know anyone looking to join the revolution, let me know." Once I figured out he was serious (he wasn't being *serious*, which gave it away), and that joining this particular cause wouldn't get me killed or even arrested (it would, in fact, get me employed), I asked him a question of my own.

"What about me?"

"Are you in the market?" he asked.

"I could be if the price is right," I replied.

"What are you looking for?" he asked.

"Make me an offer I can't refuse," I replied.

Little did he know my requirements were modest: anything that had me waking up instead of going to sleep at sunrise; anything where I could sit instead of stand; anything where I didn't have to inhale second-hand smoke for eight hour intervals; anything that had benefits extending beyond free meals and pilfered pints. His offer had all those things, plus this unfamiliar concept called *stock*. Being accustomed to using that word only as a verb, I was officially intrigued. Within a month I was out of the service industry forever (except in my dreams wherein, like most people I know who have waited tables for more than a casual summer, I recurrently have inane-to-impossible nightmares involving wrong uniforms, too many customers and virgin daiquiris.)

My suspicion of life dissolved like an ice cube in an ash tray: all those good things everyone ever told me turned out to be true! Networking worked! Being in the right place at the right time is not a sham—at least if it happens to you. Everyone loves a winner!

Only in America. Well, only in an online America could an over-educated bartender begin reporting to the college dropout he used to serve drinks to; the one who started out at a call center and, by remaining in the right place at the right times, got promoted over the course of four years to Senior Director of Some-Such. Neither of us could explain exactly what we—or anyone else in our department—did, and, in any event, no one was asking any questions. If this was the real world, I thought, I could conceivably ride this out until they put me out to pasture.

* * *

As the century ended we survived the millennial changing of the guard, then we worried ourselves silly over Armageddon, also known as Y2K. Those of us still standing (sitting, actually) had somehow survived rounds of layoffs we lost count of after they hit the double-digits. All fat-cutting, they always said. Just strategic, they also said when supplemental pink slips were inexorably passed around. If you're worried about your job, they said, you're not one of the ones who has anything to worry about. *Et cetera.* This was, in sum, a few years in the life of the enterprising dot-com underling. That was me; I was that guy. As the new decade gathered steam, it was a good time to be a Republican. It was a good time to be employed. I was not a Republican, but I loved the idea of being employed, so I was mostly content to let my employers assume what they were going to assume, assuming I didn't say what I thought, or show anyone how I felt (this part was easy because I wasn't sure myself), and perfected the compulsory expression of an anonymous employee in our post-ironic age: a bemused grin with mouth slightly agape, signifying that I had no idea how I came to be here but I sure was thrilled! This was easy enough, in part because it was more than a little true. My bills, after all, weren't going to pay themselves.

* * *

Then it happened.

The wheels were already in motion, to fall off, for over a year. Start-ups began shutting down their sites almost as quickly as they launched them, and we heard rumblings about The Big Bubble bursting. But, a few cursory rounds of layoffs aside, it remained business as unusual. Until the day that changed *everything* (ask anyone). Some people thought 9/11 was a convenient pretext for the massive downsizing that followed shortly thereafter. Some people thought 9/11 itself was a convenient pretext for... something.

It was about a month later, just about one year ago, when my boss called me at my desk. I knew it was serious since no one used phones anymore.

"Hey Byron, step into my office," he said grimly. Glumly, even.

So it's finally happening, I thought. After all the times I called in sick, all the beers I enjoyed on the company dime, after daring them to discard me at my previous job, I was finally being fired from the first place I sort of appreciated, and needed. The first job place I'd really tried to work hard; the first job where I'd really *tried.*

"It's over," my boss said.

"Just like that?" I asked, grimly. Glumly, even.

"I'm out," he said.

"You?" I asked.

"It's not like I didn't see this coming," he said.

What about me? I didn't say.

"Are you okay?" I asked.

"I think so," he said, after saying some other things about the company, himself, and me.

"So you'll be moving up to F5," he said.

"The fifth floor?" I asked.

"Yup. From the frying pan into the inferno."

"Why would *I* be on the same floor with all the executives?" "You made it to the show," he explained, after explaining that I was now reporting to the man who'd just terminated him with extreme indifference. The man who allegedly called the shots, the man I'd never said one word to in over three years.

"But I've never talked to him," I said. "I don't know him," I added. "He doesn't know me," I elaborated.

"That's good. That's exactly the way you want it."

"How do you figure?"

"Trust me."

"So…what will I be doing?"

"The same shit. Only less so."

"Should I be concerned?"

"Trust me."

"Are you going to be okay?" I asked, again.

"The package they're giving me is fair. It's competitive."

"Are you sure?"

"Well, let's just say they're making me an offer I can't refuse."

And there it was. I wasn't promoted so much as passed over, unimportant (or at least underpaid) to the extent that I could stick around, until… Until what? This hadn't been merely another round of layoffs; this was a bloodletting, a massacre. This, finally, served evidence that the company was failing. You don't write off losses like that until you write them off and see the stock prices soar. That was the secret, the anti-American Dream in a nutshell. Everyone, including the old timers like the guy who was no longer my boss, figured they had survived Y2K, had avoided sliding through the accumulating holes in this slowly deflating bubble, had baked enough investments to make them immortal. And they had. What no one understood was, just like in 1918, there was another war coming. A bigger and bloodier one.

* * *

A few words about (*insert name of company here*).

Truth be told, our business model had no business staying in business once those theoretical futures became the increasingly painful past. Like almost everyone else, we started small, got too big just quickly enough, then what we were worth on paper wasn't able to keep us from drowning in our own liquidity. After the last drops from the venture capital cask had been drawn, my company found salvation in the new rule: if you can't beat them, buy them. Dot-coms were like dinosaurs, and everyone knows what happened to the dinosaurs. But people forget there are creatures, like crocodiles, that remain kissing cousins to those alpha reptiles, and they represent our link between a new world and what went down before we became bipedal. Our company became, by process of elimination or evolution, one of the crocodiles, and we subsisted the way any crocodile survives: by hanging out in the shallow water and sneak-attacking smaller animals. We ingested every company we could swallow, and we got bigger (our heads grew as our head count shrank): we didn't reduce staff so much as we *streamlined*, worked *smarter* and explored *new solutions*. We were either enlarging our brand, by extension and attrition, or creating a bulwark, one acquisition at a time, to deflect whatever blows the free market decided to dish out.

In addition to all the little companies we procured, there was one in particular that caused all sorts of issues. Like most relationships it started out honestly, which is not to imply there was anything innocent about it. We were upstarts, *new media*, and we absorbed, or overwhelmed, a company way bigger, and older, than we were (which, considering we were dinosaurs made them amoeba, I guess). This was meant to signal the initiation of a new epoch, a reset, a realignment. Then the dot-com era decided to commit suicide and, in an unpredicted turn of events, the behemoth we killed ended up saving us. The amoeba-turned-anaconda gave us a taste of our own medicine, and now we're trapped inside a company that still uses our name but calls all the shots, waiting it out to see if two bodies are better than one or if our stomach will explode. And so, instead of being proud but unemployed we are bored and semi-productive and grudgingly grateful and sentimental and emasculated, but mostly we are still alive and get paychecks twice a month to prove it.

We had a rough few years, as a country and as a company. We endured annihilation, so there's nothing left to do but make as much money as possible until the next cataclysm, whatever it might be. Count me in. I'm a team player. I've also got nothing better to do.

Some are born great, some achieve greatness, and some have greatness thrust upon them.

You didn't say that.

You haven't lived that.

You aren't even trying to aspire *to that.*

Not yet anyway (that's your story, and you're sticking to it).

So, if greatness be the food of life… *ah, fuck it.*

Where are you?

Same place. Same person. Same problems.

The Big 3-Oh, which seemed like such a Big Deal is now sufficiently far gone it seems almost… cute to consider how much you feared and dreaded that Big Day. Especially when you should have known turning forty was a much Bigger Deal. If you haven't had kids or accomplished much by thirty it's still acceptable; it's almost expected these days. Everything leading up to that is just a test run, an audition for reality. After thirty, though, everything suddenly gets way too serious. Your body tells you this. Your friends tell you this. All the things you hoped to do tell you this, at night when you have no choice but to relive moments that never happened (also known as nightmares) or, worse, during the day when you'd rather be doing anything other than what you're doing—except worrying about the things you were never smart, or secure, or audacious enough to do. Yet.

So what do you do?

You work.

No one is expecting anything else. You show up, you do your job, you get paid.

It's just money.

Yes, it's just money to them.

It's just money to you, too.

So?

Sure, you like the idea of security. You like the notion of a nest egg. You like the idea of being a little less terrified about what's going to happen to you, financially, a few years down the road. But you also like the idea of liking your job. You like the idea of liking yourself.

So what do you do?

You drink.

Then what?

Rinse, wash, repeat.

And then?

Sick again. Same scenario: Laid low after getting high, trying to get laid. And nothing can bring your desiccated senses back to earth quicker than the meat hooks of mortality.

So.

Sulking about sad things, feeling sorry for everyone (including yourself), thinking about the people who never had half a chance (excluding yourself), all the suffering and strife felt by folks who didn't even bother to bring it on themselves.

Self-indulgent? Sure. But it's better than nihilism; it's better than nothing. *Having a conscience kick-started by a hangover has to count for* something. *Here's some truth: to remain sane you have to shield yourself from the sadism of an indifferent universe, or else grief will swallow you up, fill you in, and suck you down like a broken boat; another mermaid singing songs no one will hear.*

What's the alternative? Renounce life and sever your soul on the razor's edge? Give yourself to God and follow his Son? Pull a social worker and feed the families who can't feel heaven? Do some good things no one will ever know about? Or go all the way in the other direction, seeing things that suffocate your senses, stranding you in the streets, afraid and alone, desperate in the darkness, cold with the comprehension that there is always, in the end, only one way out?

That's your story and you're stuck to it.

So what do you do?

I don't know *(To yourself you say this).*

Two

SEND IN THE CLOWNS

OBODY KNOWS YOU When You're Down and Out.
(I didn't say that.)
Now *that's* a song, a blues song. The real item. Not to be confused with the cookie-cutter, paint-by numbers, copycat slop that most people think of when they think they're thinking about the blues. These days, it seems, anything goes. Anyone can sing the blues. And they do. It's not unlike what's happening all over the place, to all types of music: there are no prerequisites or apprenticeships; there is no perspicacity, no shame. Like so much of what passes for music today, it lacks dirt, authenticity, and conviction. There is, in short, no soul. It's clean, polished and feeble. In a word, it's fashionable.

The point being, you aren't going to find many folks who really know the blues.

Of course, you don't sing the blues to talk about someone else; you speak up because you feel obliged to account for yourself.

What's it all about, then?

Blues ain't nothing baby, but a botheration on your mind.

Yeah, what he said.

You always hear him before you see him.

Chazz is the king of the basement, as we all respectfully refer to him. In the basement of the corporate office—or *HQ*—is the mailroom, and Chazz is in charge of all that comes in and goes out from HQ. It's safe to say that Chazz, like just about everyone else in the company, is busy. The company—if you own a computer, you or someone you know has very likely done business with us, or at least *heard* of us—is successful, and it seems to gather size, power, funds and new faces every day, all in accordance with the somewhat unsettlingly Messianic sense of destiny that prevails within. Of course, once you have attained status, become what the corporate cheese-dicks refer to as a *brand*, you are ubiquitous and everyone wants a piece of you. The sheer correspondence and marketing materials that HQ generates are incalculable; the world is not entirely electronic yet, and as long as there are forests to deflower we'll find ways to waste all that white paper. I've never been down in that basement, partly because I want no part of that Sisyphean scene, but it's obvious it takes a certain sort of person to even attempt organizing, much less overseeing, the corporate mailroom.

Since part of his routine involves making the rounds several times a day, ensuring that all the confidential and otherwise urgent intelligence is being disseminated ably and accurately, I see Chazz fairly regularly. And I always know when he's coming, because his mouth never stops moving. If he isn't conversing or chatting someone up, he's humming, or whispering, or singing. Sometimes he's discreet, more often he's ebullient. I can't decide if this is by design or if it's an unconscious quirk, the result of some internal mechanism he's either unaware of or unable to suppress.

He has a peculiar habit—which immediately endeared him to me—when addressing others, of quoting fragments from songs, invariably an old blues or Motown tune. My impression is that most people—at least the uptight and extraordinarily unhip executives who hold forth on the fifth floor of HQ—have no idea what his remarks, which always signify *something*, actually mean, or where they're derived from. Indeed, I suspect this is part of the fun for him, as a black man in a predominately, even suffocatingly, white environment.

It was mutual like at first sight, as far as I can tell.

One day, about a week or so after I'd met him, he was coming down the hall and I could hear him talking, as usual.

"All right now, all right, *everything's everything!*"

"Hey Chazz," I said, not even getting out of my chair.

"There he is, say my man, *what you know good?*"

I immediately recognized the tune he was referencing, and felt obliged to acknowledge it.

"*What's Happening Brother,*" I called out from inside my sturdy, but scarcely soundproof cubicle.

Chazz stuck his head around the corner and winked at me.

"My man... say, what's your name again?"

"Byron."

"That's right, my man *B* knows what time it is!"

"Hey Chazz, I'm just trying to tell you *What's Going On...*"

"*Mercy Mercy Me,* I see you're not starvin' for Marvin!"

"You must have *heard it through the grapevine.*"

His expression shifted quickly from interest to approbation. "Oh, so you *really* know a thing from a chicken wing then?"

"I guess I try to know a thing or two about a thing or three..."

"Yeah you do," he agreed. "That album is *it,* you know what I'm sayin'? It's all in there for us all. Brother Marvin understood, he knew we're all the same, at least in the eyes of the Lord."

"Listening to that album never hurt anyone," I replied. "In fact, it would do a lot of people a lot of good."

"Let Reverend Gaye keep preachin', and you and me will keep *teachin',* right?"

After that conversation, Chazz made it a point to stop by to see me every time he was up on the fifth floor, which was fine by me. I had unwittingly passed some sort of pop-quiz, it seemed, and from that moment I could do no wrong in his eyes. He, in turn, was the first relatively new employee I could—or wanted to—have an actual conversation with since my former boss was traded for a player not to be named later.

* * *

Things tend to be tense, or at least urgent at HQ, especially in the ivory asylum of the fifth floor. This contributes to an atmosphere that is less than conducive for any type of sustained concentration. Between the shouting, the phones ringing and the unbearable cheery *pings* of real time chitchat amongst all the people for whom email conversation is not efficient enough, it's hard to get a thought in edgewise. Allow me to introduce corporate America, dot-com survivor style. For this reason, I tend to stay later in the evenings, after most of the big shots and their obsequious assistants have left for the day.

I noticed Chazz seemed to work similar hours, and he got in the habit of dropping by my desk to get (or give) the download once no one else was around. He shows up every evening after seven, and sometimes we'll sit and watch the sun set—from the fifth floor the views during autumn are extraordinary—talking about music and sports and life.

I can hear him coming, as usual. He enters singing, as always.

"Byron! Byron, Byron bo i-ron! Banana fanna fo fyron! Fe fi mo Myron! BYRON!"

"What you got going on there?" Chazz asks, gesturing to the cluster of printouts scattered across my desk.

"It's the end of the month, so I'm trying to get this newsletter finished…"

"Check you out bro, you be *runnin'* this place, yo!"

"Not in this lifetime."

"Yeah you do. I know what's up, you got the *smarts,* man."

"Who me?"

"Yeah you, you know all about this shit, these *computers* and so forth…"

"Oh no I don't, I just know how to turn them on and off."

"Shit, you have to know *somethin'*, else you wouldn't be up here on floor number five, know what I'm sayin'?"

"Well, sort of…"

"Right!"

"I'm here because the one thing I *can* do is something no one else around here can do, or wants to do anyway…"

Chazz raises his eyebrows, part Cheshire cat, part Sherlock Holmes.

"And what would that be?"

"Have you ever heard people say if you know how to write, there'll always be someone who needs you?"

"I've heard it said…"

"Well, that's me. I'm in charge of putting this newsletter together."

"See? That's no joke, Jack!"

"Well, all of the execs like to read it, because I basically tell them how great they are, so I basically write down what they want to hear, you know?"

"What kinds of things do you tell them?"

"Oh, like how much closer they are to taking over the world, stuff like that."

We both laugh, but Chazz nods his head thoughtfully.

"That's important though…"

"No, not really."

"Sure it is, man. Writing is *power*. Anybody can learn how to pound numbers into a machine, which is all I see most of these other fools doin'…"

"I guess so, but I know I can't do any of that technical mumbo jumbo…"

"Of course you could. Any *robot* can be taught to copy shit out of a manual, or a file, or whatever the hell kind of nonsense they do. But you can't teach it to *think*, know what I'm sayin'?"

"Yeah, I hear you. But they've got the power, and that's all that matters. If they ever decide they don't need me, they can always find someone else to make up good news."

Chazz doesn't miss a beat.

"Well, isn't it all good news these days?"

"As far as *we* know," I say, hoping that will suffice.

"Anyway, you can take those smarts with you, wherever you go."

And they'll be stuck here, I think. Killing each other with smiles on their faces, same as it ever was. The image this sentiment brings to mind is brilliant as it is familiar.

"Well, you know what they say," Chazz asks abruptly.

"No, what's that?"

"*I Have Had My Fun, If I Don't Get Well No More.*"

I venture my best guess: "Muddy Waters?"

"Nope, St. Louis Jimmy Oden."

* * *

A few nights later, having successfully completed the newsletter, I ask Chazz if he'd care to join me across the street for a celebratory cocktail or three.

"What do you say there, Chazz? Let me buy you a beer."

"Thanks but no thanks Buy-Ron," he replies. "I never touch the stuff."

I leave it alone, understanding he is a recovering alcoholic. Why else would he say that? No one says: *I never touch the stuff.* They might say: *I don't drink.* But *I never touch the stuff* means they *used* to touch the stuff. A lot.

Everyone gets a chance to touch the stuff the last Friday of every month, as the company hosts a *beer bash*, which is not to be confused with the *keg-kickoff*, which we have to signal the start of a new fiscal quarter. Between the beer bashes, keg-kickoffs and holiday parties, the company—with the one-two punch of free beer and casual dress—has wisely retained a few of our favorite things from the halcyon dot-com days. A simpler, more (or less) prosperous time when the company was like every other small start-up: tiny funds fueled by big dreams of world domination. And after the world? The universe, also known as the Internet. The rest of us hope we don't get tangled up in the world wide web and can survive long enough to marry this Monopoly money, also known as shares. They gave away stock options like tabs of acid at a Grateful Dead concert, and now we're all following the tour bus, having bookmarked the Wall-Street ticker on our screens, so we can see how rich we theoretically are, when we cash in our chips for mansions to be named later.

* * *

Phone ringing.

If it's long distance, it's business and I'm obligated to pick up; if it's local, it's almost always personal, so I'm entitled to ignore it.

Unless it's Whitey. If it's Whitey, I have to answer. Whitey has recently resurfaced, after another extended hiatus. Since college, Whitey has worked the irritating extremes of in-your-face ubiquity and out-of-touch apathy. It's not me, it's him—just ask him. That these sudden but explicable silences coincide with a not unimpressive inventory of new girlfriends and new jobs is not uncoincidental. Like many of us, he spent most of the last decade looking for love, looking for a job. But love and jobs always seem to see you coming, and they remember that you need them more than they need you. Whitey, like most young men who want money quicker than most employers are prepared to provide it, figured sales was a good fit for him. After a handful of successively ugly and swift sackings, he found a new frontier and boldly went where everyone else had gone. He fell down the rabbit hole, landed on his head, and had pretty much been incommunicado—lost in the elysian fields of the Internet—seeking whatever fortune had not already been found. Whitey is in continual contact mode at the moment, more so than ever, actually. As the moon turns the tides, in the unalterable cycle of Whitey's evolution, he is currently without girlfriend and hates his job. He is so ensnared in the system he makes *me* look like a pre-lobotomized patient fixing to fly over the cuckoo's nest.

So, Whitey needs me. He needs love. He needs a lot of things, and while I can promise or provide few of them, I'm better, it seems, than nothing.

So, when the phone rings, and it's Whitey, I feel obligated to pick it up.

The phone is ringing.

It's Whitey.

I pick it up.

"Good afternoon (insert name of company), this is Byron…"

"By?"

"What's up Whitey."

"Hey man, you got a sec?"

"Sure."

"Well… you know how I was explaining, you know, what I talked about with…"

"With your therapist?"

"Yeah, okay, so, I wanted to tell you…"

"Go ahead, lay it on me."

"The only thing preventing any of us from finding what we're looking for is ourselves."

"Okay."

"That's it."

"Uh…"

"Okay?"

"Okay."

"Okay, later."

Whitey's not a non-piece of work.

Like everyone, he's got his share of issues, obviously.

Like everyone, he has to reconcile them.

Unlike everyone, he is trying to exorcise some of his demons with the same urgency he sought to avoid them, and that's causing some interesting chemical repercussions, hence the frenetic phone calls.

Whitey, like everyone, is not an uncomplicated individual.

He saw the light.

He freaked out.

He disappeared.

He resurfaced.

He flailed.

He got better.

Most people do.

You'd think, after a conversation like that, I'd need to indulge heavily at the beer bash, and you'd be right.

A couple of hours and more than a couple of trips to the keg later, I'm standing in the corner with Otis, my other partner in crime. I couldn't work here without Otis, I *need* him; along with Chazz, he's a rare source of sanity.

Otis is one of the miracle men of the late twentieth century, upon whom fortune— or fruition—smiled with its unfathomable approval: he never finished college, and never figured out whatever it was that adults are supposed to figure out they'll do to make ends meet. In short, he never had a chance. Except that, in the capricious periods whereupon insurgencies occur, what had been a trifling diversion became his deliverance: he knew computers.

He's the IT guy for HQ, the systems administrator for the fifth floor, which means it's his *job* to have unrestricted access to all the executives' PCs, to ensure that their systems are updated, and to assist them when the burdens of big time performance prevent them from remembering how to manage complex tasks like saving their documents or finding the on/off switch on their machines.

Otis is—in almost every regard—like everyone I knew in college, but now that we're all thirty-something, it's equal parts refreshing and unnerving to see a grown man who acts *exactly* like an undergraduate, and never seems to give a second thought to what anyone else thinks. Not to put too fine a point on it, but the guy inspires me.

If I have enviable access to these mighty men, Otis is a (pretty) Big Brother—he can read their emails, inspect the websites they've visited, maybe even read their minds, since at least half of these people must have modems instead of hearts pumping the blood through their money-making veins.

It's always amusing to watch the rigid-assed senior staff mingle with the minions and pretend they're enjoying it. They're so insincere about everything they do: the deals they make, the worlds they promise, the charities they support, the only thing they seem earnest about is the relish with which they crush their competition and the fact that there aren't enough hours in the day to work: inconvenient obligations like eating, sleeping, wives and children complicate matters. So there's nothing better than beholding the brass, dressed down for the more-casual-than-the-rest-of-the-week vibe of a beer bash Friday. Only in America, in this corporate candy land, could you find grown men who look miserable without their coats and ties. They are professional players trapped in a frat-boy flag football tournament. There's one exception, Boyd Bender, the CFO, who I fear, loathe, love and appreciate in equal measure. He is so cliché, he is *beyond* cliché—he explodes cliché, requiring a reevaluation of how clichés are classified and what they're capable of inspiring. Look at him: He remains the only executive who insists on wearing button down shirts. In what must have been an excruciating contractual compromise, he does without the tie, but wears his solid color, conservatively long-sleeved oxfords every day, whether it's above ninety in July or on beer bash Fridays, when the other hon-chos are gamely sporting their ill-considered Hawaiian crimes against fashion.

One felt sorry for his clothes, actually. His shirt pressed and steamed into submission, the screams of pain from his slacks muted by their heavy starch, his socks self-conscious about the sweat they might need to soak up, even his shoes, exhausted from worshipping the ground he walks on. You get tense just *looking* at him; he is that uptight, that severe. He even drinks his beer briskly, as though that too was a job, another task to achieve as resourcefully as possible. I'm not afraid to say I am more than a little intimidated by him, not unlike the way I'd act in Special Ops around an agent I knew could kill me with his eyelashes, without even batting them.

"Look at that joker," Otis says, reading my thoughts—sort of.

"I could sand my deck with that shirt…"

"Thinks his shit don't stink."

"No, he *knows* his shit stinks, that's why he's so indignant."

Chazz, appearing out of nowhere, leans in close and puts things in his inimitable perspective:

"Send in the motherfuckin' clowns!"

"Oh the clowns are in full effect," I say.

"What you say there O-teece?"

"What's happening Chazz?"

"Hey man it's your world and I'm just a squirrel tryin' to get a nut…"

And so on, for several moments.

Chazz seems content to watch us drink beer, and we all have a half-decent time mocking the handful of dressed-down bigwigs taking one for the team in their too-comfortable T-shirts.

"Doesn't seem quite right though, does it?" Chazz says after a while, speaking for at least two of us.

"What's that?" Otis asks.

"All these big-time playas pretendin' to pass the time with we, the little people."

"It's all part of the act," Otis says, presumably speaking for all of us.

"I still can't believe *I'm* here," I add. "I always said I'd never own a suit, a cell phone or a computer..."

"No one can do that these days," Otis says, smirking. "You can't afford *not* to be able to afford a computer."

"Unless you're trying to be a homeless person," I say.

"Shit," Chazz says, shaking his head. "I'm pretty sure even homeless people have computers these days."

Otis and I both laugh, as that seems to be what's expected.

"Y'all pickin' up what I'm puttin' down right?"

Otis holds up his hand for a high-five.

"Whatever you say brother!"

All of a sudden Chazz is in Otis's face.

"Hey, why you have to say *brother*? What's with the *brother* bullshit? Are we brothers?"

"No, I'm..."

"What, it's cool to just call me *brother?*"

"I didn't..."

"Damn right you didn't. What, like you and me are *tight* or something..."

"Listen, I'm sorry man, I wasn't trying..."

All of a sudden Chazz is grinning; then he pretends to throw a punch.

"I'm just playin' with you partner, it's all good!"

We laugh again, as that seems to be what's expected.

After a few moments of uneasy banter, Chazz leaves us alone.

Otis shakes his head slowly and lets out a long whistle.

"I think that's his way of bonding," I offer.

"That's one tightly wound motherfucker," Otis replies.

"The funny thing is, he usually seems pretty laid back, always singing songs and whatnot..."

"You know he was in the military, right?"

"No, he never said anything about that to me."

"Well, that might explain some of it."

"Some of what?"

"Come on Byron, did you see that look in his eyes? That's the thousand-yard stare if I've ever seen one."

"Yeah but he was just joking around."

"Dude, you can't *fake* that shit."

"So what, are you saying he was serious, even though he said he was joking?"

"No, I *know* he was joking, and that's why I'm saying it."

"I don't follow."

"There is a seriousness behind that circus act. There's one angry son of a bitch behind all those shits and giggles."

Would an angry guy sing songs like he does?

I start to ask this question, and then stop.

I *want* to ask this question. But I don't, because I already know the answer is *yes*.

* * *

Friday night. Live. Lots of moving and shaking of asses. Too many peacocks and not enough parrots. Or something.

The multitude of light shirts and dark ties make it difficult to discern who is staff and who are working stiffs just off from work.

All these men of steel with their cell phones stuck to their sides like remoras, or half-assed hip replacements.

And then suddenly, salvation.

Across the room I see her: she looks exactly like Candice Bergen, circa 1970: the brown eyebrows and blonde, shoulder length locks, tall, thin, not wearing bell bottoms because they're not back in fashion—yet—but it doesn't matter, you can *buy* those, you can't buy that body.

Instantly I understand it's happened again.

And it's not drunkenness.

It's even worse.

It's *love*.

I've seen this movie before. So has she.

I would talk to her if I was capable of speaking.

I could at least get closer to her, show her that I care.

I could walk across the bar and sort of see what happens.

I could, at the last second, see the light smirking off that diamond, the cold-hearted disco ball of disappointment on her finger, that sign that says *closed*.

I could catch the glare from the big meathead moving in front of her, the guy who gave her that ring...

What?

Last call?

For the first time ever I find myself saying words which would, at one time, been inconceivable: Thank God (To myself I say this).

* * *

Saturday.

Still alive, still *drunk*. Nothing a few pots of coffee can't cure.

What did I do to be so black and blue?

Maybe if I could remember I'd feel better; then again, maybe if I could recall all the things I did, I'd feel a whole lot worse.

You can't always get what you want.

Yeah, what *he* said.

And that's from a guy who doesn't even have a day job. Although Mick Jagger, more than any other rock star, has perfected the vampiric vibe necessary for survival, sympathy for the devil be damned. Look at him, trim as a teenager with crags in his cheeks that make statues seem soft. But these are not men we can measure ourselves against; these are people who've made *careers* out of doing precisely the things so few people are able to imitate. Perhaps that's what makes them rock stars. And like the stars themselves, the lucky ones burn bright, while all around them, their hard-partying partners-in-crime are falling out of the sky, or streaking into rehab, or getting born again in a galaxy far, far away.

The only things worse than the things you do to your body are the things your body does to *you*. Payback is a bitch, especially when you don't have the sex, drugs and rock and roll to help you ignore the pain.

Wait. Am I having a mid-life crisis? Shit.

Then it occurs to me: if I keep having them, I'll never die.

Even rock stars haven't figured out *that* one. Yet.

Head ringing, just like the phone.

Annoying, but if I ignore the phone; it will eventually stop, unlike my head.

It won't stop, so my instinct for survival—or at least sanity—requires me to do the unthinkable:

-Hello?

-Dude…

-Hey Otis…

-Oh God…

-You sound as bad as I feel.

-Fuck beer bashes.

-Yup.

-Fuck (insert name of company here).

-Yup.

-Dude… have you ever had one of those hangovers where you forget to breathe?

-You mean like right now?

-I'm serious…

-*Dead* serious?

-Dude, I actually have to concentrate, lying on the couch, I am having to focus just on breathing. I'm doing those Freddie Krueger exercises like my wife did when she was pregnant…

-*Kegel* exercises?

-Those too.

-Don't forget to drink a lot of water.

-*Water?*

-Yeah, water, ever heard of it?

-Well, my body is 90% water already, right?

-Uh…

-Why would I want to go adding to that? I might drown.

-So anyway, what are you up to this weekend?

-Up to? I don't have weekends anymore.

-What do you have?

-I have kids.

-Sounds great.

-I got lucky last night, at least.

-You mean driving home safely?

-No, I got *lucky*.

-Lucky?

-I got *laid* last night.

-Laid?

-Yeah, I had sex, stupid.

-Really? With who?

-With my *wife*.

-Yeah, but you're married…

-So?

-Well, but… isn't that sort of a given?

-Hardly.

-So, that's something to get excited about?

-You'll see.

* * *

All things being equal, I feel fortunate for my penis, which is to say, I still have one, my penis is still in one piece. And trust me, I'm no Don Juan, I'm not even Donald *Duck*, but if you hit thirty and have not settled down to the squalid stability of your STD-free soul mate, you are rolling the dick dice every time you go not-so-gently into that good night, dutifully wearing the compulsory condom, as well as goggles, gas mask and scuba wet suit. Even jerking off isn't as safe as it used to be, if you don't bathe, disinfect, scrub the sheets, and spray Lysol in the room during pre-play. After all, who knows *what* types of germs you've gotten stuck to yourself out amongst the unwashed, contagious masses.

And it's not that getting married is the secret; it's that no men I know who are married have wives who let them have sex anymore. So, admittedly, marital bliss does not have much going for it, but it certainly sounds *safe*.

I don't get laid nearly as often as I'd like, but I make love to myself as much as I can, just to stay in game shape. My hand hates me for it, but we both know it's got nothing better to do. Besides, wear and tear on the body beating off beats wear and tear on the mind beating yourself up. Fortunately, my mind is fine. So much so, in fact, I seldom require the once-obligatory assistance of pornography. Of course, if this makes me less than sane, so be it. What I'm trying to say is that I'm in good enough shape for the shape I'm in, which is more than I can say for most of my married amigos. And the ones with kids? Forget it. I'm willing to bet my long-suffering bank account that any of those saps (the men anyway) would perform oral sex on an alligator, donate their dicks to science, anything short of actually selling their new souls—anything just to get back the old souls they sold for security.

So: solo, soul, sane. So what?

* * *

She had a silver car.

Here's how you know someone has gotten to you: when, a week, or a month, or a year (or more) after they've left your life, you do a double-take every time you drive past a car that could be hers.

Take a car, any car—any *silver* car—and it could be her. Even, as it approaches, you *know* it isn't, couldn't be her, you still look.

Just to make sure. Just in case. Because (you think) the one time you don't look up, you'll miss her.

And?

And the spell will be broken; it's like no longer wanting—or needing—to say your prayers before bed, once you lose the desire to believe, the magic disappears, faith dies. And? And faith in all things will die (eventually, inevitably) so you want to hold on as long as you can, hang on to all the things you can't ever control, because those are the secrets you never want to solve. Once we understand what you're seeing in the mirror, suddenly it's all so much polished sand, it's uncomplicated, explicable by science.

And so: even if one is in a different city, a different *state*, one should never not look, never not allow oneself to hope, because there's always the chance that it could be her. Could be love.

What are you seeing, exactly?

Yourself, in a tux?

Maybe marriage was *the secret. You've felt nothing at all like envy for your friends who had wedded—happily or not—and especially the ones who'd had children—willingly or not—in between, say, first job and first affair. And you could see the simpletons on the horizon from your rear-view, left behind, not knowing what hit them, not* wanting *to know: the living dead. Okay, and what were* you *doing? You were holding out (you thought) so as to avoid those foolish fates: settling, cashing in the chips, neither ahead nor behind, contemporary but cautious, invulnerable but apathetic, respectable but repressed, safe but stifled, alive but not living. Average. Equal. Indifferent.* Existing. *Okay.*

Maybe the secret is that there is no secret. People with families— real *people—look the way they do for a reason: they're real, they have families. Once kids become part of the equation, you're obliged (or allowed?) to stop worrying so much about yourself. Plenty of parents still want to go out and stumble back from a long night at a bar (and some still do); they'd all like to cut loose on occasion, they just can't afford to.*

So, was it the societally induced, cliché-laden, baggage-buried trigger of turning thirty that awakened the yearning—bordering on panic—that you'd long since grown accustomed to feeling? The clock ticking, or the spirit (understandably?) waning, human patience expiring, realistic, even healthy, skepticism about the passage of time and the consequences of inertia? Was your heart betraying you or your brain warning you, or some unkind combination of the two, shaken up in the martini tumbler of circumstance, this chemical chaos of living in the very early twenty-first century?

Were you losing faith? Or were you realizing (too soon, morbidly) what you'd be missing later in life?

Who are you seeing, exactly?

Look around; look at all these people, equally motivated or miserable or misguided, as well as the handful of hard cases, who'd somehow never figured out how not to be happy. All those people; the same person.

And, you know: Once you reach the age where you want to begin lying about how old you are (signified by the day you begin losing the hair on your head and find it turning up in places it has no business being, like your back, your shoulders, your ears and especially your nose) you want to slow down, avoid the wreckage that is ruining everyone around you. You spend your formative years cultivating your own unique set of issues and get to a certain age (some people actually become adults) where you realize you have issues, and they're the only things you own that no one else wants. Then you work toward eradicating your issues, and the strongest amongst us survive and eventually some of them make money sitting there, listening to people (who are paying them) talk about their issues. Then, inevitably, sitting around and listening to people talk about their issues helps them develop an accelerated, more complicated set of issues. No one gets out of here unscathed, and you may think you've got life beat, but it waits, then sucker punches you in sudden death overtime.

And, you think: you'll never be that guy. The guy who sits on toilet seats without a second thought; who might use the restroom half a dozen times a day and look at himself in the mirror once, or twice, tops; who actually doesn't mind—or, perhaps, secretly prefers—lukewarm coffee (or, worse, decaf, or, worst, the kind served over ice for five bucks and change); who can eat bologna sandwiches and avoid meat (even bologna) on Fridays during Lent; who believes that God blesses America and that Jesus Christ is a Capitalist; who can relate to anyone playing or providing commentary on a game of golf; who buys clothes—or food, or appliances, or fiancées for that matter—from a catalog; who is actually entertained by movies, or books, or albums, or people that put entertainment before aesthetic, or amusement before honesty; or sales before soul. You'll never, in short, be a normal person.

Three

SICK AGAIN

TO BE FAIR, there are likely a lot of people who would envy the opportunity to fly up to New York City every month. Take me, for instance. True, I fly *to* New York City, but that's not the half of it. La Guardia is ultimately an empty mirage, a revolving door I walk out to catch a cab that will take me through the city to the corporate office. I do *see* the city, and I breathe that air, during the hurried moments between terminal and cab, and in those uncertain steps between safety and the executive board rooms, which swallow everyone whole and spit us out when the dirty work for that day is done.

Anyone who gets airborne often enough to actually *use* (as opposed to merely have) a frequent flyer number can attest that it was no picnic before you-know-when, and no one else has more authority to confirm how much more awful it's become, now that everyone is a potential tragedy waiting to transpire at thirty thousand feet.

Look around: some of the pretty people, many of the mediocre, and the rest of us, all sizes and shapes: men trying to look like the human mannequins who sold them their suits, women with bodies stolen from a Robert Crumb cartoon.

I can't help overhearing the woman across from me who has not discovered her indoor voice, agitated and unabashed, wire growing out of her ear to prove she is not, in fact, arguing with herself. To tell the truth, she's yelling—there is simply no way around it.

And look at this joker, walking in purposeless circles, mouth in constant motion above the ice cream cone he's carrying in the hand not holding his carry-on. Not everything I just described is accurate, I realize, as I see how he's sizing up the innocent bystanders: his circles are serving a purpose after all—he is seeking out the amateurs. I myself am more or less an amateur, but I'm not as much of an amateur as he hopes I am. Direct eye contact is out of the question, yet I'm practically daring him to say something just so I can ignore him. After all, if 9/11 gave us anything, it ensured that all the actually dangerous people now avoid airports. But then, there's no reason to invite annoyance. Just because he can't hurt me doesn't mean he won't kill me with kindness.

Some of the people in airports are leaving town to escape their problems, some are heading toward their problems, and the rest are either unaware or unwilling to accept that *they* are the problem. These are the otherwise unknowable citizens who shout into cell phones even as they bump and grind down the unfriendly aisle.

As I edge my way forward warily, trying not to touch or eyeball anyone, I am certain the capricious airline gods have assigned me a middle seat between the ice cream man and the woman whose main problem seems to be herself.

In the air less than an hour, there's a collective, silent expression of anxiety amongst the people who can't plug something in. The second tires hit the tarmac it quickly becomes a contest to see who can turn on their phone first. How did people exist in the world before cell phones? Before email for that matter? Before *computers*? I lived in that world. Recently. And I have no idea.

There is only one way to get through mornings like this: drink heavily. Right now the coffee and orange juice are kicking in, caffeine battling c-vitamins, engaged in a Dostoyevskian struggle for my soul. Or, at least, my nervous system. A million little meetings imploded into one agenda, it becomes an endurance test to see who will blink first and ask for a bathroom break, or delegate more action items for the unfortunate underlings lucky enough not to be here. Mostly I try to maintain equilibrium with the most important people and stifle the incessant anxiety that someone might ask my opinion or a question I actually know how to answer. Not unimpressed, I watch possible futures unfolding from the projector, purgatory via PowerPoint.

Instead of taking advantage of the catered lunch at HQ, I take an opportunity to walk around a city I'd otherwise never have the chance to see.

It's strange. For starters, you can't tell who is crazy anymore since everyone has taken to talking to themselves. At least it looks like they're talking to themselves, but it turns out some people have forsaken cell phones and actually installed tiny machines where their ears used to be. At least that's what it looks like. It's a miracle they aren't being run over as they cross the streets without looking, until you realize everyone inside every car is also on the phone.

The absurdity is interrupted by an authentic exception—a real throwback—who parts the crowd before me, frantically brushing his teeth with his fingers. It's refreshing to behold someone who is at least still trying, still making an effort to stand out amongst the mostly silent psychosis. Or is he? He looks like he has something crucial to convey, but his speech is muffled by those busy fingers, and the streets are already singing with the sounds of science. Or at least science fiction. We'll meet again, I don't say, as we move on in opposite directions, having made what passes for that human touch in a post-ironic America. Mission accomplished, I take my chances on the nearest hot dog vendor, resigned to tempting mortality the old fashioned way.

These day trips ask a lot of you, almost so much that you find yourself fondly reminiscing about the good old days you never knew, the days when horse-drawn carriages were cutting edge business travel, days when people might have fantasized about a few hundred miles in less than an hour, not anticipating planes that make your mind feel microwaved.

Cooked on the surface but still raw inside, it's all in a daze work as the cab carries me home through disorienting yet familiar streets. Survival suburban-style; a metropolis in transition, trying its best to live up to the image it was designed to imitate—sprung from the minds of forward-thinking people who are trying to recreate the past. On the corner high school punks stand beside a phone booth, making no calls; a quick right turn and I'm feeling the money dread as we cruise past several blocks of four car families. Being outside the city is safer, particularly if you prefer the sound of crickets to cop sirens. Eventually, I'm deposited in the middle ground of this middlebrow town, and for lack of any other options, I am relieved.

And yet. This is supposed to happen *later*, with wife and kids and a basement to be banished to after hours. I'll deal with that later. I think.

My front door is the one mystery to which I have the key, but for some reason I still feel as though I'm sneaking up on a stranger every time I return from a trip; I'm not sure who I expect to see, who might be hiding from me, who possibly could have found their way into my modest refuge from friends and memories.

With Pavlovian precision, I make my way to the medicine cabinet and pour myself a bracing plug of bourbon. It's more than I need or deserve, I think, but I don't want the bottle to suspect I was unfaithful in another town, waiting for my return flight for instance, in a cramped and crappy airport bar at La Guardia. If this were a movie (I think, mostly in the past, but even today), I would grab my crystal decanter, filled with obviously expensive spirits, and administer that potion the old-fashioned way, needing no ice cubes, especially since I would never get around to drinking it, as it's only a prop, a cliché. No one reaches for that tumbler these days (except in movies); the question is: did they *ever*? Even in the 50s? Or has it always been part of the script?

* * *

Now maybe it's merely the hangovers, but daytime is different.

On weekends anyway.

Yes, I have to sleep off the whiskey and the damage done, but there's more than that, more than the compulsory early, mid and late afternoon catnaps. No matter how I feel all day—and I usually feel pretty feeble, thank you for asking—as soon as that spiteful sun heads over the horizon to roust and browbeat weary citizens on the other side of the hemisphere, I start to come slowly to life. As the imperious sky darkens, I begin to glow, from the inside out. I'm ready for action. Out on the town, eventually, inevitably. Obviously. And in the meantime, even coma-inducing activities like reading or talking on the phone suddenly have meaning, even promise.

Later. It's late, and I'm alive. Doing my best to defy death, dancing dangerously behind the wheel. Built for greed, the highway can't contain me. I laugh at four lanes, the entire planet is my playground, so long as I don't see the dreaded blue lights bumrushing my rearview.

Reality Check (3)

You're done, it's over.

Our minds are not unlike the universe, (you think): vast, expanding, occasionally exploding, sometimes dark, sometimes bright, flashes of light, dead stars dropping into unconsciousness, cold, empty, brilliant, impenetrable, unaccountable, inexplicable, illimitable, et cetera. Being cognizant but detached is tolerable, it is only when the actual weight of this awareness was awakened, that the fear creeps in.

This is the worst fear (you know), the most sickening obsession anyone is subjected to, at some point after adolescence. All those formative experiences you have at eighteen you so desperately need someone to share with you that, at twenty-two—and up until twenty-five—you rightly appreciate not needing to embarrass yourself by reliving or even relating to anyone (including yourself). But then, unless you have become bitter, or regressed, or are irredeemably fucked up, you long to find some solidarity, on an adult level, as you grow and learn in those tumultuous pre-thirty years.

And then, suddenly, it's over. You're done.

At thirty, if you've not already sold out (to the lowest bidder) or settled, or suicided yourself, you've made it. You've got scars, you've got skills. You have, above all—and for better or worse—yourself. And you're all you can count on, as always. You are insulated, ensnared in that human armor, how could you begin to describe to anyone (including yourself) the imperatives that catapulted you from proverbial Point A to Point B? You can't. It's too much, it's too long: to explain why you listen to this music (why this *is your favorite album, why* that *is your favorite song, et cetera), why you read poetry, which movies make you weep (or laugh, or puke). And so on. You can't recreate these moments, reincarnate that magic. You're all that you've got. It hurts, but you're alive. And so you can't begin to uncover the mysteries that have conspired to make you who you are. The person who fears it's too late to find someone else who can help him find meaning in the mess he's made of his life.*

And beneath it all, that lingering, unwelcome reminder: it's over, you're done.

Four

MEAN STREETS

A FEW WORDS ABOUT my commute: it's killing me. If you don't believe it, ask any of the anonymous near corpses suffering alongside me, their anger and impotence creating a morbid energy inside all these windshields. Let me put it another way: if my job entailed having sex with Swedish super models three-to-five days a week, at triple my current salary, I'd still wrestle with whether to willingly mire myself in this mess.

Maybe the commute causes cancer. It certainly feels like it, it's certainly causing something. Carrying stress in the jaw, not to mention my neck, my knees, my nuts.

Everyone knows, now, that road rage can kill you—or at least cause you to kill someone else (usually the asswipe who swerved into your lane and then slammed on the brakes, just to let you know he's there), so people are trying to control themselves, curtail those carcinogens, and the result is several thousand ass-cracks shut tighter than a cherrystone clam.

This commute is Pavlov, I'm a dog (that woman who just cut me off is a bitch), and a shot of bourbon is my bone. Or a beer. Or some vanilla extract, if that's all that's available. Look: as soon as this moonwalk of machinery grinds the gears of congestion, the first thing I can think of is how badly I want a drink. What the hell else am I supposed to do? It's better than some of the options other people choose, like cuddling up with a couple of quarter pounders, or (the other extreme) running to jump on the treadmill, or biting a hole in the tongue or ulcerizing holes in their heart, or kidnapping and killing the kids from the milk cartons, or (the horror) going to *church*.

This is my life: welcome to the occupation. College already an unattainable memory, the farthest car back in my rear view mirror, all of us going nowhere fast, a million tons of muted machinery. We have to stick together, socialize to survive, roll with the punches or become road kill.

The sweet smell of manure holds sway. The hills are alive; at least the deep green and nervous grass seems to be, eager to stretch out and show the world what it's been up to all summer, sensing the cold nights coming, afraid of hunkering down, dying and waiting in line to be reborn in the spring.

The fuck are you staring at? I hiss at the stranger staring at me in my rearview. Oh, wait, that's me.

I'm not sure what I'm staring at, exactly, but it's definitely not healthy.

Quick catalog: eyes too honest—or too surprised—to lie about what they behold; dark patches of hair in all the wrong places, sagging shoulders that seem to point in different directions, a lethargic slouch from hours spent slumped in office chairs and twisted around myself in nervous nights trying to sleep.

I wish there was some sort of spa I could enter—somewhere where all the CEOs go so that they can emerge, actually appearing *human*, although we all know they're not fooling anyone.

I, on the other hand, could come out my old self again. Or, at least go all the way over to the other side and run with the pack where the wild things are. Where the law of the jungle is clear: kill anything you can, subsist on everything smaller than you are, all parties understanding it's nothing personal, it's strictly business.

The business section looks up at me, as if it's actually innocent of the crimes everyone commits each day in its name.

Each day I read a little bit less of the newspaper. I've been through the cycle, it seems: starting with the comics, then moving up to the sports pages, then slowly grappling with the local news, then the arts and entertainment and finally, after college, world news. Nothing changes except this one constant: everything gets worse, always. It's nothing personal, the world seems to say. It's strictly business.

I recall, in high school, being vaguely afraid of the random sociopaths who may or may not have concealed switchblades in their skin-tight jeans (no one, to my knowledge, ever did) and mostly I was just afraid of getting my ass kicked. Until a few years ago the height of high school anxiety, for males, was getting beaten up in the locker room, in front of all the girls you beat off to. How endearing, how outdated. Now, you have to pass through a metal detector and armed S.W.A.T. teams patrol the hallways. And that's just the nursery schools.

This is why movies are so miserable and no one bothers to buy books, if they ever actually did: because no work of imagination is ever going to equal the show playing outside, everywhere, inside, all the time. The world is a blockbuster and the final cut can never occur because there's no budget and we've lost count of the cast.

You hear about embittered old burnouts who hang their Sunday papers in effigy, sacrifices to the gods that failed them, worn down by the information overload we've created (in our own image). If you're lucky enough to actually live a long life, you've inherited the accumulated burden of memories: all that suffering, all those mysteries, all the injustice, all this *pain*. It only gets worse so you ask yourself eventually, inevitably: why did I bother?

So I'm reading a little less, each day, of the newspaper. I'm beginning to suspect that I'll just cut out the middle man of middle age and stop reading altogether. A preemptive strike; apathy before annihilation, don't let them take me alive, cash in some of this awareness for sweet, beautiful bliss.

Listen:

"Come on, stay green! Come on! Stay, oh you motherfucker…"

You know you've got troubles when you start talking to traffic lights.

Life is all about the routine, right? All of us poor, conditioned creatures go through those same motions. The light turns red, my foot taps the spinal cord of my car which tells its overheating heart to pause, and we exhale, taking a moment to take in a familiar sight. Look at the youngish man, who didn't bother, or couldn't afford to figure out that there is safety in numbers. All of us are uncomfortable together, in our inoffensive groups. There's no advantage to seeing through our charade, when it means you're washed up before you even began, alone at the stoplight, asking for crumbs from the folks you were too proud, or scared, or smart to connect with.

"Hey brother can you spare a life?" (To himself he says this).

Shit, he's younger than *me* for God's sake.

Come *on*. It can't be *that* bad.

What are you trying to tell me, what have you got to say for yourself? Have things gotten that discouraging that you find yourself out here, working this crowd like a tragic clown? Or are you simply getting a head start on humiliation, having seen a vision of what our future holds?

Here's what we haven't realized yet: at some point the past tense is going to become the present tense. We're moving too quickly—the future never had a chance: it can run but it can't hide, it's always out there, just watching (whether it knows this or not), just as the now is always hurrying to catch up, quickly falling behind, into the past. The future ain't happening, it already happened.

Denial is like a dyke—the water is wide, waiting, impassive. You're never certain but most of the time you know, you sense the security of that invisible shield; it's only when you stop and look that you see the cracks, circling up slowly from all sides, that you become concerned. It's only then that you look at the stranger in the street and struggle to avoid his eyes, because you're actually seeing yourself.

Cars slow down across from me, a car anxiously stops—too close—to the car in front of it, a door opens slowly and an older man slowly, oh so slowly, gets out. He appears angry and out of sorts, hopefully he knows he's not alone. He's taken it upon himself to not *take* it anymore; he feels obliged to confront the brazen bastard—who looks all of eighteen—who probably just cut in front of him, or tailgated him for a few miles before passing him on the right, or flipped him the bird, or fucked his wife—who knows these days.

Please grandpa, get back in your car, I plead.

It's not just that I don't wish to see a senior citizen get his ass kicked (I don't), but I'm aware of some things that have transpired in the decades gone by since this stooped-over street fighter had any business trading blows. I'm even vaguely aware of some of the tectonic shifts that have occurred in the last few hours, for that matter. For instance, kids don't bother with tire irons or antiquated concepts like *fists* these days. They don't have to. Gramps is correct in his certainty that these sissies don't know how to fight like *men;* he's right. But I know something he would never be able to bring himself to believe: kids don't fight anymore because they don't *have* to. They don't have the numbers, or the knuckles. They've got the guns. So please gramps, put your walking stick down and get your tired ass back in your cautious car, before you find yourself starring in an unrehearsed rap video.

You can practically pen their obituaries: here rests another old fart who thought the old rules still applied.

Get a load of *this* guy.

Laying low at the stoplight, I have no choice but to consider this specimen strolling down the sidewalk, inscrutable grin stretched across his face. Immediately, instinctively, I roll up the window.

What a shame, (to myself I say this).

What kind of sick-ass world are we living in when the sight of some happy-go-lucky idiot, who actually seems to be *enjoying* life, arouses a feeling of fear?

And yet. It's always the smiling psycho with a sawed-off shotgun in the supermarket, or taking hostages at the playground. It's *never* the guy grimacing in line behind you; it's never the sketchy character with the five o'clock shadow and fedora who shoots up the 7-Eleven—those faces only exist in films. Besides, *no one* smiles when they're walking down the street, not in real life, not these days. Anyone who does is already living in the future; beaming at visions of the bomb they just detonated, causing a fifty-car pile-up on the freeway. Or else they're smirking in silent acknowledgment of the helpful voices in their head admonishing them to be ever vigilant for anal-probing aliens, or eavesdropping federal agents, or the guy in my car looking at them with envy in his eyes. No, it's infinitely more refreshing, and routine, to observe a stranger swearing and scowling his way down the street. That's a person you can trust, a person hiding no secrets, a person ensconced in the painful prison of the here-and-now.

Now: a crimson blur encroaches, in one fluid moment, coming from nowhere, from behind me, beside me, and abruptly in front of me. *What the fu…* Loud report, reverie ended (*oh my God it's a bomb, he really had a bomb!*), back to reality and this jackass who is already moving ahead, maneuvering around the next car. *What are you, an asshole?* Exhaust, acceleration, unconcern. *This isn't the Indy 500, motherfucker!* I speed up and read the personalized plates with disgust and disbelief: CEO 2B. *Oh Christ. Are you fucking kidding me?* Damn it, where was the justice? God, please, where are the cops to pull this imbecile over? Just one time, I'd give anything to be able to watch someone like this get nailed. *Hey! If you pull in front of one more person I'm gonna run your ass off the road. No, don't worry, that light isn't for you, red means run!*

Okay: red light, relax. Look up, look around. Look at *that!* Now here's something that might help: heaven, bliss, a blonde.

And just like that, I'm in love again.

In a few seconds that last forever, I'm able to envision our entire lives together. I compose sonnets and visualize entire operas dedicated to her beauty, I make elaborate plans, starting with the wedding—we would definitely elope, probably to the Caribbean, because she would want to be somewhere *warm* to keep that amazing tan… I'll marvel at how she provided me with one boy and one girl (each one stunning, each entirely, miraculously, in her image and not mine) and still retain that figure, no pounds to shed, no cosmetic surgery necessary; if anything she gets progressively *more* gorgeous, and somehow finds me intriguing and endearing, even as I dedicate my days to developing a golf game and a beer belly, even as I lose hair on my head and grow hair on my back…

Then, as always, it's over: green means go (no, stay!) and we're off, on our way elsewhere. Typically, tragically, I turn left while she goes right, speeding out of my life forever.

***

"I can't afford to get drunk tonight," Whitey says as I order the third round.

"Why, you have to be at church in the morning?"

"Worse, class."

"Whitey, you *have* a job, what are you taking a class for?"

"I need to learn more about computers."

"Why?"

"So I can get a *better* job."

At moments like this, there is nothing to do but take a drink.

"So," I say. "What should we toast?"

"A new job for the new year."

"A better job?"

"Just a *good* job!"

"Haven't you heard? A good job isn't good enough anymore."

"As long as it makes me the good money."

"Ah, fuck the money."

"That's the thing, I want a job that actually enables me to make love to money."

"Okay, but you can't let yourself *love* the money."

"Why not?"

"Because money cheats on everyone; money will always break your heart in the end."

"I'll try to remember that."

Whitey got the last round, so it's my turn. As I make my way to the bar I see someone. The same dude I see every few months. When we are drunk. And we have the same stupid conversation, then exchange numbers, and forget all about it until we do this dance, again.

Oh shit. Avoid eye contact... too late.

"Hey, I *thought* that was you..."

Hey! Nice to see you, hope all's well, and all that good stuff, but for once let's not pretend we're going to get together and *do lunch* or *grab a beer*, because even if we really want to do it, it just ain't gonna happen and we both know it. I never have enough free time to hang out with the friends I've managed to stay in touch with, and time as tight and what, you're married now, and a couple of *kids* too? Well, it's obviously out of the question then. So, I'll see you next month, same time, same place.

(To myself I say this.)

"Hey dude!" I say.

"What's going on? Great to see you!"

(One beer it's a handshake, two beers a high-five, five beers an embrace).

"Where are you working now? How they treating you? Still married? Wow, you've got *another* little boy? Nice! Look, give me your number, I lost it last time, again... oh, you have a business card? Check you out! Yeah, hook me up, cool. Let's grab some beers one night this week, or at least do lunch. Yeah, sweet. Hey, me too. No, seriously, I'll call you, yeah I'm putting your card in my wallet. Okay, it's good to see you too man. Say hi to the wife, yeah I'll talk to you later this week…"

I finally make it to the bar and see that Whitey is already there.

"That looked awkward," he says, smiling.

"Yeah, thanks for helping me out."

"I *did* help you out," he says, handing me a beer.

***

I'm beginning to understand that professional athletes and country/western musicians from the 70s are the only ones who actually managed to work hard and play hard. The rest of us pay up front, and then keep paying on the backend.

A request:

I need, in ascending order of importance: a safe place to stay, a good night's sleep, aspirin, H2O, antibiotics, a blood transfusion, forgiveness, and faith in something inexplicable or, failing that, myself. An identity. In short, a life.

And so I ask myself: What happened? What *hadn't* happened.

See: someone has already forgotten everything that happened. Same old story.

Actually, I remember all of it, and that's why I need to forget. Sometimes the mind won't let you forget and that's why you have to work with it, to help you help yourself. Another night: what had someone seen, smelled, said? Who had someone insulted? Where were the keys? Who called the cab? What time was it? Still dark: dark outside, darker inside. The way someone likes it, the way someone *needs* it. Going, alone, into the darkness, for someone who has no guilt is gratifying, an escape or release; for someone with stifled sadness, it is a shuttle into silence, where an empty room is the agent of unwelcome memories.

Alive, alone: another night.

It's only you, making love to a memory, which is always better than almost any other option.

You think:

Here we are: the sex may happen, or, it's already happened, and we're in the post-coital intensity of close, searching conversation, that most soulful exchange of intimacy (or, the intimate exchange of soul).

Then it occurs to you: why is this working—or worse, why should you want it to work?

(You know: Love is a game. It's not a sport, because in sports you win or lose, in games you live or die, at least in the sorts of games that matter, like love. It's so much easier, alone. Relationships, unlike death and taxes, are optional. Love is a habit. If you can go it alone, get out early, get out often, and taste the pain of solitude. It might sting a little, at first, but it's addictive as all hell. Consider this: people will do anything to persuade themselves that what they try to feel is real; they need to believe it and know they have nothing to lose. That's how insane schemes, like wars and religions, get started. And people fight the bad fight, convincing anyone they can, and they keep on fighting, or die trying. Eventually, they may actually sway everyone around them, but not themselves, never themselves. That's why religion keeps living and wars keep people dying. It's good business, that's all.)

The only thing more enticing than a fantasy you can never have is a fantasy you've already had, but can never have again. Mad or married, bad breakup or broken ties, the ones you did or could or should have loved are history, moved on, they're out of reach, untouchable, unavailable, already gone. A memory.

Five

FIELD STUDIES

I T'S NOT NECESSARILY that I enjoy talking about the men's room, but the fact of the matter is it's where a surprising amount of action occurs.

It's here, in this sulfuric-scented enclave that little people like me can rub shoulders with big people like *The Don*. I'm proud to report that on several occasions I've stood alongside this man—who has helped create this company in the image of the image he once created of himself—and exchanged mutual splatterings from the faux-ivory urinals that even the most wealthy dicks are obliged to visit a few times a day.

It's no big deal if I've already established my position (far right, farthest from the door) before he comes in and joins me. Otherwise, I've been known to walk in, see him, and turn right around. You don't drop trou alongside a man of his stature if you can possibly avoid it. When I'm already in there, it's an unremarkable event, no macho codes to concern oneself with. I know the drill: attempt—with every iota of willpower in my possession—to avoid sideward glances (direct eye contact is out of the question) and remember that whistling, speaking or passing gas are simply non-options.

The Don, which is what everyone calls him behind his burly back, is generally considered by all the highest compliment, an unironic affirmation of his status. He isn't *the* number one honcho, but unlike our mostly reticent and unobtrusive CEO, it doesn't seem accurate, or adequate, to call him number *two*. Being number one would only put him first in the line of fire if bullets ever fly; we all know who calls the shots up on the fifth floor. Listen: he pulls more money out of an ATM for beers at the ballgame than you make in a month, and he'd be the first to tell you so. But he doesn't have to, he's *The Don*.

He stands confidently, purposefully, *aggressively* over the steaming commode, as though he might mount it at any moment. It is, quite frankly, frightening. If he slipped, his cufflinks could give me a concussion.

He is *The Don:* he laughs at the inanity of our informal environment, and unlike our unsmiling CFO Boyd Bender—his direct report—who is simply uncomfortable unless he is not comfortable, *The Don* has more difficult decisions to make each day. In short, there aren't enough occasions to facilitate the threads he owns, so the workplace will have to do. Each time he trims his beard he's made another grand. What's he going to do, wear *T-shirts*? No, he's going to wear suits, like a boy band's pimp. Looking at him, you don't envy or begrudge his sartorial excesses, you find yourself appreciating the fact that he's doing his part to keep the sweatshops solvent, or at least spending all that bread on clothes instead of buying *people*. Would you tell Castro he couldn't wear his camouflage? Would you try to deny Caligula his debasement? Not if you want to keep your job, not if you want to keep on breathing.

* * *

Politicians and military officers pray for trouble, as it provides them with otherwise elusive opportunities: the chance to shine, to focus their energies on enemies they do not need to know, and ascend in ways not imaginable in times of peace.

Conversely, entrepreneurial types, being neither courageous nor useful when the going gets tough, thrive primarily during times of prosperity, lapping up the liquid assets that, like cicadas, spring out of the ground in their chaotic precision. It is axiomatic that bugs and businessmen know enough to enjoy the fruits of nature's labor. And only the suckers fail to realize that the good times won't be around forever. So: there's no time like yesterday to make the types of decisions that can't wait until tomorrow. When you are on your way toward owning a scared new world, there is not enough time for luxuries like *today*.

The rest of us still find the time to sleep at night and occasionally we even let our guards down and take a lunch break.

I bring my own lunch on occasion.

It's always a mistake.

I enjoy eating with Otis, and I tend to look forward to his commentary more than the bark-dry burgers and chlorine-flavored chicken breast sandwiches they serve in the cafeteria. As usual, Otis tends to business before pleasure, and makes sure to get his daily diatribe regarding Jean, his highly motivated and annoyingly ambitious co-worker, out of the way.

"I keep holding back, but she's going to force me to unload on her, and then I'm going to have to make her cry… she's leaving me no choice."

I've never had the misfortune of watching a grown man trade punches with a grown woman, but if half of the email exchanges Otis shows me are true (and how can they not be—they are right there, embossed in electronic memory like insects in ether), then he and Jean are going to brawl eventually, inevitably.

Jean (pronounced *Jean* to her face, *John* behind her back) does what Otis does, only she does it on the fourth floor. They are each expecting to be promoted before the New Year. Only one of them is likely to get the nod, hence the subtle and occasionally explosive tension boiling between them.

Jean is two years younger, so Otis figures she can wait her turn. Otis didn't finish college, so Jean figures she is demonstrably more qualified.

Jean feels that since she administers twice the staff Otis oversees, she clearly warrants consideration; Otis is of the opinion that since the hot shots he handles are ten times more important than the idiots Jean obliges, he obviously is first in the pecking order.

Otis swears the friction can be explained easily. Not surprisingly, he suspects that she wants to sleep with him, even though he's married (*dead*, he calls it) and she is an unconfirmed but obvious lesbian (*dyke*, he calls her). If he'd just suck it up and fuck her, he claims, his problems with work would be solved and her problems with her head would dissolve. I envy Otis the bliss of his ignorance—however willful or at least useful it happens to be—but I don't envy his jaw the day Jean overhears him talking about her.

"If you two go toe to toe, the smart money's on her…"

"She just might drive me to start smoking again."

"How's the cold turkey treating you, anyway?"

"What does it look like?"

"Still craving?"

"Are you kidding?"

"Hang in there man, I'm proud of you."

"You know what I miss most about my Marlboros?"

"What?"

"Everything."

And then, Otis's beeper, which has been suspiciously silent—which more than likely means that the people who always need him are also eating lunch—starts to shriek and just like that, playtime is over.

That's the thing, I think as Otis dashes off to douse another fake-virus brushfire on F5: it's not that he affects a slacker pose, he really *is* undaunted. And, I think (I'm on a roll), it makes perfect sense; a tightly wound person would snap like a snow pea with all the daily crises that occur in this fast-paced but slow-witted arena of world (wide web) domination.

I feel for Otis. He played baseball in high school, therefore he chewed tobacco. He never grew to love it, but that didn't matter because he put it in his mouth long enough and the nicotine took care of the rest. In college he stopped playing baseball but he did not stop dipping.

He got married, had his first kid and figured it was time to put away childish things, so he decided to give up the dip. But that nicotine was a real bitch (shouldn't they *warn* people about this stuff?). It was an ugly month or two, and it led to all sorts of problems at work and at home. Especially at home. But eventually he was able to overcome the desire to stick a golf ball sized wad of powdered snuff between his cheek and gum, and this was not an inconsiderable achievement, considering how long he had been hooked. How did he manage? Easy: he took up smoking.

That worked for a while (which isn't to say his better half was *happy* about it), but his wife finally put her foot down—and he agreed—that it was time to stop the madness.

Now, miserably nicotine-free, he settled for the shitty substitute of sucking on just about anything all the moments he was awake. Chewing gum, mints, candy, toothpicks, peppermint leaves, cough drops, sunflower seeds, pens and pencils, his fingers, his fingernails, paper clips. Sometimes all at once. And he'd put more stuff in, if it would fit.

* * *

As much as I enjoy listening to Chazz's stories, after a while I became wary of his moods, which caused him to be uncomfortably predictable. During the days, he is usually upbeat and affable, but as the interminable afternoons wind down into languid evenings, a somber burden seems to press down on his eyebrows.

"What's the good word?" I ask.

"Shit man, it's a cracker's world and I'm just tryin' to catch a crumb."

"Everything okay?"

"Just one of them days. I got another migraine tryin' to keep a good man down."

"There must be some kind of medicine out there to help with that, right?"

"No man, there isn't," he says grimly. "See, this has been happenin' since I came back from the war—some kind of post-traumatic shit or somethin'."

"You were in Vietnam?" I quickly calculate what his age must be, and it dawns on me that this man, who I regarded as a big brother of sorts, is actually old enough to be my father.

"Yes sir. *Semper Fi*, and all that good stuff."

"Oh, you were a marine then?"

"*Am* a marine, son. Once you're a marine, you're *always* a marine, dig?"

I nod my head and offer a sardonic, but respectful salute.

"Well, isn't there something the service can do for you? I mean with your headaches?"

He smirks.

"I mean, if you're a veteran, they *have* to help, right?"

"Shit man, they don't give a care—less you're an officer."

"Really?"

"Listen, don't make no difference what anyone says, a nigger is still a nigger, 'specially in the corps."

Every time I talk to Chazz I tend to catch myself actually paying attention to what's going on around me. His soliloquies serve as unintentional pep-talks, and when I walk away from him, it's as though I've slipped on secret glasses that enable me to see through the horseshit for a few seconds.

Look: stalled soldiers entrenched in their cubicles, taking work breaks. It's enough to make you want to take up smoking. Why the hell shouldn't we all get to enjoy the bi-hourly five-to-fifteen minute reprieves? When you add it all up, these rebels are doing up to twenty minutes less work an hour than non-smokers; it's the sort of thing you'd be obliged to complain about. Then you realize: it's best not to make mention of other people's productivity unless you're willing to risk calling attention to how little work *you* are actually doing.

* * *

In the elevator we all become imbeciles.

If two people fall on each other in an elevator, does it make any sound? No.

Condo living, if you're lucky, allows you to avoid annoying things, like stairways. On the other hand, if you're unlucky enough to get stuck in the elevator with someone else, you can't escape. To speak or not to speak, this is the question.

I work with people and find I'm seldom at a loss for words; how hard is it to bullshit about anything unimportant, including business, sports, sex, politics, the economy, the environment, or the Internet apocalypse, *anything*? But for some reason, no matter how many times I stand there with people who share the same space (we call ourselves neighbors), the only possible topic of conversation is the one thing we all care the least about: the weather.

Even when I consciously resist it, some gravitational force, some irresistible element, something inherent in my nature takes over and before I realize I hear myself saying those unbelievable words:

Hot out there, huh?

Or, in winter:

Sure is getting cold!

And then we panic, pause and smile nervously at each other for the remainder of the ten-second eternity until one of us escapes the steel cage. And these aren't strangers, they're *neighbors*! Why is it that I can roll with the smiles and frowns and talk smack with just about anyone I encounter: on the streets, in the men's room (only when appropriate and mutually consented, of course), at concerts or sporting events, even in my godamned *dreams*, but here, only in the elevator, I become a sweaty, stammering deaf-mute. I find myself wishing for scandalous things, like, say, situational Tourette's Syndrome. Anything to inspire something approximating small talk.

Thank God for my dog. He is usually with me at these moments, and in his inimitable, honest (and wordless) way, he can defuse several seconds of silent agony. He lets his tail do the talking, and with the absence of agenda or guile, he conveys what humans have spent many millennia unable to imitate.

* * *

I may not be dying, but I'm most definitely getting older. My body is turning on me, endlessly amusing itself with new ways of betraying my trust.

It's been a long day—on the couch. (That's another part of getting too old too soon—the beers you drank are still sticking around long after they have served their purpose. Wouldn't it be nice to simply pay to make them go *away* as easily as you pay to acquire them?)

Fortunately, I am able to distract myself from the horrors of my hangover by focusing all my attention on the water that has inexplicably gotten stuck in my ear. At least I *think* it's water. At least I haven't reached the point of worrying whether it's blood leaking from my brain. Or something.

So: I'm leaning my head to one side—compounding the agony because I read that the cause of hangover is dehydration—you don't have enough *water* in your body, and the reason the room spins is because your dizzy brain loses the juice that otherwise keeps it floating in gray complacency. And here I am, with fluid in my fucking ear. Maybe if I could just transport *that* water into my brain it would all even out.

Then: should I lean the other way to get the fluid back in?

Then: hot, sticky, unsatisfactory sleep.

Teasing me: a few false starts. I can sense the slightest movement, but it's only a shadow, nothing is going anywhere. I remember, as a kid, putting peroxide in my ear after swimming and with a few seconds of miraculous tingles, it was dry as the Pope's dick. I could use some now but I don't have any peroxide handy, as, after all, I am no longer a kid.

Asleep. Dreaming?

Almost there: and then my breathing becomes one with the ear canal and slowly, seductively, a honey drip of fragile motion.

Awake.

I sit up carefully. It starts to trickle, glacially, a fever breaking, a thousand babies' burps, burnt-out batteries firing with life, a dry tsunami crashing over a skyline of cotton.

"Oh God," (I whisper).

"Is this it?"

But I *know* this is it. I just can't do anything to disrupt it. I sit still, ecstatic. Finally. It pops like a silent explosion.

"Oh God it's coming! Oh God!"

My poor neighbors. They must be amused or else appalled, hearing me, visualizing the sordid deed, a young man masturbating so shamelessly. So brazen, so loud. If only I could tell them the truth. Tell them how much better this is than beating off.

Reality Check (5)

Check you out.

Sober, sane, smiling. A saccharine coated reverie, dissolving in the light of day, awake and alive in the darkness. And more: you see yourself, doing what you once thought you might do, in front of students, talking about the artists who inspire us or ameliorate our collective angst, somehow. Not giving two shits about salary, not associating with the types who measured their worth by the things they could theoretically own if they theoretically had any interests outside of accruing 0's at the end of the theoretical checks they might theoretically write anytime. And more: feeling connected to lives outside your own (again), leaving a mark, intimacy above and beyond those occasional encounters, that fleeting human touch, seeing yourself (someday) inside a separate set of eyes. And still more: eventually becoming a character in one of those books you admired so much but no longer found the time to read.

It's not too late.

To yourself you say this.

Six

DAYDREAMS AND NIGHTMARES

THESE DREAMS ARE trying to tell me something:
I find myself back in high school. Often. At night.
The bell rings, students scurry, locker combinations
are unscrambled. Except mine.

What is my fucking locker combination?

All around me doors are opening and slamming shut, my buddies all about business, the pictures of pin-ups inside their lockers replaced by pictures of their kids. My homeroom buddy, with the beer gut, easily fitting his briefcase into the small space, and here I am, imploding in this typical teenage crisis, attempting to be cool while the anxiety escalates on the inside: high school redux.

I'm going to be late for class—again!

And then, this: Shit! This is the math class I haven't been to in two months (who could blame me, what with a full time job during school hours—a fact conveniently ignored in the insanity of this recurring scenario), more than two months, an eternity in dream years, and I'm not even sure what room it's in. So here I am, unable to open my locker, again, realizing I'm late for the class I have already failed.

And that's the least of my worries. I still have to contend with what's-his-name, the African American (I would have said black, but I was old school) class bully who is built like a brick shit-house, the one who is admirably open minded in his ability to democratize the art of ass-kicking. He plays no favorites; anyone smaller than him (and *everyone* is smaller than him) is fair game for his cinder block fists, and he takes each day one kidney punch at a time, a shove here and a trip there and a pulled, almost *loving* punch to the caved in chests of his favorite targets. There was one rule, sacred as it was incomprehensible: show no signs of pain or fear, and take your beating like a pretty-big boy. Any words, any wincing, whining, or outward signs of being affected—including the ultimate catastrophe: tears—and a real beating might ensue.

But it wasn't the brothers you feared, it was the black girls— the sisters—that one avoided at all costs. (You saw what they did to *each other* when they fought, you could only imagine what they'd do to you). True, the boys could *kill* you, but males often use only guns to kill one another, their weapons of choice being intimidation, and its close cousin, humiliation, which every teen-ager knows is worse than death. But the sisters meant business, and they didn't do half measures. They talked big, they laughed big, and they *hurt* big.

The last thing anyone ever wanted to do was allow them to notice you noticing them, no matter what they were doing.

"The fuck *you* looking at home slice?"

Or,

"You *know* I'll slap the shit out of you. Right shorty?"

Shorty. Home slice. Punk. White boy.

No worries.

But if you heard *motherfucker*, that was your ass.

Here was the thing: if push came to punch, and one of them really tried to hurt you, you had to take it. Take the beating, the embarrassment, the medicine. Because if you dared to defend yourself—and only then—the brothers got involved. And those were the kinds of beatings that tears and time could not cure. If the brothers decided to beat you, you stayed beat. Beat down. And heaven forbid the beating made you a target: you might as well quit school and go work in the coalmines or on the farm in 1880, or enter a monastery, because nothing good was going to come out of the rest of your high school life.

These dreams are trying to tell me something, I know. I'm just not sure what it is.

* * *

Daydream notion. Sitting on the porch on a Sunday afternoon. Too early to start drinking, too late to stop myself from the too many drinks I had last night, wondering things like: how seriously should you consider the expiration date on a jar of mayonnaise?

Hungover. Overhung. Hung out to dry heave. Name it. If it's bad, that's me.

Inhaling fast food (obviously), wondering how much my liver will let me push it around before it stands up and says *I'm not going to take this anymore!* It's too hard to think and eat, so I concentrate on the food, trying not to acknowledge how incredibly awful this crap is (bad for me, bad for the environment, bad for the people who make minimum wage selling it, bad for the people who make less than minimum wage manufacturing it, and especially bad for the miserable animals whose synthetic lives are sacrificed so that we can do all these bad things).

Every time I eat fast food it's like having sex with an old girl-friend. I'll start to think about it: lustfully, then obsessively, then violently. I need to have it, and when I'm finally enjoying it there is nothing better, nothing else in the wretched world exists while I'm getting it on, getting it in me, devoting every iota of my being into the sullied enterprise. Eventually, inevitably, it ends, and the second it's over those intolerable feelings of guilt begin. The sloth, the lack of control, the sickening pangs of self-loathing. *Et cetera.* And I promise myself never to do it again. Then the whole room reeks of what just went down, and it hangs in the air, imploding like an enraged cloud until, in my defiant fashion, I get hungry again and the smell starts to distract me until I can't take it, and I need more. Immediately.

Later: it's late, we're alive, and I suddenly wish I were alone.

It was as good for her (I hope) as it was for me, and after, we lie down in darkness, with no choice but to talk since neither of us happens to smoke.

-Tell me about it, I say.
-Tell you what? she asks.
-What's your story? I ask.
-I got laid off, she says.
-Shitcanned? I ask.
-No, downsized, she says.
-Everyone gets downsized, I say.
-They do these days, she says.
-Unless you're lucky, I say.
-You've been lucky so far, she says.
-Yes, that's why I'm so miserable, I say.
-Tell me about it, she says.

* * *

Listen:

Some are born to sweet delight;
Some are born to endless night.

I didn't write that.

Look:
Jim Morrison, I saw you today at the Chinese buffet.

And I couldn't help noticing how you weren't dead. Even worse, you are alive: old, enduring, human. Mysterious no more, all that messy magic evaporated. Exhaustion in your eyes, a stumbling gait imitating your once svelte Lizard King prowl. A resigned beard, an indifferent slouch, a southern drawl softly supplanted your butterfly scream. And here are some things I was afraid to ask:

How was it?

To grow old and die at twenty-seven—then, to start over again: a plaything of the gods and their fickle fantasies.

How did it feel?

A lifetime of summer Sundays in only six years, a papier-mâché soul, a black and blue brain, dying nightly and living only to die.

How is it?

Burned inside out, counting yourself unlucky among the living and this banana peel reality: church on Sunday, a dream deferred to the safety of TV dinners and insipid re-runs before bedtime.

This is the end, my friend.

Stop. (Look, listen):

I can't stop spending; money runs through me like a sieve, I bleed green bills. And those are just my bar tabs.

And yet. I'd rather eat well than accessorize. Who gives a flying fuck how much my bed cost? Just give me a so-so night's sleep. Your dining room table cost you *what*? Did it make your breakfast taste any better?

Give me fuel. Allow me life. Light my fire.

These idiots with their Mercedes muscles, their stock-optioned Swiss savings accounts, their Ivy League egos; or even worse, the dumb luck got rich quick goofballs, of which there must be more now—after the eve of the millennium turned out to be a bust and our stock turned into the snake in the Garden of Eden—than ever, what with the ephemeral oil fields of the Internet.

And yet.

I'll be honest. I make more money than I know what to do

with, and that's coming from someone who spent two years *after* college speculating about all the ways he might someday spend his money.

More honesty?

I don't feel the least bit ambivalent about it. This is America, I'm an American, I am addicted, and that's the end of it. It's the money dread: you can draw a line in the sand connecting money-lenders in the Temple to fat-cats on Wall Street to tightfisted towel-heads inflating the prices of oil sold to robber barons in high rises looking down on schizophrenics sprung from asylums, sleeping under newspapers proclaiming that the rich are getting richer. It always, in the end, is about the haves and have-nots. But that has nothing to do with me; telling me to *think* is like asking me not to breathe.

I make money. So I spend my days inventing new ways to give myself nightmares and the only thing that matters is that the game began long before I got here and it won't even be halftime a hundred years after I'm gone. The world will turn a billion years after the big players in the here and now crash and burn like so many miniature suns.

* * *

Question: Do you ever think you drink too much?

Answer: Every time I wake up with a hangover or beside a woman whose name I can't recall, I'm obliged to reassess my commitment to this mess I'm in.

The catch is, while I'm thinking it over and evaluating my issues, I invariably pour myself a drink—just on principle.

Delirium Tremens.

What kind of bullshit is *that*?

Thinking man's hangover; a fancy term for people who can't handle a little adversity. Just take your medicine like a man and stop whining about your shaking hands.

DTs? That's why God invented Gatorade. If you're really in a bad way, accidentally slip a little vodka in there and you're good to go.

I guess that's the whole point though. Your body lets you know it doesn't expect to get you through this without some *pain*. Now it's a matter of seeing whether sobriety wins out over winohood, your spot already squatting for rights on the street corner. It ain't pretty, but it's a living. For some folks. For the folks who can't afford country club incarceration, a nurse with an IV injecting over-the-counter ambrosia, restoring your precious bodily fluids. Fight fire with fire, or go down in flames. A made for TV mini-series, one martini at a time. A few beers Monday night, a few beers Tuesday night, a few dozen beers Wednesday night, and the obligatory Bloody Mary aftermath, followed by stoic, strictly administered sobriety, for twenty-four hours. Then, amazingly, it's the weekend. Again.

* * *

-What's up Whitey.

-Hey man, you got a sec?

-Always.

-Okay. Uh, well you know…

-Talk to me.

-I was thinking…

-That was your first mistake (To myself I say this).

-Well, I was thinking about that the other day, because I have an amazing new strategy I wanted to share.

-Oh? What's that?

-I tell chicks that I've decided not to have sex for an entire year, kind of clear my head or my system, a purifying philosophy, or some shit like that…

-Uh…

-You know, turn the tables, I don't want it, I'm not even *looking* for it.

-Sounds very faux-Zen…

-*Exactly!*
-Does it work?
-Like a fucking charm.
-Or, a non-fucking charm (To myself I say this).
-How can you tell?
-Trust me.
-Be careful bro.
-Why?
-It could become a self-fulfilling prophecy, you tell women you won't do it, it might come true, you know, bad karma and all that...
-Karma shmarma, it's all an excuse anyway.
-Excuse for what?
-Ever since I started this medication I can hardly ever get it up anyway...
-Uh.
-I mean the drive is dissipated...
-Uh.
-At least that's what my doctor said. So, you know, if I have to put my libido in a footlocker anyway, I might as well *get* something out of it, right?
-But what are you getting?
-I'm getting *laid!*
-I thought you just said you *weren't...*
-That's just an act.
-I thought you just said you *couldn't...*
-I can't, but *they* don't know that.
-Uh.
-The thing is, these women *want* me.
-But you can't *do* anything...
-Yeah, but it still counts. If they still want *me*, it counts.
-Counts?
-You know, if you *can* get laid, it still counts for getting laid, right?
-Uh...

-The bottom line is, I'm en fuego!

-Whitey, I'm glad to hear this medication is working such wonders for you.

-Hey, thanks man.

-Anytime.

-We're still on this weekend, right?

-On what?

-Our tee-time is eight sharp.

-How are we going to golf in the dark?

-Huh?

-Eight o'clock?

-Yeah, A.M. That's eight o'clock in the *morning.*

-The morning?

-Obviously!

-Whitey?

-Yeah?

-I don't get to *work* that early…

-I'm telling you, you're going to love it!

Whitey freaked out.

He got better.

Some people don't.

* * *

"You'll learn to love it," Whitey says, and while I'm not a gambling man, I feel certain this is a bet he would lose.

I drink too much and exercise too little, and—based on what I see all around me—I can't figure out if I should feel grateful or dejected.

Grateful because half of the people I see are disgraceful: tomato-jowled fatsos huffing and puffing their way to a first heart attack. They're dressed identically: khaki slacks and double extra-large polo shirts that are still three sizes too small, tucked in so that their guts—marvels of sheer mass, spherical monsters poised to attack, or at least make a break for it, restrained only by those tireless belts, heroically strapped in their holding patterns—can do everything in their power to hold gravity hostage.

The other half are the opposite end of the spectacle, and cause me to question why I can't summon the desire to stop treating my body like a temple of doom: these carb-counting, cardio-conversant, protein shake pounding members of the bionic boys club. These are the men who have nursed crushes all their lives, but are only now ready to commit and confess to the world how much they truly love themselves. The kind of men who had sex with their wives and felt like it was an act of betrayal. Men supremely confident to grow mustaches without irony, men who washed their cars more often than most people wash their sheets, men who never heard a compliment they couldn't improve upon.

Only in one place could one find so seamless a pairing of extremes: the golf course. Obviously.

"Wow," I say. "This is even worse than I imagined."

"You better get used to it," Whitey says.

"How do you figure?"

"You better learn to love it if you want to get anywhere in this business."

"In this business? What business do you mean, the asshole business?"

"Hey man, I'm just telling you like it is."

"So what's next, you're going to tell me that I'll need to fuck my boss to get promoted?"

"You should be so lucky," he says, jokingly. I think. "If only it were that easy," he adds, jokingly. I hope.

"Whitey, please do me a favor."

"What?"

"Say something that doesn't make me want to beat the crap out of you."

"I'm serious dude, this is how business gets done!"

"Business?"

"Doctors, lawyers, businessmen. Deals get closed on golf courses more often than offices."

As is too often the case with Whitey, I can't help but wonder if there is a book people have to read in order to spout this sort of shit, or if it's simply a result of assiduously *avoiding* reading in the first place.

"Whitey, have you ever heard of H.L. Mencken?"

"Who?"

"Never mind."

"Did he win the Masters or something?"

"Not exactly."

"Look, if you want to get your colleagues to trust you, do it out here, on the links. This is how you *bond* with the big boys."

Why the fuck would I want to bond with any of those imbeciles? I don't ask.

I only need them to trust me as far as they can throw me, I think.

"If you say so," I say.

"I know so," says Whitey.

He's right about one thing: *everyone* plays golf. I was almost surprised when I discovered that *The Don* and the rest of the honchos couldn't be bothered to blow off six or twelve hours every week. Then again, they're probably too busy playing with money to goof around with golf; they are too busy *buying* golf courses to play golf. Myself, I usually sleep on Sunday mornings. Everyone else, it seems, is either on the golf course or in church. As far as I can tell, I haven't been missing much. As far as I can tell, golf affords grown men the opportunity to accomplish two things: get out of work (or, if they are married, out of the house on weekends) and drink beer. Not that I'm necessarily opposed to either activity, but I usually don't have to dress up like a frat boy from the early '80s to make it happen. And I certainly don't have to shell out sixty bucks to ride around in a cart and occasionally jump out to whack my ball into the woods or in the water.

"Couldn't we at least have brought some *good* beer?" I ask.

"You have to bring cans," he explains. "That way you can cram them into your golf bag."

We could always not drink, I don't say.

"You learned to love it," I offer.

"Eh…"

"You don't love it?"

"I used to love it, then I got better…"

"So?"

"Now I'm just good enough that I hate it."

"Oh, so it only gets better from here." I sigh.

"You'll see." He smiles.

Here's the real kicker: a lot of these dudes will get up while it's still *dark* outside so they can squeeze in a semi-quick eighteen holes before heading into the office. I can't fathom it. And yet, I have no option but to admire that level of lunacy, disguised as dedication. Myself, I feel pretty confident that if someone offered to shovel free money into my car, but I had to show up before six A.M., I'd happily hit my snooze button a few more times instead. It's already getting chilly in the mornings and early evenings, so I wonder what these sportsmen do with themselves during the winter months. Sleep? Watch TV? Get to know their children again? Anything, I reckon, rather than spending more time at work. And on that score, finally we find some common ground.

"Lookit," Whitey says, iron in one hand, can of (awful) beer in the other, unlit cigarette dangling. "*This* is America!"

Reluctantly, I have no real choice but to agree with him.

* * *

Look:

More death and destruction. On TV, obviously.

Only this is the worst one yet, the most gruesome, uncomfortable competition I've ever made myself suffer through. Worse than football. Worse than hockey. Worse than *golf* even—for me, the viewer. Even worse than crocodiles sneaking up on poor, parched zebras that may or may not know death is waiting in the water, but they'll die if they don't drink, so they take their chances. Something's going to get them, sooner or later. This is worse, because these are humans. And they're well fed, intelligent and entirely willing to engage in the war of attrition that will leave all but one of them deposed and defeated.

The national spelling bee.

This shit is unbelievable. This is not something I need right now, but I can't turn away. I'm a nervous wreck, watching these overtaxed adolescents putting their brains on the line just to make their parents proud. I can't console myself thinking about the lucky kid who will eventually emerge the winner; I'm stuck feeling sorry for all the other saps that have to lose, one by one.

I'd help them if I could, but none of them can hear me. Then there's the unfortunate fact that not only can't I spell most of the words. I've never even heard of half of them.

I watch, and I wait, and think about all this useless beauty—the simpler things I turned the TV on for in the first place.

Who won?

I have no idea.

I can't take it anymore. I don't have any more tears to shed. I want to see who will win, but not as badly as I want *not* to see that second-to-last kid lose. The close-up on his parents committing Hari-Kari as the cameras roll. I can't handle it. I turn it off.

Suddenly, my dog becomes very excited, as he is known to do, and I (nicely) ask him to shut up, as I'm known to do. When I can't convince him to calm down I finally survey the scene outside and see what he is so enthralled with: two small squirrels, rolling around beside a tree.

So what? (To myself I say this).

Then it occurs to me that I honestly cannot ascertain if these creatures are fucking or fighting. Then I wonder, briefly, if I should be disappointed with myself. And then, this: am I *supposed* to know? Haven't humans made sufficient advances over the years so that

I *don't* have to know this type of shit? Certainly, I could be more acquainted with the earth, and the ecology, and the types of slow, studious observations that enable one to determine the difference between two squirrels fussing and two squirrels fornicating. But then, I could also be a lot more acquainted with cold, and hunger, and polio, and tuberculosis, and child slavery and the myriad anti-blisses our ancestors' ingenuity afford me to remain ignorant of. I didn't make this world, but this world most definitely made me.

In that moment you forget who and where you are: slowly closing your eyes to escape the sunlight, suddenly you are eleven years old, standing in your basement, smelling the dank linen and dusty, discarded boxes of books—alone in the darkness. Standing over the sealed glass jar, an inadvertent god surveying a world you had unwittingly created, catching your breath as the stench closes around you, indicting you: that dark mass of slowly moving forms...

Quickly, you force the memory away and you are back—yourself again—opening your eyes to cars on every side, to the synchronous sound of slowly shifting gears.

You look up tiredly at the makeshift billboard hanging beside the road, a solicitous beacon calling out to the commuters:

ONLY 5 REMAINING!
STARTING IN THE LOW 500'S
COME SEE THE DIFFERENCE!

What difference? (you think). Construction of this project coincided with the then semi-tolerable commute to your new job. Now, only a few years later it's completed, proving that if there's money to be made, houses and highways and buildings can sprout up in no time at all. Maximum occupancy, you think, measuring these methodical lines of brick townhouses. They called them town homes *now. The more congruent and indistinguishable modern homes became, the greater an effort these canny developers exerted to create the illusion of autonomy—wistful compensation for the fact that these particular models were stacked to utilize every available square foot of space.*

CONVENIENT AND CLOSE TO
WHERE YOU NEED TO BE!

How inviting, you had thought. All that stood between the houses and the highway was a broad granite wall, which was at once a decisive and dubious boundary.

This is the spot where the traffic comes to an inexplicable stand-still each morning. You catch yourself clenching and slowly retract your jaw, running your tongue along the roof of your mouth. This habit you developed in college, when the introduction of stress was accompanied by the grinding of teeth while you slept. When you took this job, that compulsion reared its irritating head again, only now you were doing it (often) in your waking hours as well.

"You're going to grind them down to chalk," your dentist warned you with the smug authority of a man who had so mastered his profession and personal hygiene that such imperfect habits were beyond his comprehension. As a remedy that seemed remarkably state-of-the-art despite its almost comical simplicity, the doctor had fashioned a plastic mouth guard, designed from a mold of your bite imprint, which was to fit comfortably in your mouth, effectively impeding the activity of those overzealous reflexes. But you could not bring yourself to wear the expensive apparatus. It was too ridiculous, too embarrassing a concession of weakness.

Unconsciously inserting your tongue between your teeth, you stare at the gray wall, which seems, the more you see it, an extension of the development rather than a barrier. Had it been designed to lull these new homeowners into forgetting that they were practically spitting distance from one of the most inefficient highways in America? Breathing the fumes of a million cars. Perhaps this was the payoff for living in the suburbs, ensconced in the cocoon of oak trees and manicured lawns and shopping malls, away from the squalid strain and strangeness of the city.

How do they do it?

When you pondered this question, it usually bolstered a certain disdain: an awareness that you were not one of them. *Increasingly though, you've found that this reassurance was necessary in order to assuage a creeping disenchantment: uncertainty about the job, enduring this commute, and the unnerving sense that somehow you were missing something—that you had failed to attain what everyone else seemed to be in possession of. So you repeat to yourself, like a mantra, that you know who you are, that the choice had been* yours, *that you had control over the decisions you made; that you were, in short, your own man.*

Staring at the gray wall, it occurs to you, seemingly for the first time, that there were actually real *people inside those houses, people who* wanted *to live there, and who very possibly were at that moment looking out their fashionable bay windows, watching you in your car—inseparable from the infinite array of shining steel shapes—scoffing at your participation in this tedious ritual. And to your sudden, not quite disbelief, you find yourself entertaining the viability, the practicality of these houses, and the sagacity of the folks who chose to live in them.* I bet those people don't have to wake up an hour earlier just to get to work on time! *The voice rings mockingly in your head.*

The forward progress lasts for a few minutes and then stops again. You look in your rearview mirror at the endless line of cars, speculating how many tons of machinery presently surround you. A carbon monoxide factory, you think sardonically, measuring the dark shapes that stretch back as far as you can see. A factory that produces noise. And pollution. I'm probably dying right now, you think, abruptly rolling up your window. Every man for himself. *That voice, again. Taunting you, as always.*

"Every man for himself," you repeat out loud. Bottlenecked on the freeway each morning, like a bunch of crickets *(and again you recall that afternoon and the stench that greeted you as you descended the stairs)...*

"No," *you shake the recollection away.* Ten more minutes. You'll be out in ten minutes.

Seven

NICE WORK IF YOU CAN GET IT

"PUBLIC SENTIMENT IS everything. With public sentiment, nothing can fail; without it nothing can succeed."

The man running the meeting looks approvingly around the room. "Does anyone know who said that?"

No one volunteers an answer, but if I had to wager on it, I'd guess it was a politician, probably a president. I am not mistaken.

"That's Abraham Lincoln, ladies and gentlemen," our leader informs us—though, ironically (or not) there are only men in this particular meeting.

I look around the room.

One of the wonderful things about working at (insert name of company here) is the casual environment. *The Don*, who is even smarter than he dresses, has inculcated an atmosphere that manages to be loose and yet almost fascist in its conformity. How? The T-shirts, which serve as everyone's unofficial uniform. It's an anti-dress code dress code.

Unfortunately, one of the advantages of working on F5, surrounded by the supermen who keep (insert name of company here) safe from the competitors that no longer exist, is that I am unable to sport the khakis, polos and T-shirts like all the worker casual mannequins who populate the comparatively laid-back cube farms on the floors beneath me. No one, of course, ever said I *couldn't* dress like the others, but I feel awkward enough each time the industrial overhead track lights ricochet off *The Don's* platinum tie clips into my dutifully averted eyes that dressing, like any other employee, would only accentuate how much I am just like every other employee.

* * *

Question: What do I do for a living?

I work, that's what.

And whoever said you were supposed to *like* your job?

My father worked over forty years as a repairman, and I never heard him say a good word about it

What did he repair?

He fixed anything, refrigerators, air conditioners, washing machines, name it. And he had to spend his days, his entire adult life, going into other people's houses to fix their things. His job was to make broken things work, the things people were too cheap, or too stubborn to replace, or too damn ignorant to fix themselves. So he had to spend his days inside of houses he could not afford and would never live in, being reminded of all the things he did not have. He hated them all, and said it was only the job itself, the process of fixing things, that gave him any satisfaction. Doing the job right, he'd say, is something you can hang your hat on. And so, even though he despised these people whose patronage he depended upon, he went out every day and made their broken things unbroken. He did his job.

Me, I'm just biding my time until somebody figures out that I somehow earned tenure without even completing the coursework. But is there coursework anymore? Everyone knows the drill: if you can sell, you'll find work; if you can write, it's like having an inexhaustible supply of get out of jail free cards.

Check it out:

Thank you for contacting the office of (insert name of CEO here). Your concerns are very important, and while the volume of correspondence prevents me from personally responding to each letter, I have a staff dedicated to…

That's me, I'm that guy.

If you've ever emailed (insert name of company here), you've received this response.

I wrote it.

And I'm that staff, I'm the go-to guy for these issues that are deemed sufficiently important to warrant a staff to address them, to ensure that they are communicated to the powers-that-be, so that they can promptly do nothing about them.

Listen:

Thank you for bringing this matter to my attention. While we recognize that our business would be impossible without your support, we also strive to keep the best interest of all of our customers in mind…

Real people used to recite those lines, using real words on real phones in real time. Now I simply *write* them. One advantage of running a corporation in the electronic age is not needing to waste money on stamps, and you can theoretically reply to any complaint the same day you receive it. One disadvantage of the electronic age is the otherwise unthinkable volume of correspondence free postage encourages. Five years ago my job could not have been created, or even imagined.

Nice work if you can get it. Of course, five years (or five weeks, or five minutes) from now my job might be eliminated. So I've got that going for me.

Thank you for taking the time to write us! If you didn't I wouldn't be able to respond. In fact, I probably wouldn't have a job.

To myself I type this.

Mondays are always challenging, especially in the men's room. Lots of asses cashing checks their stomachs wrote over the weekend, emboldened by the beer, the burgers, the televised sports, disappointed by ill-timed turgidity, zigged and zagged by dreams of money and nightmares of privation, all combining to produce this consolidated omen of ill scents, a very modern and unfortunate aromatherapy.

Everyone poops. Ask Otis's two-and-a-half year old son and he'll tell you. But only executives poop on F5, and I do my best to keep it that way.

It's not that I feel awkward emerging from the stall; after all, everyone poops. But I'm acutely aware of the discomfort it causes leaders of men like Boyd Bender to step up to the sink and see someone like me seeing him. Never mind the fact that most of the honchos on F5 are too busy, or too rich, to impart their cherished time to such uneconomical considerations as bodily functions.

So I do the trite thing. I retreat to the anonymity of other floors, eager to imitate one of the blithe, liberated nobodies who don't know how good they've got it.

And yet. Everyone *pees*, too. Even me.

The people who pay me might not be mortal, but the smells they create are very human. And so: I've adapted; I can hold my breath for over thirty seconds. Just like the bridge builders grew comfortable being underwater for ungodly periods of time, I too am sucking it in and holding on for dear life. As always, there is nothing quite like necessity to assist one in overcoming otherwise unobtainable obstacles.

But thirty seconds is never enough. And then, even if I could find the wherewithal to break world records: three seconds to the stall, the fastest piss in history, half second to zip up (Ouch! Careful there), two seconds to the sink, five seconds to lather, rinse and wash, a furtive grasp for the towel dispenser and then desperation sets in. At this moment I realize that it's too late, the smell has already begun to seep in through my ears, assaulting my hair, assailing my eyes, embalming my body.

Everyone poops, I remind myself. But not everyone is lucky enough to smell the shit these great men produce on F5.

* * *

The first Monday of the month means another workweek, means another flight from here to there. I never used to travel and still am unsure why suddenly so much money is being spent so I can sit in meetings where everyone stares at their laptops. I know things are changing, and all of these meetings are starting to make me think bigger changes are about to belly up to the bar. The types of changes that are going to dislocate many of my non-traveling colleagues, of which more later. During the plane ride I am, as usual, in no mood for casual conversation, especially when I see that the flight is nightclub capacity. Now, if your job is one that requires even moderate air travel, then you know that my disdain goes much deeper than a simple lack of elbowroom. Which is to say, if you have a low threshold of tolerance for idle chatter with happy-go-lucky head cases or irredeemably bitter creased-collars who, like yourself, can't afford first class (in other words, if you are *normal*), then it is imperative to minimize all interference.

I'm not in the big city yet, but I'm in big city mode. And the more you travel, the more imperative it becomes to armor yourself from the soft thoughts that accompany life in the outside world. Give me the city any day, and as many different cities as possible. Enough so that, after a while, all the places look the same, and the faces all blend into one another. Everyone knowing what's expected of them and going about it, living their lives.

And yet. I spent enough time in church growing up that, no matter how hard I might try; I can't quite clean the Catholicism out of me. Invariably, as I try not to look around, I catch myself thinking things. Such as, should I at least make myself available, at least open my eyes to whomever might be in need, some stranger who is seeking me out? (Always, on the subway or the airport shuttle, or any of the daytime nightmares unfolding each second in every city on the face of the earth, you find yourself avoiding those eyes but thinking: *In heaven this won't matter.* And yet. If eternity holds the promise of, among other delights, a steady diet of semi-retarded soliloquies and deficient dental work and the desperate need to crack the code of secrets that never made sense, all of a sudden the prospects of oblivion—that long, uninterrupted nap—hold a previously unimaginable appeal.)

Then, of course: the only thing less clichéd than looking for Christ amidst the least of your brothers is searching for a savior amongst the double-breasted pretty boys sitting in business class. It's more comforting, more sane, to blend in amongst the apathy—those pursed lips concealing professionally polished fangs—and eyes that only look inward, unable to find a soul and not particularly anxious either way.

Reality Check (7)

You're listening to the old woman again.

This is another part of your daily routine: every time you enter the building after walking your dog, or if you're stopping to get the mail, or anytime you are anywhere between your front door and the main entrance, this woman (you have no other option but to say she is an old *woman) whose name you of course cannot remember, appears like a mosquito at a campsite.*

She is there every time—every time—if you're walking out (you've learned not to step out of your door in only your boxer shorts) to throw your trash down the chute, she's there; if you are coming or going to work, she's there; if you open your door (you've learned not to open your door without your boxer shorts on) to get the newspaper, she's there; and especially if you're returning with rapidly cooling carry-out food, she's there.

You had half-seriously begun to consider whether or not she had rigged your door to some sort of homing device, and then you slowly started to notice, over time, it isn't just you (of course *it isn't just you)—it's even worse than that. It's everyone, it's anyone: anyone she can see or talk to, anyone she can make that human touch with, however fleetingly, any excuse she can find to escape the oppression of her immaculate isolation.*

Eight

POETRY & PORNOGRAPHY

"SO WHAT DO you *really* want to do?"

As usual, Chazz has waited until everyone else on the floor cleared out, and then come calling. As usual, I don't mind his company.

"I don't know," I say truthfully. "I guess I'd eventually like to put my degree to some use. Maybe teaching or something."

"Yeah, I could see that…" he says. "See, now that makes sense to me, man. I can see you workin' with people, lightin' them minds up."

"You can?"

"Aw man, that'd be a good look for you, talkin' about books and stuff, like you do with me up here…"

"Some days I have a vision of what I need to do."

"So what's stoppin' you?"

"Other times I'm not so sure what I need to do."

We both laugh, but then he looks at me and points his finger at his head.

"You'll do the right thing bro, I know you're good people. I got faith in you."

Question: What do you really want to do?
    Answer: Not what I'm doing.
    What do you do?
    I'm a poet. And I know it.
    I'm a poet for the wrong people.
    Do they know it?
    Do they care?
    Do I?

Listen: the world doesn't owe you a living. The world doesn't owe you *anything*.
    Take Chazz.
    He's a lot sharper than he lets on, and I'm not even certain how much he's even letting on. He talks a good game. And I believe him. Or, I *want* to believe him. Or: all the jive talk is an indirect way of conveying that he isn't jiving. He is dead serious. So much so that he has to make light of it. He simply, or sadly, is lacking the ways and means to instigate the types of action a more radical acumen—in another time, or place, or person—might otherwise engender.
    I can easily understand where some of that scarcely-concealed frustration springs from: if he'd been unsuccessful, even unable, to find a suitable channel for that acerbic—but often astute—assessment of our world, he's had that much more time to stockpile his ammunition. His ability to communicate, his arsenal, could be gunpowder: rife for enterprise, and explosion. His dispossession simply did to him what it does eventually, inevitably, to everyone else: obstructs agency, leaving one ineffectual, an observer.
    Like myself, he could have eaten up like so much angry candy all of the lightweight, part-time agitators and anarchists I'd once run with. If he had been let loose on the facile battlefields of some college campus, he might have attained a proper—and positive—outlet for those passions and the ire that fed them. He easily would

have rolled with the earnest students who dive headfirst into the incendiary screeds of the ever-underground revolution: DuBois, Fanon, Ellison, Baldwin, Baraka, whomever. He could speak and people would pay to listen—even if they were only other students.

And then? And then it's up to the individual to take it to the next level, whatever that might be. Stop reading, writing and talking. Time to act, and time ain't on your side. And then: if you no longer have the drink, or the drugs, if you don't have the big bucks, and all you can come up with are excuses, what the hell are you *supposed* to do?

Send in the clowns.

* * *

I surf the net.

Everyone does. And just about everyone is looking at porn all day. And that's only counting the ones who'll admit it.

"What is your *problem?*"

Otis is standing next to me, pointing at my computer.

"What?"

"Well, every time I come in here to sneak up on you, you're reading, like, *book reviews* and shit…"

"Yeah?"

"Well… what the fuck?"

"It's better than working."

"That's not the point."

"What's the point?"

"Porn is the point."

"Uh…"

"What part of nudity do you not understand?"

"Don't get me wrong, I enjoy beautiful women as much… well, maybe not *as* much as some, okay, *most* people… well, anyway, I have no problems with soft porn."

"So then what's the problem?"

"I suppose I'd rather approximate reading a book…"

"What the fuck are you talking about?"

"I'm talking about *fucking*. When it comes to having sex, I'd much rather have the real thing, that's all."

"So would everyone, even people who actually have it... hell, *especially* people who actually get it. Trust me."

"So?"

"So, *that* is the appeal of porn."

* * *

You know it when you see it, someone once said about pornography. With good music you know it when you hear it. And when it comes to sexual harassment, you know it when you do it, which is why you don't do it. So who does it? The usual types of people. People who don't know better, people who don't know they are doing it. People, in other words, who are not here today.

"So," our grim-faced facilitator begins. "Can someone give me an example of sexual harassment in the workplace?"

No one says anything.

"Anybody," the woman standing at the front of the room says. A question, or a dare.

"Do you mean like from personal experience?"

Otis, obviously.

"Do you have an example from your own experience?"

"Not that I could share with the group," Otis says, mirthfully. He shoots me a wink and then subtly shifts into business mode. "No, I'm just kidding. Obviously, being a man, I've witnessed all sorts of questionable stuff... I've always wanted to know the best way to expose it."

Otis, I am beginning to understand (and appreciate, and envy) is a genius. He has figured out—or, even better, instinctively understands—how to straddle the line between disgraceful brown-nosing and distracting banter. Sometimes they are the same thing, but an effective employee can't perform the former without a facility for the latter. As such, he is always the uninvisible elephant in the room: his mostly jovial irreverence provides enough entertainment value to keep any meeting, or mandatory training session like this one, from hanging itself with the rope of its own awkward self-importance.

Where would we be without an Otis amongst us?

Listen: "I feel there needs to be more accountability from upper management…"

"Which will…" the facilitator facilitates.

"Which will create an environment of more open exchange."

I'm sure the person saying this despises herself a bit for being so shameless, so *unoriginal*. But that's what it takes; that is what's required. Average (and especially the original) worker ants continue to ignore this imperative at their own peril.

"Ah, so buy-in from the people making the big bucks," our facilitator, who may or may not be on autopilot at this point, explains.

Buy-in. Another word, along with *bandwidth* and *brainstorm*, that completes the Bermuda triangle of contemporary corporate lingo: the killer Bs that cause any sane person's ears to bleed.

Then, the compulsory flip chart comes out and we go around the room (*round robin*, as the facilitator is compelled—and paid—to say) unburdening ourselves of ways we could foster a more open and unguarded work environment.

Take sexual harassment, please.

Like any other fad, the parameters of this quite serious infraction were forever altered as soon as people figured out they could make money off it. Good for them. This would seem to be yet another instance, unfortunately, where we can count on lawyers enacting the necessary changes a hell of a lot faster than politicians. Probably because politicians are too busy sexually harassing their young staffers to focus on the issue at hand—or in their hands, as the settled-out-of-court-case may be.

Take our facilitator. What a racket. Even if it was conceivable, I can't fathom how anyone could earn their paychecks peddling this stuff. Unless, of course—as always—the person in question actually believed it. In fairness, there have to be a handful of facilitators as well as preachers who are wholly invested in the prepackaged platitudes they invoke at every opportunity. But to actually find work, talking to workers, about ways they can enrich their work experience? How can anyone hawk such bad medicine, knowing that, at best, it's akin to shaking incense over a decomposing corpse: the air may smell interesting for a few seconds, but after the smoke clears the body is still beyond repair. Everyone knows this, so how could anyone convince themselves to make a living attempting to convince anyone else? Of course, as always, there is only one possible answer: money.

"Okay, next we'll do some role playing," she says, obliterating the illusions of anyone in the room who hoped this session would unfold unlike every other one all of us have attended. A little role playing goes a long way. More than a little (and there is always more than a little) quickly makes me wish I was anywhere else, doing almost anything, not excluding the obscene image of being sexually harassed by Boyd Bender.

"Okay," the facilitator says, after we have all (poorly) played the roles none of us will ever be important enough to enact in our lifetimes. "Before we break out into discussion groups, does anyone have any questions or observations?"

"Hypothetical question?"

Otis again.

"What if you feel there is a case of harassment in your office, but the perpetrator, say a woman, is doing it as a desperate ploy to disguise her own conflicted sexual feelings... does that count?"

Silence. Otis *has* to be doing this for my benefit because, by the looks on all the faces around the room, no one can believe their ears.

"The reason I ask is, I have a friend who has confided in me... and I've really been at a loss for what to tell him. I hope this is the appropriate venue to discuss it… it would be so helpful for me to be able to advise him, you know, in an appropriate manner…"

The flip chart immediately comes back into play and, as always, I am unsure if I want to hit Otis, or hug him. As usual, as the session drags on, I acknowledge that it is a bit of both.

* * *

So many rules in the corporate world. So many rules in the real world as well, and the unreal world, for that matter.

But rules, of course, are made—or at least *meant*—to be broken.

The golden rule: never date a woman you work with.

Only a fool would fail to heed this edict, only a fool would fool around with a female in his office.

But that doesn't necessarily mean you can't partake in some consensual sexual relations with them. Indeed, you can almost kid yourself into half-believing that this type of behavior is encouraged, *expected*.

Look: a lot of people work at my company.

Correspondingly, a lot of *women* work at my company.

Subtract the married ones, the ones unattainable or too easily attainable for all the obvious reasons, then add in the smattering of married ones who actively instigate extracurricular encounters, and you've got a talent pool that only a blind man or a bishop could indefinitely abstain from.

Every day it's possible to fall in love with a fresh, unfamiliar face. That's reason enough to keep coming to work. It's reason enough to keep living.

After a month or two this remains wonderful, another few months and it's peculiar, several more months and it remains magically inexplicable, but after a few years of finding new faces worth fantasizing about, it begins to almost insist on action. It also dares you to defy its weird, wanton ways.

So what am I doing here?

I've got a tail between my legs and an ass in my face. Normally, this might not be an altogether disagreeable (or unlikely) arrangement, but the tail in question—not to mention the ass—does not belong to the woman I fell asleep on top of.

I am spooning and being spooned by two stinking felines who collectively weigh more than I do. I'm not exactly what you'd call a *cat person*, which is to say I'd prefer if they generally weren't around. But I especially dislike sharing a bed with one; I dislike it even more if there are two of them, but I draw the line when I start hacking up fur balls in the middle of the night.

The worst part is that this is my own fault, sort of. She asked me how I liked sleeping over, if the cats (she said *her babies*) bothered me, and I truthfully told her each time I stayed was like a trip to Disneyland. She liked that very much. One small detail I left out of my lowbrow allusion was the fact that in the course of the evening, she got to be Snow White and my roles alternated amongst Sneezy, Grumpy and Sleepy.

I am; needless to say, desperately allergic to these flea-flinging curs, which is my problem. But she thinks my efforts to find room on the mattress between her and her babies is a sign of loyalty, or maybe even love, which is her problem.

Sick again, I slink home to my unsoiled sheets.

I try not to think of amusing, immature puns concerning the pros and cons of having no pussies in my bed. Surprisingly, I am unsuccessful.

A little forehand-play before falling asleep is just what the doctor prescribed.

As I said, I don't service myself as often as I want to, not nearly as often as I *need* to. And, as usual, when I absolutely *have* to, my boy suddenly gets all shy with me, like we've never met before. And I'm not above a little small talk, some sweet nothings, a bit of reinforcement if need be. But the softer I speak, the softer I get.

Therein lies the rub, so to speak. And on these insufferable occasions when I can't talk myself into it, I grudgingly concede that all is as it must be in my own weird world: so long as tomorrow while I'm standing innocently in line at the grocery store, I'll suddenly be able to hold up the joint with an untimely hard-on. Then, later, when I'm home (at last) behind closed doors, classical music in the air, champagne on ice, candles on fire, I'll come up short in another unfortunate effort to wine and dine my own dick.

My dog is mad at me.

I can't blame him.

He knows the rules: I don't come home, I'm in violation of the contract (two meals, a bowl at least half full with half-clean water, and a minimum of three walks a day), so he is entitled to cut loose all over the kitchen floor, or even the couch.

But my pal is a team player; he has character. He held it. For me. And, I reckon, for himself; after all, it's *his* house too.

His tail does its thing; I'm surprised he doesn't take flight, and he is happy. Dogs cannot suppress that genuine love and honesty. But then, after the walk (and a piss that would make a drunken mule proud) he recovers and reverts to character: not taking the treat ("Who wants a biscuit?" I say. Not me, his back says), sitting on the other side of the room. Normally this would be my opportunity, my obligation, to win him over; shower him with affection and praise, but I can't. I just don't have it in me. The poor guy, he probably thinks *I'm* ignoring *him*. But I'm simply too hungover to address this injustice.

Eventually, inevitably, he comes around. The little wags every time I look over, the overtures of amiability, his minuscule capacity for indignation already exceeded. He follows me into the kitchen, and as I look around—still too ashamed to directly acknowledge him—searching for a diversion, the oddly recurring thought once again arises: Can I possibly be the only person afraid to utilize the self-cleaning function of my oven? I don't trust it. I don't trust anything that makes promises it can't keep. Then again, if I actually used my oven, this admittedly might be a more enticing feature.

In no time my dog is all over me, drunk from love as well as the fumes seeping through my skin.

I don't mislead him: the best I'll be able to offer is space beside me while I doze in and out of recrimination and self-pity. As usual, he has no complaints; happy to receive whatever I will give him. Dogs, after all, are not unlike humans: they need food and water, shelter and support. But they also need love.

* * *

Long story short: man and woman meet, man and woman fall in love, man and woman marry, man and woman move, man and woman have child, mother and father move (again), father goes to work and mother stays home with son, father meets other women, father falls in love (again), father moves (again), mother and son do not see father, father marries new woman, mother marries no one, mother and son hate father, son grows up, mother moves on, son worries about mother, mother grows older, son sets off on his own, mother worries about son, and so on.

Not everything I just said is the truth.

For instance, I'm not sure my old man ever *loved* his second wife. He had a way of falling out of love with the things love leads to. Like love. What's not to love? Or, rather, for my old man, the *not* was what he loved. One type of man might feel that the world owes him a living; another type might think the world owes him an explanation. Both are bound to be disappointed.

Listen: my old man was a real piece of work. He cut out of the picture early enough so as to do us both the favor of not having to put any effort into our relationship for the rest of our lives. I used to feel pretty sorry for myself, though I never admitted it. Boys don't admit to feeling pain, they just learn to deflect it by inflicting it. So: they get into fights, step on ants, throw eggs at strangers' houses and generally embark on a mission to make the world as miserable as they are.

And then they grow up and come to understand that everyone, for the most part, does the best they can. Or that people would do better, if they were able, or else could imagine, in hindsight, how much they might have done differently, given another chance. And sometimes these feeble justifications manage to persuade.

Reality Check (8)

*When you remember the ones who got to you, the ones who still war-
rant a third thought, it's always about the ones who got away (the ones
who let you get away). The ones who won't leave you alone because
they left you, alone. The ones you find yourself searching for, on the
highway or at the shopping mall, in magazine ads or movie trailers.
They could be anywhere; you might see them anyplace except where
you think you want them. The ones who months or years later still
make you think: we didn't have enough time to fuck as much as we
could have; we didn't give each other enough time to fuck each other
up. Et cetera.*

    Here is something you never want to tell anyone:

Today was the worst day of my life.

    *Especially if the next day is even worse. And so on, until after a
while each day is dueling with the one that preceded it, each shoving
the next shadow into the spotlight.*

    You can only endure so much of this before you have to
do something.

    Today was the worst day of my life, you might say.

    But I thought you loved me, they'll say.

    I do love you, you'll insist.

    Then what's the problem? they'll ask.

    The problem is that you seem so happy.

    So?

    And it's showing me how empty my own life is.

    (To yourself you'll say this.)

Nine

DELUSIONS OF MEDIOCRITY

EVERY SATURDAY MORNING I have a hangover and Whitey has computer class. He is getting certified as a *real* smart computer guy; in other words, he's one of the myriad party crashers paying good money to become what Otis unwittingly accomplished in between high school hand jobs. Apparently, if you can sell *and* you know more than a little about computers, you are unstoppable in this new world disorder.

I'm trying to turn him on to the wonders of Vietnamese cuisine.

"How's the class going?"

"I finish one book and open the next one."

"Sounds awful."

"You can't keep up, each time you get proficient, they've gone to another version, they can't fucking fix version 2.0 and all of a sudden it's 3.0 or 2.5."

"Sounds exhilarating."

"And they're not kidding anyone, right? It's all about making money! It's the same with cars and appliances, once you've paid for them the fuckers break on you!"

"Condoms too." (To myself I say this.)

Our steaming bowls of broth arrive (reminding me, always, of Ramen noodles and yet another thing American co-modification, in the name of cost and convenience, has managed to mangle) and Whitey looks at his bowl, then me, then the waiter, who is already halfway back to the kitchen.

"I'm not sure about this," he says.

"It's better than it tastes," I offer.

"What's that supposed to mean?"

"Can a billion Chinese people be wrong?"

"But this is a Vietnamese restaurant..."

"Exactly."

"Well if they're so right, why the hell are they all coming over *here*?"

"Here?"

"America!"

"Well... why did *your* great grandparents come over?"

"Potato famine."

"Right. And now we have French fries. Congratulations."

In spite of myself, I'm not unimpressed with Whitey's chopstick skills.

"When did you learn to use those things?"

"What are you talking about?"

"You look like Mr. Miyagi over there."

"Oh, these? I *had* to learn, my boss takes our sales team out for sushi each week."

"Don't tell me you like sushi all of a sudden?"

"No, I hate it. But what choice do I have?"

Our waiter returns, but his attention is focused entirely on the tables around us, which he is attacking solemnly with spray bottle and rag.

Whitey glares at him and shakes his head.

"What's your problem?"

"I wish your boy would lighten up, I'm not trying to get Windex misted in my soup..."

I motion to the boiling broth. "You think that shit is stronger than *this?*"

Whitey is unimpressed.

"A little ammonia never hurt anyone."

The waiter returns to the kitchen, but Whitey is unconvinced.

"That's ridiculous, you'd never see anyone pulling that shit in a *real* restaurant!"

"What's a real restaurant?"

"McDonald's."

"What, you think that kid in the drive-through washes his hands before he handles your chicken McNuggets?"

"Well at least I don't have to *see* it, at least he doesn't contaminate my food right in front of me!"

"Do you think he's doing that on purpose?"

"Of course!"

"Check your head Whitey, you're acting too white for your own good."

"Whatever you say, Ho Chi Minh."

"So what are you up to the rest of the weekend? We hanging out tonight?"

"I have my godamned study group tonight."

"Study group?"

"Yeah, for this class…"

"What are you studying?"

"We have weekly projects."

"Projects?"

"Yeah, we need to figure out how to handle certain scenarios…"

"Scenarios?"

"Yeah, if you're going to be a network administrator, you have to be ready to take care of viruses and shit."

"Viruses?"

"Yeah, one infected email can shut down a whole system."

"Ah, you mean like the *Y-2K bug?*"

"Well, we're talking about brush fires, that's the full on towering inferno."

"Yeah, but that was all horseshit, right?"

"Horseshit?"

"You know, a total scare tactic to whip everyone into a frenzy…"

"It worked."

"Exactly."

"So you're talking about the *post*-Y2K bug?"

"Whatever makes people most afraid."

"Are you afraid?"

"I don't know."

"Do you believe the hype?"

"I will if they pay me."

"Uh…"

"If they pay me enough to fix it, I'm prepared believe in *anything*."

Mental note: remember that no matter how bad things may get—even if I have to go back to bartending—it could never be as bad as trying to make sense of (much less get ahead in) a world that was like a greased pig at a southern picnic, unattainable, impossible to get your arms around, even as another one just like it has already been dissected and smoked and served on paper plates that wiser folks are stuffing into their mouths.

* * *

She is perfect.

She does not quite walk in Beauty, but she does not exactly walk in Ugly, either.

I could write poems for her; I would write poems *on* her, if she'd let me. A few key takeaways from our Dutch treat dinner: She's not afraid of sushi, she drinks beer, she seems to enjoy sports about half as much as I do, she apparently pays attention to politics even *less* than I do. She is pretty close to perfect. Plus, she's agreed to come home with me on the second date. What's not to love?

"What's this?" she asks.

"Junior Wells," I reply.

"Oh, blues? How about some Eric Clapton then, he's king of the blues!"

Are you fucking *kidding* me? (To myself I say this.)

"So… you like music?"

"Rolling Stones or Bob Dylan," she says. "I could live with just those two if I had to."

"I'm more of a Beatles and Neil Young man myself."

She shrugs.

"You ever heard Miles Davis?" I ask.

"Who?" she says.

Nothing.

Then she reaches into her purse and pulls out what appears to be an expensive cigar. I know it's expensive because it's enclosed in an official looking silver case, like a sex toy from the 70s, a miniature chrome cannon. Before I can signal my astonishment she kicks it up a notch: it's not a cigar, but a spliff that would make Bob Marley blink.

"Mind if I smoke?" she winks at me.

Is that a joint or a palm tree? I don't ask.

It's obviously a hand-rolled number, but it's difficult to determine if *she* rolled it, because it looks like a sticky, cylindrical wasps' nest.

"Here," she says, handing it to me.

"No, I'm good," I say.

"Are you okay," she asks?

"I'm working on it," I offer.

"Do you want me to put it out?" she frowns.

"No, not at all…"

She raises an eyebrow.

"You don't smoke?"

"Not lately…"

She wrinkles her forehead.

"I'm in sort of a monogamous relationship with booze at the moment; it makes me feel better about myself."

"Are you afraid to smoke?"

"I'm afraid *not* to, actually."

"Well then, what's the problem?"

"I figure I need to confront my fears at some point…"

She does not say anything.

This isn't going to affect my chances of seeing you naked, is it? (To myself I say this.)

"I don't know," she starts.

I don't say anything (wondering if I accidentally *did* say something).

"I don't know if I can trust a guy who won't smoke with me…"

"You can if it's a guy like *me*," I promise.

"No, that's the thing; a guy like you has no business not smoking with me."

Question: At what point does pride enter into an equation like this?

Before I can answer, she saves me the trouble and lets herself out.

* * *

Not only does someone wake up, alone (of course) but he wakes up with a boner that could cut the earth's crust.

Not even a wet dream? You couldn't even do that for me?

A new low.

Another nightmare, the worst kind, the kind you can only have when you are awake.

I need to lay off the hard drugs. Wait a minute. I haven't done hard drugs in years. Shit. I need to *start* doing hard drugs again.

A series of similar, increasingly self-pitying mini-epiphanies follow, as usual.

Sunday came, and without slowing down to let anyone notice, it went. Sundays have a way of doing that.

On the dissolving horizon the sky looks good enough to eat: orange sorbet on a dark purple plate; overhead black birds want in on the action, circling one another, entwined in their autumnal ritual.

My dog punches the clock, chasing after creatures he has no chance of catching. He chases squirrels the way his owner chases women: blindly and brazenly, but with no idea what he'd actually do if he ever caught one.

* * *

The TV is talking.

Listen: there are people who actually believe that the moon landing never happened. *Lots* of people. Not that it didn't happen, necessarily, but that it was an elaborate, carefully staged scam; that it happened out in the desert, secret film crews capturing the entire thing. Unfortunately, most of the people who agreed to be interviewed all happen to live in trailer parks, which tends to undermine their credibility.

But I'll be damned if, fifteen minutes in, I'm on board, buying just about every argument. After twenty minutes I'm talking in increasingly agitated tones to my TV. A half hour later I'm ready to make a down payment on a used trailer.

Listen to them: these people might not be crazy, but they are playing the part to perfection. Wide eyes working to wash away the one-two punch of alarm and indignation, creased foreheads wet with the weight of their weird worlds, the insistent outlook of the converted Christian or polished politician, the unburdened body language of a puppet who has finally plucked the wires from its back.

And, I think: Please!

Please let this be true. Imagine: all the churchgoing, flag-waving, right wing radio listening, free market following, see-no-evil simpletons (and that's just Whitey) if they found out?

And then, this: No!

Nothing, it eventually occurs to me, could conceivably be worse than if those astronauts actually landed on Earth. Because it's marginally acceptable, or at least *comprehensible*, that in a time when millions of people are starving and dying of decades-old diseases, we'd have the effrontery to float billion dollar babies in space—*that's* enough, that confirms all we need to know about priorities and good and evil and the fact that there is, of course, at the end of the night, no chance whatsoever that *God* is watching over all this. But to think that the suits who call the shots arrived at the decision that it was ultimately to their advantage to take the time and imagination choreographing a made-for-TV miracle to propagate compliance, or boost morale, or whatever mendacious busywork those men who don't work for a living get up to when they are hard at work behind those fortified doors.

If *that* is even a possibility, then all bets are off. Then suddenly even the cynics are shit out of luck, and things like fake wars and flying planes into buildings begin to seem like a rather ingenuous part of the program. See: it's conceivable that money gets spent every day on scientific charades that serve no practical purpose. Or conceding that God obviously doesn't exist, so it can't be *His* fault (because He never existed). But finding out that *we* are capable—and worse, willing—to pull off that kind of crap? It's almost enough to make you join a militia. It's almost enough to cause you to cash it all in and start looking for the alien transmissions in your fillings. Or hunker down in a trailer park on the outskirts of Area 51.

* * *

Here's a vision:

I'm not drinking.

Two of us finish eating, and then pour off the last of the wine (a bottle of wine doesn't count, does it? Wine isn't *drinking*, is it?).

Maybe it could have worked.

Maybe you and she could have figured things out.

Maybe there was life after years of killing yourselves in order to live.

Maybe a little moderation was not the end of the world, like she always joked.

Maybe she wasn't joking.

Maybe you could have given her more time, another chance.

Maybe you could have helped her help herself. Or just helped.

Maybe you both could have been people you never envisioned.

Maybe everything could have been different, only more so.

Maybe it could have worked.

To yourself you say this.

* * *

Another vision:

I'm not looking.

My eyes are closed, but it doesn't matter because the lights are out. She has taken me to the shower and our hands are doing all the talking. Eventually we are sitting while the indoor rain falls warmly over us like corroboration; anything could happen. She starts shampooing my hair—in the dark—but it's all a ploy to get my head where her fingers are, moving me closer—in the dark—until eventually I feel what she wants me to find.

No vision.

I'm not seeing.

My eyes are open, but it doesn't matter because it's dark out. Late.

Awake. Alone? Hard to say since I can't see anything.

Sober but not asleep doesn't seem like much of a trade-off, not at a moment like this.

Listen, I don't say, unwilling to reach out and see if she's still beside me. If you hit thirty and you're still single, either you've found some strategies for survival or else gone insane. Or, if you're lucky, a little bit of both.

Know what I mean?

Lying still in darkness she doesn't say, whether she's there or not.

* * *

Unfortunately, I can feel it coming. Instantly, I am aware of what I'd hoped to avoid, since the phone is about to ring.

I wait and listen, listen and wait. Eventually, inevitably, it rings.

"Hey Whitey…"

Once that's over with I feel better and hope Whitey does as well. It's not that he hasn't recovered from his setback, he has just convinced himself that talking about it will make it less painful, or more manageable. It wasn't such a big deal, I always tell him: everyone has some scars from mistakes they made. But when we go over the same story, it occurs to me that he not only doesn't want to be alone, now, he doesn't want to be alone, *then*. It is not enough to remember a rough time in the relative safety of a friend's confidence, he needs me to be there, to live it again, with him.

Whitey freaked out.

He's getting better.

Most people must.

If you're looking for satisfaction you'll be disappointed; if you're looking for money you'll be miserable.

I didn't say that.

But I should have. Whitey needs to hear it, now, although he really needed to hear it, then.

"What the fuck do you know about it?"

Whitey did say that, more than once, to me, then.

Then: I didn't necessarily disagree with him. I was holding drinks hostage from drunks until they handed over the money. I made money doing this but I wasn't making *money*. Whitey wanted to make *money*, and the sooner he could go from semi-broke to sports team owner, the better. I was making small talk with big players and Whitey wanted to be one of the guys making big decisions, earning big paychecks, running up big bar tabs, and leaving big tips.

"I'm all for it," I told him.

What the fuck did I know?

I had segued seamlessly, if expensively, from undergraduate to grad student while Whitey began wearing ties and paying taxes. While I was reading Russian literature in translation, Whitey was committing no crimes and enduring the punishment of sixty hour work weeks.

"This is what it takes to get in there," he explained. "This is how you get noticed."

What I tended to notice was that Whitey was burning through jobs the way I had burned through thesis topics. I couldn't decide if I wanted to focus on an examination of "the other" in Dostoyevsky or a critique of capitalism seen through the collected works of F. Scott Fitzgerald. Whitey struggled with whether he was meant to be in banking, procurement or marketing.

What the fuck did I know?

I demurred on the yellow brick road to tenure and became a Barthes-quoting bartender. I suffocated on my student loans and viewed my professional prospects with a fear and loathing only the over-educated could afford. By this time Whitey had turned at least three tropical rain forests into business cards, each new endeavor another dart seeking a bull's eye.

"What the fuck do *you* know?" he asked as I strained his second Martini.

"I know you aren't exactly a Martini man," I said.

"How do you figure?"

"Well, for starters, extra dry does not mean pouring more vermouth in."

"To tell you the truth, I can't stand these things."

"Oh, well so long as you know where you stand..."

"Listen smartass, you *have* to be able to drink a Martini. If you're ever rolling with one of the execs, you have to be ready to throw down, old school style."

"Rolling with the execs?"

"I wouldn't expect you to understand."

"Are you sure you don't just want a light beer?"

"Don't try to change the subject. I'm trying to explain to you that I've finally figured it out."

"Okay, lay it on me."

"Look, I know it sounds crazy, but only someone willing to risk *everything* can take it to the next level..."

Take *what* to the next level? I didn't ask. I also didn't press him to explain exactly what the *next* level consisted of. What I did want to know was how taking a job, with practically no pay, could possibly equate to anything approximating the proverbial big time.

"If you just shut up and listen, I'll explain it to you!"

It took him a third Martini before he outlined the trajectory that would bring him from the boiler room to board member. As I was to understand it, Whitey was making a solid (possibly ingenious) strategic decision to accept a job that would pay him nothing until he produced. What I saw was a white collar pyramid scheme, sucking time and energy from ambitious (or greedy) acolytes who were looking to suck on the surgically enhanced boob of big commerce.

I had heard about this scam before, of course; everyone had. A sales gig selling something (not stocks necessarily, but not actual products either) that earned commission, over time. Which sounded like any other sales job, except I had never heard of an arrangement that required the sucker to wear a suit (not coat and tie, *full* suit) each day, take lunch at his desk, and study for three months—on his own time—to pass the exam that would give him a license to do what he did, before he was ultimately hired, on a conditional basis, to sell a certain quota each month. Actually, I *had* heard about this type of gig, but I thought it was a cliché, a joke. Maybe an energetic punk right out of undergrad (maybe), but a dude who'd already been in the workforce for a few years?

It sounded masochistic, and more importantly, it didn't sound like a lot of fun.

"Fun? Are you kidding me? Look, if you want to have *fun*, stay in the service industry for the rest of your life. No offense."

"None taken. So, how much did those suits run you?"

"Huh?"

"You heard me."

"A few grand, but…"

"A few *grand?*"

"Look, these suits are an investment."

"Okay."

"Listen Byron, don't worry about the business world, just pour me another Martini."

"I think you've had more than enough my friend."

"What the fuck do you know?"

Six months later I was still dispensing cocktails and ingesting second hand smoke, and Whitey, unable to pay rent and more than a few grand behind on his credit card payments, had moved back home with his parents. I can't say it hurt me more than it hurt him, but it would have been preferable not to see Whitey humbled so… predictably, so efficiently. Suffice it to say, celebrating his twenty-seventh birthday in the same house he grew up in was not part of the original plan. Sleeping in the same bed he occasionally soiled as a child did not exactly work wonders for his faltering confidence; getting 86'd from the job that set him up to fail was a final straw of sorts.

It was around this time that the Internet exploded, and a little while later I too was earning a paycheck and paying taxes. I didn't even have to wear a tie. Whitey withdrew, and for the better part of a year I talked to his parents more than him: no matter how many times I called or dropped by, he never picked up the phone or opened the door.

I didn't speak to him until he invited me to my old place of employment, to tell me he had a new job and a new apartment. He ordered a Martini.

* * *

I'm surprised when I don't get any calls or emails or faxes or out-of-breath office visits from Whitey the next day. In fact, I'm somewhat disappointed. I could use some of Whitey's scorched-earth soul searching to help me put my own fetid affairs in perspective.

I decide to give him a taste of his own medicine and swing by his apartment, unannounced, that evening.

He is unshaven, in his underwear, huddled under a blanket on the couch, eating what appears to be SpaghettiOs.

"You okay?"

"I called in sick today…"

"You okay?"

"Yeah. Just a bit hungover."

"You got banged up on a work night?"

"I had to."

"What did you do?"

"We had some folks in from out of town, so we all went to that steak house, on the company's dime."

"Say no more."

"I mean… I've never seen that sort of gluttony. Beef, wine, the whole eight yards."

"Or nine yards," I offer.

"Exactly."

"You okay?"

"Red wine and cigars, that's all I could taste this morning."

"Say no more."

"Six of us, and I think our dinner tab was more than I make in a month."

"That's America."

"You ever wonder where all this money actually *comes* from?"

"It's generally better not to think too much about that stuff."

"I guess."

"Whitey?"

"Yeah?"

"What the hell are you eating?"

"What's it look like?"

"They still *make* SpaghettiOs? Did they card you?"

"Card me?"

"To make sure you weren't in college."

"What?"

"Isn't it *illegal* to eat SpaghettiOs if you're over twenty-one?"

"I would have preferred some Mickey D's, but I didn't have the energy to go out and get it…"

"Well, next time call me."

"You'd have done that for me?"

"I'd much rather pick up fast food for you anytime than see you like this."

"Like what?"

"Eating SpaghettiOs. I'm going to have this image with me forever now."

"Don't worry, I don't have many dollar-fifty dinners left in me."

"I certainly hope not."

"It's all gonna change soon, you'll see."

"How do you figure?"

"Because I'm paying dues now, but if you pay dues long enough, the dues begin to pay you back, you know?"

"I certainly hope so."

"Byron," he says, after he's gone ahead and said all sorts of other things.

"Yeah?"

"A few years ago… you know."

"You sort of freaked out."

"Yeah."

"And it kind of fucked you up."

"Right."

"But you're cool with it."

"Pretty much."

"Whitey?

"Yeah?"

"Stay white."

"Always."

So. Key takeaway from a life engaged in as little introspection as possible: the only way to be content is to simply be *yourself.* Fine. The major drawback involves the fact that just about everyone, it seems—at least the ones who could be said to think about it—are more or less miserable with who they are.

And some people aren't even *that* lucky.

So? You help who you can, including yourself.

So: why is it that you never feel more alive than when you are reaching out to assist someone who is having a tough time? It's not that you feel better because they feel badly, or that it makes you celebrate—or recognize—your relative health or comparatively amicable existence; it's more that, when called to action in the name of doing *good,* knowing that your efforts might make a difference (and not in the abstract, but a real, discernible difference: the kind you can measure in the eyes of someone you love), you feel some of the things any of us should be more capable of. How often does that actually happen? *How* does that happen? Because. Your true friends are the ones who allow themselves to believe the white lies you tell about yourself and can't bring themselves to believe the unfortunate truths other people tell about you.

* * *

Phone ringing, or is that just my head?

It doesn't stop (the phone *or* my head) so I quit kidding myself and pick up.

-Dude.

-What's up Otis.

-Did you see that cat?

-What cat?

-The cat that came and pissed and shit in my mouth during the night.

-Oh *that* cat...

-Was it at your house too?

-Oh yeah.

-Can we sue (insert name of company here)?

-Yeah, but then we'll have to find *real* jobs.

-Good point.

-Jobs where we might have to wear ties...

-Ouch, stop it, not when I'm this hungover...

-You sound as bad as I feel...

-What are you doing?

-Nothing, reading a book.

-A book?

-Yeah.

-Like, for work or something?

-Uh...

-I mean why are you *reading*?

-Because... I want to?

-Are you serious?

-Are you saying you never read books?

-You mean like a whole... an actual *book*?

-Yeah, you know, a book with a table of contents, a beginning, a middle, an end... something other than the phone book I mean.

-The last time I read more than ten pages of anything was when I signed my mortgage papers.

-They didn't have Cliff's Notes for you to use?

-Shit, if they figured out a way to do that, they'd make even *more* money.

-For God's sake man, how do you live with yourself?

-Me? Hey buddy, I fucked Angelina Jolie last night!

-Huh?

-You heard me.

-How do you figure?

-How do you *think?*

-Oh. You still jerk off?

-Are you kidding?

-You still feel the need to service yourself?

-Sure, why not?

-You're *married!*

-Yeah?

-Dude…you don't jerk off when you're married…do you?

-You'll see.

-Ouch.

* * *

It's not supposed to happen. You're obliged, by the unwritten codes of corporate illogic to ensure that it does not happen. Sometimes, however, it is unavoidable; eventually, inevitably, it is going to happen.

Stuck solo in the elevator with Boyd Bender, the unsmiling CFO.

As the doors close with their guillotine precision, it is difficult to determine which of us is more uncomfortable.

Don't play the game (to myself I say this).

We're both human beings, we're both men, we're both employees of the same company, the same *team*, there is no reason—other than the unwarranted, unspoken imperatives of pie-in-the-face propriety—to act like anything other than a normal person, doing normal things in a normal situation. It's only life. Don't play the game, I think, realizing (too late, as always) that this half-second internal soliloquy is all part of the game.

"Hi Boyd."

"Hi."

Hi.

He knows my name; or, if he doesn't, is it more insulting that he knows it but won't say it, or that after more than a year of aloof hallway encounters and hasty urinal drive-bys, he hasn't bothered to entertain the slightest interest in obtaining the name of the bathroom buddy he'd never bond with?

The five-second ascent to the fifth floor is frozen in time, centuries unspooling in invisible waves of awkwardness.

Then, just before the steel screen sets us free, out of somewhere—some perverse, irresistible impulse—insult is added to injury:

"How's it going?"

In the milli-moment before he springs himself from my polluting presence, he offers the half-smile, half-nod, the gesture that is not quite close to actual speech, or the unthinkable commitment of emotional attachment on any level, which says, all at once: Yeah, fine, great, whatever and by the way, who the fuck do you think you are, encumbering me with your semi-coherent, feigned familiarity when we both know I don't have the time, energy, interest, or *capacity* to associate with you, and while I've got your attention, let this serve as a reminder that in case you're too witless to realize it, your requirement is to wait for the *next* elevator, or in the unfortunate, unavoidable exception when we're stuck together for a few seconds, find the self-respect necessary to allow me to suffer in silence and under no circumstances are you to ever interrogate me with imbecilic inquiries like *How's it going?*; in fact, don't acknowledge me in any way, okay, and by the way, I've already forgotten more about life, and business, and what it takes to oversee a corporation than you could ever imagine, so *it's* going in ways you wouldn't understand even if I bothered to explain it to you, so jam your head back up your ass, be happy that the hard work I do on your behalf is going to translate into ten times the money you'd ever hope to make in your life, and the least you can do is extend me the courtesy of avoiding eye contact at all times, unless I go out of my way to give you the time of day, which is never going to fucking happen in a million years so make a mental note of this and let's not waste any more of my life and incidentally, my dress shirts are dry-cleaned by Satan, and it's lonely at the top and it's a tough job but someone's got to do it and I'm never going to die...

To himself he says this.

* * *

Every now and then I bump into Otis's least favorite adversary, Jean, in the hallway and I can't help getting excited. Not about her so much, but about what she will do. Not for me, for my computer. When I see Jean on F5, I know Otis has called in sick, again. Otis is not afraid to use those sick days; he calls them sick-of-work days. No one feels secure about their jobs these days and here's a guy with one kid at home and another on the way, making damn sure he enjoys every day off he's legally entitled to take. Sometimes I reckon that with balls as big as his, he must walk around with a semi-permanent hernia. Anyway, when I see Jean, I immediately pray for some sort of personal computer problem. Why? Not so I can enjoy her delightful personality—though Jean is always nothing less than *professional* in my presence, and that's all I ask for, that's all I need—but I know she will actually *fix* whatever issue I have. It's not that Otis is incapable; he can work circles around Jean (I imagine seeing the two of them in action simultaneously would be like watching the natural grace of a professional athlete versus the gritty ambition of an amateur.) But Otis can also *talk* circles around Jean, and the only time I tend to discourage this is when I actually need help refueling or delousing or reinventing my computer, or just sweet-talking it so it will come around and do what I tell it.

"Hi Jean, Otis out today?"

"What else is new…says he got food poisoning."

"Food poisoning?"

"That's what he said."

"I guess he hasn't used that one before, huh?"

"Oh he's used it…"

"But that's such a… that's the old standby!"

"Well, I guess it could be the truth this time."

"Still… even if you *have* food poisoning you should never say you have food poisoning."

Jean's look asks me three things, in descending order of urgency: Why are you standing in front of me? Why are we still talking? And, was that supposed to be funny?

Dutifully dispensed with, I go on my merry way. I'm not saying Jean is intimidating, but I wouldn't want to meet her in a dark alley. Or a parking lot. Or a church. Or a bedroom. At least here, at work, if she kicks my ass I can probably sue someone.

* * *

There are worse things than meetings.

But since I'm not a dishwasher, a janitor, a flight attendant, or basically anything that requires me to actually *work* for a living, I'm still entitled to feel a little bit sorry for myself.

There are, I continue to be reminded—no matter how hard it is to believe—people who *enjoy* this shit. They are invariably the ones who schedule the meetings, which achieve the impossible by causing me to actually feel nostalgic about high school. At least in those desperate days, when stuck in a small room and irredeemably bored, I did what I had to do: I doodled and I daydreamed. And that usually does the trick; a little lack of reality will usually pull you through. Retreating into your mind is an acceptable alternative for people who are comfortable inside their own skin. The problem is, these agenda-driven dipshits want nothing less than to be alone; if the only company they can keep is their own, they'll resort to anything, including calling meetings. Every other option is optimal so long as they don't have to deal with themselves, and whatever inadequacies they're unable to ignore when they can't hide inside the straightjacket of a spreadsheet, or the enablement of a power-point presentation. Muzzled by their own mediocrity (what other reason could there conceivably be?), they don't think twice about dragging the rest of the world down with them.

And so I sit here, unable to draw stick figures, obliged to keep my head up and my eyes open, in case anyone has the impudence to ask for my input, feeling like a kid again during those interminable hours spent in church, the Holy Spirit staring down at me, daring me to seek distraction.

* * *

Look: even here it happens. The obligatory booger on the wall above the toilet.

If you're a man and you've logged even a modest amount of time in semi-sterile public stalls, you're accustomed to this sight; you practically come to count on it. And yet. Even here? Even *here* this happens? Who does this and why do they feel compelled to contribute, childlike, in this unfortunate fashion, these pieces of themselves?

It's not that I actually believe these founding fathers up here on F5 are innately more mannered, or in any way superior to the foot soldiers on the floors below; indeed, I often go out of my way to envision the ways in which these superheroes, when they discard their capes and return home, are every bit as uncouth and uncivil, are every bit *American* as everyone else. And yet. When they are *here* they owe it to us—they owe it to themselves—to constrain the impulses that remind people like me that all of us are more alike than we'd often care to admit.

So: who is it?

I can imagine Chazz, with his festering resentment for the men he imagines are keeping him ever on the outside, envious and apart, wanting to leave a sardonic calling card, his sticky middle fingered salute for the preening prigs. But I know it isn't Chazz, since I know as well as anyone that he only comes up here when he has to, and he never lingers on F5 unless it's after hours, with me.

Otis, of course, is another obvious option.

But Otis only comes up here when one of the execs calls him, or if he has to take a dump—the irony of which is certainly not lost on me—and while I can see him sticking nose nuggets under his desk, or on his pants for that matter, I can't see him doing it here. Even *he* has enough decorum, enough respect for the rules (or enough disdain for the clichéd gesture), to avoid such self-indulgent statements.

And since I'm almost positive it isn't me, it has to be one of the hotshots who can't shake a latent affinity for their inner-adolescent. Maybe it's *The Don*; because, after all, when you are king of the jungle isn't it your right, your obligation to mark your territory, to remind anyone else who is sitting on the throne? And more importantly, if it *is* his, should I preserve it? It must be worth some money; everything else he touches seems to turn to gold.

* * *

A few words about the geese that have set up permanent residence all over the increasingly unkempt corporate lawn (and, it would seem, every other office building, golf course and playground in America): I'm not saying they're everywhere, but seeing them everywhere I go makes me wonder, where the hell did they *come* from? Or, where did they all exist in the good old days, before deciding that the entire world was, in fact, their oyster?

Other than eating the grass and shitting on top of anything they can get their asses over, and hissing at any human who happens to encroach on their personal space, they're mostly an inoffensive, if ubiquitous part of the landscape.

Seriously: where did all these fuckers come from?

Is this corporate candy land so beyond belief that even the *animals* are trying to get in on the action? Come to think of it, a million geese surfing the Internet for a million years could never come up with a scenario as improbable as this fin-de-monde fantasy: look around the parking lot, there are an awful lot of expensive cars; cars people under thirty have no business driving. Only in the bad movie we occasionally call America can customer service reps, who couldn't cut it in college, cash in their stock options and retire at twenty-five. Who knew these surly underachievers, who mastered the digital dialogue of computers to escape the wretched reality of the *real* world, would turn out to be the robber barons of the early 2000s? Who knew an unhealthy penchant for fantasy (Dungeons and Dragons, anyone?) would actually provide on-the-job training for jobs that didn't exist—yet? Who could imagine that knowing how to navigate a simple office network would make them all-powerful players in the new weird order? Listen: I may work in the executive office, surrounded by self-aggrandizing decision makers, but we all know who really runs the show—these antisocial anarchists who look like second-rate rock band roadies, commanding higher salaries than Ivy League MBAs.

Welcome to the machine. The ATM machine.

Looking at the well-fed and ill-mannered geese who strut around me on all sides, I get the feeling that they quite clearly would love to wring my neck if only they could get hold of some hands. I can't get to my car quick enough, as always, and it occurs to me: there is a moral in here somewhere, but the harder I look for it, the less significant it seems to be.

* * *

Business dinner.

Ten of us, fifteen, twenty. Whatever. We'll eat enough for fifty, drink enough for one hundred, tip enough for a small country, and generally do our best Henry VIII routine on a restaurant that never knew what hit it.

This is the new money, my friends. Get on board or get out of the way.

It's not as though all this happened overnight. Not exactly. I started seeing signs of the surfeit to come in the mid-90s, when I was standing obsequiously in front of these tables, not sitting behind them with this self-conscious smirk on my face; serving the drinks, not swilling them. At least then all the assholes I served had the decency to be older than I was. Now, I feel uncomfortable, I almost feel *sorry* having my plate cleared by a waiter old enough to be my uncle.

Look around the restaurant and you'll see them: the people who can't understand what the hell happened and want an explanation. Now. It was bad enough when businessmen old enough to have kids in college made deals and lots of noise in the bar, under soggy clouds of cigar smoke. But who told these interlopers—who looked like they weren't even old enough to have graduated college, if they ever went—that they could cross over this obvious line? Who said it was all right for them to sit *here*, fine young savages amongst the old guard, upsetting a balance that was always sacrosanct? Until now.

So: why order food you can't possibly finish, run up a tab capable of giving itself indigestion, and ensure that everyone else in the establishment understands that you are eating, drinking, engorging, *spending* more than anyone else? Because. It's good business. Or, it's bad business not to. Why let this hardly-earned excess drip down the national drain when it can be written off, an explicable expense? That's America. Those are the rules and they were never conceived by or for anyone who can't understand or appreciate them.

Listen: humans are all greedy.

But some humans are greedier than others; some are a lot greedier than *that*. Often, the more rich they are, the more greedy they become. And the more easily they get rich, the more easily they get more greedy. And so on.

* * *

I still have hangovers, thank God.

Everyone who has known an alcoholic knows that as soon as you stop feeling the pain, it's because you are no longer feeling the pain; you are no longer feeling much of anything.

So, I welcome the horrors of the digital cock crowing in my ear at an uncalled for hour, am grateful for the flaming phlegm in my throat, the snakes chasing their tails through my sinuses, the smoke stuck behind my eyelids, the shards of glass in my gut, and the special ring of hell circling my head. Because if it weren't for those handful of my least favorite things, I'd know I had some serious problems.

All of us can think of a friend whose father (or mother for that matter), we came to understand, was in an entirely different league when it came to the science of cirrhosis. The man who falls asleep fully clothed with a snifter balanced over his balls, then up and out the door before sunrise—like the rest of the inverted vampires who toil during the day in three piece suits. Maybe it was a Martini at lunch, or several cigarettes an hour to take the edge off. Whatever it was, whatever it took, they always made it out, and they always came back, for the family and to the refrigerator, filled with the best friends anyone can afford.

Our friends' fathers came of age in the bad old days that fight it out, for posterity, in the pages of books, uneasy memories and the wishful thinking of TV reruns: the 50s. These are men who have never opened a bottle of wine and have no use for imported beer, men who actually have *rye* in their liquor cabinets—who still have liquor cabinets for that matter. These are men who were raised by men that never considered church or sick-days optional, and the only thing they disliked more than strangers was their neighbors. Men who didn't believe in diseases and didn't drink to escape so much as to remind themselves exactly what they never had a chance to become. Theirs was an alcoholism that did not involve happy hours and karaoke contests; theirs was a sit down with the radio and a whiskey sour, a refill with dinner and one before, during and after the ballgame. Or maybe they'd mow the lawn to liven things up, tinker under the hood of a car that had decades to go before it could become a classic. Or perhaps friends would come over to play cards. Sometimes a second bottle would get broken out. This was a slow burn of similar nights: stiff upper lips, the sun setting on boys playing baseball, mothers sitting on the couch watching TVs families did not yet own, of forced smiles battling bottled tears in the bottom of a coffee mug, of amphetamines and affairs, overhead fans and undernourished kids, of evening papers and a creeping conviction that there is no God, of poets unable to make art out of the mess they'd made of their lives.

It was a hard time where people did not live happily ever after, if they ever lived at all. It was a time, in other words, not unlike our own.

* * *

Phone ringing.
    I'm not answering because I know who it is.
    Machine picks up.
    No message.
    Thank God.

    Phone ringing.
    Still not answering.
    Machine picks up.
    No message.
    Your call (To myself I say this).

    Phone ringing.
    Whoever it is, it's no one with good news.

Machine picks up.

I hear myself, again, telling someone I don't wish to speak with to leave me a message and I'll get back to them as soon as I can.

No message.

No problem.

Phone ringing…

Ten calls, no messages.

Now I'm beginning to get indignant.

Phone ringing.

I have half a mind to snatch up the phone and shout, "What's your problem? Don't you think if I was home I'd *answer*?"

Machine picks up.

No message.

Just as well, since there is no one here to hear it.

* * *

Sick again.

All the way back to college it's been this way: every time I push myself too hard: studying, partying, talking, everything but *sleeping*, the body invariably breaks down. Combine bad genetics with a predilection to make the same mistakes, and this is one of the unanticipated things I graduated college with. And then—and now—I always remember: it's nice for the body to tolerate what it can, but after push comes to punch, it hits harder, as if to say: How do *you* like it? Do you *see* what you're doing to me? And then, there is a nice symmetry here: the body lets you know, even if you forget, but always that fear: what if it didn't? What if you got yourself to the point where your body got tired of telling you, and removed itself from the equation?

It's not unlike the way I've always viewed hardcore, but fully functioning alcoholics. How can they *do* it? I've always wondered, eventually coming to understand, when you cross that line, you don't feel hungover anymore, you are just biding time before the next binge, your body wants no part of it, figuratively speaking. You've trained yourself to take the pain. And that is when there is no turning back, *that* is when it is time for some time off, the type of vacation where they don't count the days.

Unless.

And then, this (always, inevitably, this): unless you don't have money or family or friends to place between yourself and the ailment. *Those* are the people (or some of them anyway) that you see sleeping in the streets, chronic bronchitis coupled with illness and booze and the elements and a whole *dim sum* of ugly maladies to choose from.

Question: What was worse: the ones who had been somebody and lost it, had it taken, or otherwise tossed it away? Or the ones who never even had a chance? Did the ones who used to be different remember? Did the ones who didn't know the difference? You see people in the streets and all of them have one thing in common: a story.

Reality Check (9)

There is a man who sits near the pumps at the gas station you drive by each day. The man is very obviously from somewhere else and has about him a certain look—the meek, awestruck eyes, the apprehensive gestures—that indict him as someone who speaks little if any English. A stranger.

He remains respectfully distant from the customers—who incessantly fill their tanks, like bees returning to the nest before heeding the urgency of their instinctual obligations—but near enough to the action to remain in plain view. He sells flowers. Actually, he doesn't seem to sell *anything; he pretty much sits there, on an upturned milk crate, often from early morning until well in the evening, after the rest of the weary warriors have commuted past him, home from work and their worries of the wicked world. He silently plies his wares, content to play his part in the charade: he is not accomplishing much, he is begging, and the milk crate and collection of fading flowers at his feet communicate his inexpressible anguish.* Please help me, *his unscrubbed face, his unlaced sneakers, his oversized slacks, his filthy, fidgeting fingers—everything but his voice—all ask, saying what he cannot, and will not, say for himself.*

Ten

THE SHOW MUST GO OFF

THE SHOW MUST go on. Bills must be paid. This work isn't go to do itself. *Et cetera.*

Here's the thing about having a job: it's a blessing of sorts to be busy, to have that routine to return to. That busy-work that makes you too busy to worry yourself into doing nothing with your days. It's the lack of something to do that kills people; it's the lack of any compelling reason to wake up in the morning that ruins rock stars more than drugs and booze. Wasting your days in the corporate grind has this much going for it: it prevents you from wasting your days doing *nothing.*

* * *

I can milk a mixed drink on a cross-country flight (if you order a mixed drink on a flight that does not cross time zones, you need to do some possibly uncomfortable self-examination): it's not that I can't afford a handful of $7 scotches on the rocks, it just seems… *indulgent* to have more than one. Or two, tops. Unless it's a rough flight. Or, say, you are sandwiched between two super-sized ugly Americans on a five hour flight. It's odd, though: the airplane cocktail costs about the same as it would cost on the ground, in a bar. They just *seem* so expensive, lined up alongside the free diet cokes and bottled waters everyone else is pretending to enjoy.

A slow burn of melting spirits is the secret. Finally, one purposeful sip at a time, the drink is enjoyed in a way that does both the drink and the occasion justice. This is a drink you imbibe not to quench thirst but to inspire sensations unrelated to primal imperatives. In this way, a transfigured ice cube sluiced over the tongue can reveal the salvation of the universe. At least it will feel that way, so long as your headphones are blocking out the babble and blather. Through the distilled physics of solids compressing, something approximating peace is achieved. At least the type of nirvana one can only hope to achieve a mile in the sky with no flight attendant or sexy stranger involved. When all you've got are frazzled mothers, noisy offspring and bilious businessmen, that plastic cup can become your gateway to a brave new world, a flashing chance at bliss.

When it's over you are arguably no wiser or richer; you've gained nothing that can be quantified by the root of all evil, which perhaps is the point. The point is, you are still alive. All things being equal, this is progress.

* * *

God bless the beer bashes.

Hey, I read a textbook or two in college and am not unaware of what's actually going on here. Complimentary brews, casual dress, superficial amity, kinder ways to kill us while they profit from our pains. Throwing us our bones so that we'll work longer and wag our tails when they walk by. They've replaced the whips with pieces of paper promising an uncertain piece of the imaginary pie. They shower us with free beer so we don't have to bother going to a bar to bitch about our jobs. I *get* it, and with all respect to Karl Marx, I'd rather be a slave with sneakers on and unlimited access to the keg.

Sensing my thoughts, or simply sharing our unspoken solidarity, Otis raises his Styrofoam cup.

"Cheers."

"I think I'd be more upset if they canceled a beer bash than if they forgot to give out paychecks one week."

"You and everyone else."

"Glad to know I'm not alone."

"Where's your boy."

"Who, Chazz?"

"Yeah."

"What do you mean, my boy?"

"You guys are thick as thieves."

"Whatever."

"Are you saying he's not your main man?"

"I think he's good people, if that's what you mean."

"Good people? You guys are tight like a jimmy-hat on John Holmes."

"I think these beer bashes make him uncomfortable, since he doesn't drink."

"Shit, these beer bashes make me uncomfortable and I *do* drink."

"I know, I always feel weird standing around with these executives."

"They shouldn't be here; they should all be out smoking cigars or at a massage parlor or something."

"I mean, look at *him…*"

"What's his title?"

"Head council."

"Council? Not *lawyer*?"

"Head council."

"Well what the fuck does he *do*?"

"Do? He exists. That's what he does."

"Right. But, I mean, what's his *job*?"

"To be around. To make sure anyone who might be interested know that he is there."

"Has anyone tried to sue us?"

"Not that I know of."

"Have we tried to sue anyone?"

"No one sues anyone anymore. It's the new millennium."

"What the hell does that mean?"

"Suing is so *90s...*"

"It still *feels* like the 90s."

"We're the last of the dot-com Mohicans."

"So what does that mean?"

"We have bigger fish to fry."

"You mean like the Y2K bug?"

"Right. Remember how everyone was afraid to talk about that?"

"Talk about what?"

"*Exactly!*"

"Because it's all a bunch of bullshit."

"Really?"

"Of course."

"So it wasn't for real?"

"Of course not."

"So what was it then?"

"Smokescreen."

"Smokescreen? For what?"

"Whatever."

"What do we need a smokescreen for?"

"Y2K was like the terrorists, we just need to make up shit to make ourselves worry about."

"So there is no threat then?"

"Of course there's a threat, there's always a threat."

"Well, what can we do about it?"

"Hope that there is no real threat."

"But what if there is?"

"It's a win-win."

"How do you figure?"

"Easy. If there *is* some new bug and it paralyzes the servers, I'll have enough work to keep myself employed for at least another year. In fact, they'll probably have to promote me and I'll have a whole team of college grads working under me trying to keep up with the disaster, and of course people like Mr. Head Council over there will be afraid of *more* shit going wrong, so we'll be working extra hours and getting overtime. Either way I laugh all the way to the bank."

"Okay, but what if there is no bug at all?"

"Even better. It just proves how on top of things I am, lets everyone know what a great job I'm doing."

"I need a drink."

"You already have a drink."

"What's your point?"

* * *

Phone ringing.

Eventually, inevitably, I answer it.

"Great, another fucking addiction."

"Otis? What are you babbling about?"

"Listen."

There are several seconds of slurping sounds.

"What the hell is that?"

"What do you *think* it is?"

"Candy?"

"Not just candy, *jolly ranchers.*"

"Yeah?"

"I've avoided these fuckers like the plague for... I don't know, at least ten years."

"Why?"

"Why? Because they rot the teeth right out of your mouth."

"Not if you use them in moderation."

"Moderation?"

"Yeah."

"Have you ever *had* a sour apple jolly rancher?"

"Um…"

"Exactly. That's what I thought Mister High and Mighty."

"Uh…"

"I'll give you one on Monday."

"No thanks."

"Why not?"

"I don't want my teeth rotting out of my mouth."

"Shit. I may as well just knock mine all out right now with a hammer."

"Why would you want to do something like that?"

"Save the time, save myself the trouble."

"Well, if your teeth are going to rot out of your skull, you may as well *enjoy* the ride…"

"Hey, you're right! That's a good point."

"Of course it is."

"Thanks for that."

"Anytime."

"You know something By? I love our little chats."

"Me too, there's just one thing…"

"What's that?"

"You do realize that most people stop eating jolly ranchers in the fifth grade?"

"Look man, don't destroy my will to live."

"I'm going back to bed."

"You know what *I'm* doing today?"

"What?"

"The same thing I do every day I'm at home: change shitty diapers and listen to my pregnant wife yelling at me."

"Otis?"

"What?"

"Remind me why I want to get married someday?"

"Because you're smarter than I am."

"Am I?"

"No."

In seconds, I'm back to sleep, dreaming about the dirty diapers, arguments and money worries that await me if I'm lucky enough to ever find the one I'm looking for.

* * *

Check me out:

I'm black.

It's a costume, of course, but *I'm* convinced.

Actually, it's at best a half-assed effort, as I only decided a couple of hours ago, at Otis's insistence, to attend the company party.

"Come on!" Otis implored me. "Free drinks, all the grub you can eat, what more do you want?"

"Costume required," was the best I could offer, but it was good enough for me.

"Look, I don't care what you wear, you can tell people you are going as the cool guy who is hanging out with the married guy who needs to have some fucking beers!"

I'm a team player, so I went with the one option that has been my prop for every costume party I've attended the last five years: the all-purpose Afro wig. It's less than original, it might even be offensive, but at least I didn't lose my mind and fork over fifty bucks for an adult costume at the mall. Any man over the age of eighteen who buys a costume in a store needs to have a serious talking to, with the employment of physical force if need be.

Rolling down the road, it seems important, or at least appropriate that my stereo is playing *Doing It Do Death*, the JB's succeeding at something all the gods that wailed could never comprehend: sweet music.

Listen: a million honkies banging on a million drums could never produce the works of soul music's Shakespeare, James Brown.

At the intersection, I roll up on a brother blasting a bass guitar in the shape of an SUV. He turns and has the effrontery to give *me* a funny look. Don't look at me with that tone of voice, I think, and then remember: the wig. I smile and nod my head, keeping time with the booms and baps assailing everyone within a two-mile radius. Don't worry my friend, I know what's what. *Say it loud: I'm black and I'm proud!*

Know what I'm saying?

Neither does he.

* * *

This company claims to do many things correctly, but for two things in particular they are unimpeachable: they make money, and they can throw a party. They've rented out a building down-town, which I didn't even know was possible, and they're practically daring us to drink all this beer, which I know is not possible. And yet. It's not enough to have a party these days, there has to be a *theme*, and the 70s theme has not quite played itself out—yet. A company as big as this one should not need a theme, but it is part of the SOP: it provides people with something to talk about, it provides running impetus for conversation and comradery that otherwise would not exist at an event that, without the free booze, no one would want to attend.

The scene inside is carefully orchestrated anarchy: anything goes. It's like Boston on St. Patrick's Day, or New Orleans on Fat Tuesday; or New Orleans *any* day for that matter. Everyone is in costume, so coats and restraint got checked at the door—no one can do anything incriminating, because no one knows who anyone actually is. It's almost unnerving, a sort of freedom not felt since a college keg party, but this time the cops have already been called, and they are here to protect while we get served.

* * *

Otis informs me that the night is far from over, although he could have fooled me. He swears he's fine to drive, though he's not fooling me. Then he tells me he'll take us to an old school party, and who am I to object?

"You're gonna meet my *peeps*," Otis says.

"Your peeps?"

"These are some of the dudes I used to run with!"

"Run with?"

"You know, back in the day!"

"The day?"

"I made *history* with these motherfuckers!"

"History?"

"You'll see…"

So…Otis has taken us to a party where everyone is dressed up as a drug addict.

These characters, these costumes, are all very convincing. I'm not saying the scene is shady, but there is more paraphernalia here than a Merry Prankster's reunion; the air is thicker than Snoop Dogg's recording studio.

"Have a puff," someone dares me.

"No thanks bro, I'm semi-retired," I reply.

"It's all good," he says, holding out his hand. "This stuff will make you semi-*retarded*."

"Nope, I quit the heavy stuff when I got kicked out of the priesthood."

"Heavy stuff? You never smoked shit?"

"The only chronic I feel comfortable with is back pains…"

"You wanna buy some ecstasy?"

"Uh, not for me… I get nervous when I'm too happy."

I'm impressed with my restraint, but since self-abnegation is not my style, I realize I'm on borrowed time.

* * *

Here's how you know you've got problems: when you're standing in the corner (you were standing in line for the bathroom, at some point, but either got lost or else lost interest), trapped talking to some clown in a canvas smock (naturally) and what appears to be pajama bottoms, and the hand sewn hemp hat (of course)—and he's not dressed up for Halloween. You think of something, anything, to make yourself feel better about yourself (I mean just *look* at this guy) and then it (painfully) dawns on you, like a slab of bacon hitting the skillet: this gentleman makes more a year than you do, and that's before the taxes he doesn't pay.

But he's got what the girl you're with is looking for and you hope he's feeling like sharing the wealth, which he might be inclined to get around to doing if he can remember to stop talking for a few seconds.

So you wait. Patiently. And for your troubles, you are treated to an interminable barrage of pothead patois and dumbass observations.

"Dude," he says, interrupting himself, again. "Dude, do you know the *real* reason they won't legalize it?"

Who's they, you don't ask, because you know he's about to tell you, and more to the point, it's a fair certainty that your reasons are not exactly in accordance with the ones he's about to lay on the table.

"Dude," he says (and you begin to wonder if you should tell him your name isn't actually *Dude*, just in case he's trying to be cordial, or has you confused with someone else).

"If it was legal, then all these slick-ass politicians couldn't pretend they weren't the biggest blazers of all!"

You smile and nod your head, hoping he'll bust out the bong before your brain cells get wise and make a break for it.

* * *

Having that dream about being outside the party, naked. Only (this time) it's not a dream, and it's cold.

Think, you think.

I've got that naked Afro wig thing working, which is something, but since this isn't a porn movie, I'm starting to suspect I'm in deep shit.

"There you are!"

I never thought I'd be so happy to see Otis.

"What the hell happened to *you?*"

"I'm not sure… I was in a room with some chick…"

"What chick?"

"At least I *hope* it was a chick… she *felt* like a chick…"

"Come on, let's get out of here."

"Help me stand up."

"You're already standing."

"What do you mean?"

"Are you okay?" Otis asks, although he's the one driving.

"Just get us home in one piece."

"Man, you're a mess. Listen… how did you get alone with that girl in the first place?"

"She made me take a hit off that pipe… remember that stoner guy?"

"Stoner guy?"

"Yeah, the guy who kept trying to *sell* me shit…"

"That wasn't pot, that was *tobacco* in his pipe."

"Well what was it laced with?"

"*Laced* with? Listen dummy, it was fucking Prince Albert in a Can, not the Chronic! That guy doesn't do drugs."

"He just sells them?"

"What are you talking about? It was his *costume*; that guy is a godamn tax attorney!"

"Tax attorney?"

"Right."

"Tax attorneys smoke dope too…"

"No they don't, they just *need* to."

"So that pipe wasn't tainted?"

"Maybe it was the Absinthe…"

"*What?*"

"Nothing."

"Otis?"

"Yeah?"

"Are you okay to drive?"

"Of course not!"

"Good, I was getting worried for a minute there."

Asleep.

Awake.

An important question: "Am I home?"

"Almost."

"Why did we stop?"

"I need gas."

"You've got half a tank."

"No, not that gas, *this* gas."

"Is that what I think it is?"

"Extra chili and extra cheese."

"Oh baby, death dogs! This is just what the doctor ordered."

"We'll pay for this tomorrow of course."

"I don't give a shit."

"Oh yes you will..."

Home at last, home at last, thank God almighty…

Well, no need to get carried away about it.

I did not get arrested, I did not spend the evening (or the rest of my life) in jail, and I did not even drive home. Now I can only hope for a night's sleep that is equal parts restful (with the cold sweats and hot flashes) and restless (with the hot sweats and cold flashes) which, for me, is an agreeable alternative to the usual options.

* * *

Hangovers are overrated. Why can't they just cut to the chase and get right to the *death* part?

There was nothing half-assed about this hangover: it was both cheeks, smelly, sweating, situated right in the face, suffocating, smug and entirely serious about its intentions. It was the full-on Fatso Elvis, that never-dead angel of doom, avenging all those idiotic movies from the late 50s, as if they had anything to do with *me*.

Speaking of movies, here is one way to measure how much you drank the night before: the types of movies you'll allow yourself to see. The more insufferable the movie, the more wretched the hangover.

Here, look: *Lone Wolf McQuaid* for Christ's sake.

A reflection: this flick was horrific when it first soiled movie theaters in 1984, and it's safe to proclaim that not unlike Boone's Farm wine, it has only gotten less refined with time. Also, how is it possible that every Kung Fu movie actor (Chuck Norris conveniently leaps to mind) and World Wrasslin' Federation fool (Hulk Hogan anyone?) looks younger *now* than they did two decades ago? I'm not sure, but I'm fairly certain it has something to do with their souls, the devil and the deep blue sea.

See: speaking of Satan, now I'm watching one of the John Hughes movies that is on every weekend, that one where all the actors are playing high school students but are still older than I am now, fifteen years after I first saw them when I was in high school myself. In fact, it occurs to me that one of these brat-pack bozos is actually Chuck Norris's father.

And on that note, it's back to the business in hand, followed by my big plans of making long, lonely love to the couch.

* * *

Phone. Head. Hurt. Stop. Won't. Loud.

Finally:

"Hello?"

"Oh God."

"Hey Otis."

"Let's go get some food."

"I'm too hungover to eat."

"Shit, you're too hungover *not* to eat."

"I'm just going to inhale my own fumes... keep this buzz going."

"No man, we need to eat some *bad* food for this type of hangover."

"Bad food? Those death dogs not enough for you?"

"No, I'm not talking about normal stuff, like fried chicken or tacos... I'm talking about something *nasty*, like a grease sandwich, or deep-fried monkey brains, you know what I'm saying?"

"Uh."

"Come on man, something that's got a little *kick* to it."

"Uh... why don't you just eat some *shit*? You know, cut out the middleman."

"Come on, I'm buying."

"I can't, I'm *paying*."

Speaking of shit, this one's gonna be a double feature.

My ass is kicking my ass. Or, my ass is kicking itself.

I'm not sure exactly what's going on in my gut, but I have a hunch it is a decidedly *avant-garde* affair. I visualize multicolored mushrooms and paisley wallpaper lining my liver, as though Salvador Dali got turned loose in my tummy. If they put the old scope up my sphincter, it would reveal a dedicated team of little microbe guys sniffing glue and drinking whiskey, then whacking piñatas and tending to the snow-cone machine churning up the gut rot and foul fumes that it ingests (Willingly? Warily? What difference did it make?) on a semi-daily basis. There I go, again.

Phone. Please. No. Hope. Hell. Hello.

Silence.

"Otis?"

Nothing.

"Whitey?"

Finally: "It's me."

Me? Who's *me*?

Yoo-hoo! (To myself I say this).

"You who?"

"You don't know who this is?"

Oh. No.

It's *her*.

"So… what's up?"

"What do you mean what's up? *You* called *me* last night, late."

"I did nothing of the sort!"

"You wanna see my caller ID asshole?"

Ouch. How did I get myself into this mess?

Quick: Otis, drunk dialing on my cell phone. That fucker.

"What, you don't remember?"

"Uh… of course I do…"

Mental note: kick Otis's ass.

Listen: there are certain situations you long to experience until you are unlucky enough to actually find yourself living them.

Take a guy. Me, for instance, and two co-workers: Caryn (*with a C!*) and Carrie-Ann, both in their early forties and extremely attractive and extremely divorced and extremely available and anxious to find new love; or, in the meantime, just get laid. Ask them, they'll tell you. They are both executive assistants on F5, working for hot shots who are everywhere on the planet except in their own offices. One is blonde and the other a brunette, like comic strip or sit-com heroines from the 80s, and like the accommodating guy that I am, I lust after both of them with neither preference nor prejudice.

Add six months and a few happy hours, and that is how I find myself here, at a bar I have no business being at, alone with them after everyone else with a reason has gone home. In other words, the place is packed.

I'm out of here, I don't say as the waitress brings a final round of dirty Martinis. Everyone in this bar, including the women, smokes cigars. There is a sugar-free jazz quartet confidently excoriating standards in the corner. Older men in expensive chimp suits eye me grudgingly, maybe even enviously. I got what they want, and if they only knew how eager I'd be to give it up they'd be even more bitter.

You'd think I was in heaven.

And you'd be right, if *you* were me, but I'm stuck being myself, wishing I were anywhere but here. Why? One simple reason: I've *been* here before, recently, and I've seen where this leads, and it's nowhere I'm trying to return.

Unbeknownst to Carrie-Ann, I've spent the night—twice—at Caryn's crib. And worse, I haven't so much as laid a tongue on her. By choice. And worse, this has somehow encouraged her, or reaffirmed her resolve. I have assumed unprecedented empathy for what women go through, because in this instance, I've become one.

Here's the scoop: happy hour, a few weeks ago, we're the last two at the bar (funny how that happens when you only leave happy hour after it's become unhappy evening, and they are kicking you out at last call), and I'm too drunk to drive, meaning I want to cab it back to her house and try to get lucky. So we stumble back to her apartment, and I'm practically pinching myself to keep from shouting out the sweet words repeating themselves in my head: *It's on!*

On the couch, the lights out, the candle lit, the obligatory Barry White album on (I don't have the heart to insist on Isaac Hayes), a couple of nightcaps kicking it on the coffee table. It is, as they say, on. And then the worst thing in the world happens.

She starts speaking.

A lot. About everything. Things I would not, under any circumstances, deserve or have any desire to hear (and considering I am almost certainly about to have sex that's really saying something).

Look: I overlooked the alarming assortment of teddy bears on her bed (alarming in the sense that it must require some type of performance art on her part to slide under the sheets without suffocating on fake fur); I didn't think twice about the George W. Bush bumper sticker on the refrigerator; I even turned a blind eye to the collection of movie musicals stockpiled next to her TV, like a modern day Tower of Babble.

Who cared? It was *on*!

But then, I'm hearing more than I ever needed to know about her ex-husband who (naturally) left her for a younger woman and (obviously) she doesn't hate him, she actually feels sorry for him, you know? And (apparently) she'd always been unsure about wanting kids, but fate had pretty much settled that dilemma for her, doncha think? And, well, I can't believe I'm about to tell you this, but to be honest, I haven't had an orgasm since college, I mean, that ex of mine made a *ton* of money and it all went right up our noses and let me tell you something, all that blow used to turn his prick into a pretzel!

And whatnot.

Fifteen minutes, or five hours later, I had to go deep into the bag of tricks, reaching for the exceedingly seldom-invoked pretend-to-pass-out sham. It worked.

It worked *too* well, because I found myself on the same couch the following Friday night. This time, she didn't say too much—she didn't say *anything*. That silent expectation, that all-too-rare (for a reason) opportunity to have at it, have your way, work yourself into her pretty-good graces, pull her wool over your eyes, and so on.

It's just as well, I thought as I pretended to fall asleep just outside of her arms for the second time. After all (I thought), I work with her, and I have to see her *every* day and this might be the time to act responsibly, for a change.

And so on.

The third time is no charm, especially since I actually learned my lesson (the soft way). This time, I tried to avoid being left alone with Caryn. And it worked. The only problem is, Carrie-Ann is also on the case, like a kid sister who can't stand being left out of the fun. Now, the last thing I want Caryn to think is that I've avoided the almost inevitable with her because I secretly prefer Carrie-Ann, especially since, at this point, it's probably the truth.

"I *love* Martinis," someone says.

"The dirtier the better!" someone else adds.

"I could do with more dirty and less Martini," some idiot who sounds a lot like me remarks.

"Should we ask for the check?"

"Don't worry, they'll bring it around when they're good and ready; they're very reliable that way."

"I'll get your drinks, I owe you from last time."

Ouch.

That was Caryn, and that was intentional.

Last time? Carrie-Ann does not ask. She does not need to.

Score: 1-0, Caryn.

"So, you made Byron buy your drinks? Let me guess, you forgot your wallet, *again?*"

Score: tied.

"I'm hitting the ladies' room," Caryn says, standing up.

You sure you don't want to hit one of us? (To myself I say this).

Score: 2-1, Carrie-Ann.

"So..." she says, once her nemesis is safely out of ear shot. "When did *you* buy *her* drinks?"

"The last beer bash sort of spilled over here last week, and we were the last two sitting."

This excuse comes easily, and sounds remarkably convincing. It also has the novelty of actually being the truth.

"Hmm... I guess I wasn't invited to that party," Carrie-Ann says, but she's smiling.

"You're *always* invited," I say, and so far, I haven't had to lie about a single thing.

"So… don't tell me she tried to get you back to her place?"

"Actually, she succeeded," I say. Still not even a small lie. Even worse, a big mistake.

"Well, I suppose nothing good happened, or else you wouldn't be telling me," she replies, recovering nicely.

Score: 10-1, Carrie-Ann.

"Are we getting one for the road?" Caryn asks as she rejoins the party. "Or did Carrie-Ann get cut off again?"

Offsides, but effective.

"Let me see if I can stumble to the little girls' room," Carrie-Ann announces. "Don't try to take Byron home while I'm away!"

The fur is officially flying, forget trying to keep score.

"I shouldn't tell you this," Caryn says, once the woman she works an office away from is out of sight. "But you should know…"

"Are you sure?" I ask, and that's only the half of it.

"It's just that I'm so *irritated*," she says, squeezing the life out of her Martini glass.

"Why's that?" I offer encouragingly. If I'm already soaked, I may as well start swimming.

"Well… earlier when you were in the bathroom, *she*…" she pauses (for effect?). "I probably shouldn't tell you this…"

"Of course you should," I say, because now I want to know.

"Well… she waited until you were gone and then asked me which one of us was taking you home."

"Are you serious?" I ask, and it occurs to me that one reason fantasies are seldom fulfilled is because their whole rationale requires remaining outside the realm of actualization.

Conveniently, the less-than-attentive cocktail waitress has decided it's time for us to take our melodrama elsewhere, and drops our incriminating check in front of us. It remains upside down, as though it's ashamed, either of its amount or merely being associated with the likes of us.

Caryn pulls platinum out of her purse and pins down the self-pitying tab. Like a grown-up game of musical chairs, she stands abruptly the second Carrie-Ann returns.

"I think I'm going to be sick," she whispers, all the fight—and a great deal of the color—suddenly absent from her face.

"Yeah right," Carrie-Ann hisses once Caryn has hurried in the other direction. "I'll bet she isn't even *puking*," she adds, as though no possibility could make her less pleased.

"I think it's time to call a cab," I announce, the truth having apparently become a habit.

"I don't know about *you* two, but I'm definitely driving my own car home."

Before I can offer my (honest) opinion of this development, she leans in and places her lips inches from my innocent ear.

"Are you coming with me?"

A long silence seems to ensue before I hear myself speaking.

"I'd better take a rain check."

I understand that this decision will more than likely put a permanent lock on the door I never got to open.

"Suit yourself," she says, making sure I don't see her face as she high-heels it out of the bar.

"I can't just leave her here, sick in the bathroom," I say to a table of Martinis so dry they are, in fact, empty.

A few minutes later the lights come on, making it official that this establishment is no longer responsible for our behavior, if it ever was. I add a grudging twenty-percent tip—on principle—and sign Caryn's name, which technically isn't a lie, under the circumstances.

I hang out on the wrong side of the women's room, each second adding to the solemn sum total of my discomfort. Just then the cell phone I pretend to never have on me does the twist in my front pocket and I immediately scan the caller ID I pretend to never pay attention to.

It's her.

"Caryn?"

"Hi."

"I'm standing outside the ladies' room…"

"Why?"

"Why? I'm waiting for *you!*"

"But I'm at home."

"Home? How?"

"I called a cab."

"When?"

"When I left."

"I thought you went to get sick!"

"I had to say *something*."

"Why?"

"Because… I figured you were leaving with *her*."

"But I didn't."

"Really?"

"She just left, alone."

"Is she upset?"

"I'm not sure." (Still, technically, not a lie).

"So you waited for me?"

"Well, I'm waiting outside the bathroom right now…"

"That's sweet."

"Are you okay?"

"I'm going to sleep."

"Okay."

"Byron?"

"Yeah?"

"I'm sorry. I wish things had worked out differently tonight."

"Me too."

If she were here I would smile reassuringly, but she is asleep so I'm not obliged. Not entirely innocent either, as I realize I saved my only lie of the evening for the very end.

* * *

Awake. Alive. Alone.

I've caught myself in the act, again, in the middle of a dream.

Good grief, I feel like I just finished running a marathon, or found myself transplanted in a Tom Clancy novel or something similarly dreadful.

If I'm *this* busy when I'm asleep, no wonder I'm exhausted while I'm awake.

Then I realize, I'm not alone.

My bed is crowded with the company of a surly hard-on and a caustic headache, a horrible combination under any circumstances.

First thing in the morning and last thing in the evening are the best times to tell you how you are living.

If you are in a good place—well-rested is a good place to start—you might identify with those birds, yapping happily at the sky before it even knows what to make of itself, before it's had a chance to decide if it will rain or shine.

If you are in somewhat of a less savory place—hungover is the obvious first option—you might feel like the worms, harried and hidden, hoping the light won't expose their soft spots to a world they're never quite ready to face.

Mostly, you should avoid making serious life decisions unless you are sober and showered.

* * *

"Take off all your clothes," I say.

"No," she laughs.

So: sober, there are no easy excuses. Excuses make it easier, and the easier it is, the easier it is to make excuses. Conversation can kill everything: access, intimacy (which is ironic), and mostly it can provide a good enough excuse. Stuck between a rock and a not-hard-enough place.

"Be careful," I say as she gets down on the carpet to entertain my dog's playful overtures. "He's a lady-killer."

"Like his daddy?" she asks, making it too easy, or not easy enough, depending on how it all undresses.

"Hardly," I say, reaching for the bottle of wine that is equal parts incriminating and exciting—mostly, and most importantly, it is empty.

"You two make a cute couple," I say, equal parts innocent, honest, envious.

"Why don't you join us?"

Put on all your clothes, I do not say.

"Are you drunk," she says.

"Never," I lie.

"Am *I* drunk?" she asks.

"Not enough," I sigh.

"What did you say," she whispers.

"Nothing," I lie.

"Take off all your clothes," she laughs.

"Okay," I say.

* * *

"Well?"

"Well what?"

"Was she wearing panties?"

"What are you talking about?"

"Don't give me that shit," Otis smirks. "I *know* what you were up to last night!"

"What do you mean?"

"Don't bullshit a bullshitter, you have that raspy, late night out in a bar with smoke and drink scratchy voice from talking too loud in a crowded room thing going on."

"So maybe I went out for a few drinks…"

"Yeah, but you also have the post bar back to your place up all night tapping some ass no sleep look in your eyes."

"Really? I thought I was masking it okay."

"No way. You are obviously a shell of a man this morning."

"Damn. I took a twenty minute shower…"

"Yeah, well, you smell fine, but you can't shower that mess out of your system."

"A shower can do a lot, but it can't give you the sleep you should have gotten."

"So… was she wearing panties?"

"What are you talking about?"

"Whoever you took home… was she wearing a G-string?"

"Of course. Doesn't everyone these days?"

"Dude, let me explain something to you. I'm married."

"So?"

"So? Do you know what *my* wife wears?"

"What?"

"Underwear."

"Ouch."

"Come on man, give me something to live for."

"Well, it got ugly early."

"Did you close the deal?"

"Probably."

"Come on man, don't mess with me. I *need* this."

"Okay. She said '*Oh God*' so many times I thought I was at a church revival."

"That's what I'm talking about…"

"I thought she was gonna start handling snakes and shit."

"Oh you gave her a snake to handle."

"Exactly."

"What else?"

"She's only twenty."

"Oh God…"

"And she has a twin sister."

"Oh God… wait, are you bullshitting me?"

"Probably."

"You asshole."

"What?"

"Wait until you're married, you'll understand."

"Well, I was almost married once."

"Shut up."

"No, really."

"*You?* No shit!"

"Yup, I almost did the deed."

"What happened, she came to her senses?"

"Actually, she's the one who proposed to me."

"Shut up."

"I'm serious. I mean, it wasn't any sort of formal proposal…"

"Well, what *was* it?"

"She asked me to come away with her, she wanted to get married and elope to Mexico, or maybe California."

"Was she hot?"

"Sure."

"Really?"

"Better than I had any business having."

"Well… what was the problem?"

"This was a long time ago, back when I was bartending."

"One of your customers?"

"No, she was a waitress."

"Oh."

"Exactly. Things were pretty insane then. More so than now, if you can imagine."

"Big drinker?"

"Yeah, but everyone drinks in that scene. She sort of had her hands in everything."

"Drugs?"

"Yeah."

"Heavy shit?"

"Nothing out of the ordinary—at least for the restaurant business. No needles, no pipes. A little bit of nose candy, a lot of weed… the usual suspects."

"Were you digging it?"

"Not nearly as much as you'd think."

"Didn't like the action?"

"No, I was afraid I *would* like it, so I generally avoided it."

"Why Mexico?"

"She was getting burnt out… everyone gets burnt out sooner or later."

"Yeah, but why *Mexico?*"

"I don't know if she ever gave it much thought. She just wanted to get out of there; get off the east coast. Mexico, Mars, whatever."

"So what happened?"

"She went west, she made a clean break."

"Did you keep in touch?"

"No, I haven't gotten a call or a card since she split."

"That's fucked up."

"It is what it is."

"You don't know where she is now?"

"No idea. Maybe Mexico, maybe Mars."

"Any regrets?"

"There's always regrets."

"But I mean, do you think you did the right thing?"

"Yeah. We'd both be bartending in San Diego or something…"

"So?"

"I think we each needed to grow up… find ourselves and so forth."

"Have you *found* yourself yet?"

"Sometimes I feel like the harder I look, the more lost I get."

"Don't worry, once you get married and have kids you won't have time to worry about silly stuff like happiness."

"Some days that's what I look forward to; some days that's what I'm afraid of."

"You can't think so much about your life, it'll be over before you figure out what you want to do."

Isn't that the point? (To myself I say this).

* * *

"Let's get married," she said.

I didn't think we were the marrying type, I didn't say.

"Are you serious?"

"Well… what else are you looking for in life?"

"You mean in terms of a relationship or… when I grow up?"

"Fuck growing up."

"You know what I mean."

"Yeah, I do. Look at all the *regular* people we see every day in the restaurant. Do any of those assholes seem happy to you?"

"I don't think happiness really factors into it."

"Well, it should. It's *supposed* to."

"But, I mean… do you see yourself doing *this* five years from now?"

"Why not?"

"Ten years?"

"Well, I don't see myself sitting behind a godamn desk, if that's what you mean."

"I don't either."

"Besides, it's easier for you."

"How so?"

"You can go teach if you want, you've got a degree. You're never going to have to worry about getting a real job."

"Are you sure it's that simple?"

"It is unless you make it more complicated."

"Okay, so where are we in five years?"

"I don't want to worry about five years from now… I don't

want to worry about five *months* from now. Can't we just, you know, exist?"

"We've been existing our whole lives."

"So let's mix it up then. Let's make something happen!"

"Like what?"

"I don't know... head west. California maybe."

"I didn't think we were the California type..."

"Screw it, we could go to Mexico. You know, live on the beach."

"I don't speak Mexican."

"Neither do they."

"Well, it would certainly be a change of pace."

"We could *use* a change of pace. Don't you want a change of pace?"

You have no idea (To myself I said this).

"Goodbye," she finally said, after we'd both said many other things, most of them equal parts honest and unfortunate.

I still recall that last conversation and wonder if I'd made a big mistake. With my decision. With my life.

* * *

My dog has had enough.

When he was a puppy, he'd whimper anytime I was out of sight. All through his infancy, all he seemed to want was to share space with me, inhale the air I exhaled, flirt with my feet with his nose. As he settled into the dog-eared years of adolescence, we got into a good groove: aside from the inevitable, and understandable, teenage tantrums, he was everything I could ever have hoped for. Once he was old enough to drive he would sometimes scold me: if I stayed out all night or stumbled through another substandard evening stroll, or when I collapsed from exhaustion after throwing a toy once or twice, he conveyed his disenchantment by setting up camp across the room, safely out of reach, to put his head between his hands and sulk. And stare. You can always tell when a dog is unhappy because the rest of the time they are either ecstatic or asleep.

It just doesn't happen; it goes against all the everyday angels of their nature. And yet. My dog is ashamed of me.

Enough, he says, slouching on his padded island in the corner.

"Okay, I understand," I say, comatose on my well-fortified, more than half comfortable couch.

Now that my dog has finally grown older than me, he takes it upon himself to express his disapproval, and occasionally even his disappointment.

It's time, we think, to begin asking ourselves some complicated questions.

Midnight is the cruelest hour, causing saints to sin and sinners to sing, shrieking when, besotted with spirits and spirits spiraling, impaired and incoherent, they realize they're lost with no safe way home.

The bar beckons. Bars, if they are good for nothing else, are good for that: bars beckon. Watering holes for weary warriors who want what they got and get nothing they ask for (they could pray but they know better). Swinging down accustomed streets, a humid mist sweats under the streetlights and clings to the faces of these silent, suffering souls. You wade through the haze of colorless ties and colorful perfumes. Familiar sights and sounds: laughter, screams, secrets and seductions, spilling out of mouths that come to places like this, killing themselves slowly in order to live.

So what happens? What doesn't happen. The same old story: You don't go looking for trouble, but trouble has no qualms finding you. And it finds you, as always. Trouble is so reliable that way. You work toward being a lover and not a fighter. The only problem is, it is usually the loving that leads to the fighting.

Not working, but there is a lot of work to do. You go above and beyond the call of duty. And the harder you work, the more you seem to pay. Only in America could you do so little and get paid so much, then work so hard and pay so much. Someone makes the rules, and it's not you.

(It is easier than anyone would imagine.

When you are falling down a hill, you pick up speed, and pretty soon momentum carries you. It does the work for you, and after a while you begin to feel accountable, even a bit lazy. So you decide to help out a little, pull your weight, be a team player, take matters into your own hands. And so on.)

There's nowhere good this can go and everybody knows that driving blind with deafened senses is dumb. Shifting and stuttering but smart enough not to pray (you know better).

Avoiding eye contact, the street refuses to speak—it will not willingly partner this perpetration in progress. Overhead, the fully dressed, deep green oak trees on either side lean down low, eager to eavesdrop. Here's what they hear:

   "Please help me."

Part Two:
THE MONEY DREAD

One

STRICTLY BUSINESS

L IKE EVERYONE ELSE I know, I grew up—*really* grew up, if I've ever actually grown up—in the Reagan 80s. Take my childhood, please. Actually, it wasn't all that bad. During the extreme periods of boom and busted, pro and convicts, the majority in the middle seldom feel the pain, they rarely see the cocked fists and hoisted heels. It's the people on the poles, the haves and haven'ts, who taste the changes the have lesses can afford to ignore.

But now, after the 90s—on the verge of oblivion, as always—we have anti-inflation. We've got more money than we know what to do with; we've gotten so good at counting it we need to make more just to keep up, we keep making it so that we will still have something to *do*. Capitalism isn't wrong, but neither is intelligence: you cannot spend money and make money—someone is always paying the tab (and it's usually the poor suckers who can't spend it who get fucked, figuratively if not literally, so that anonymous, ancient bored members can pulverize their port-folios). In other words, working where I work, with neither the best nor the brightest bulbs in the professional firmament, I can see for myself that this has nothing to do with *talent*, necessarily. It's about numbers. Like an army, like America. Whether you're a company or a cult (like an army, like America), you simply want to amass enough manpower so that nothing else matters. Quality? Integrity? Originality? Nice, all, but they've got nothing on the numbers. When you're big enough, you don't have to beat anyone up, your rep precedes you and quells all contenders. You don't have to fight anymore. Safety in numbers, sure, but there's more at stake than simply survival—people are trying to make *money*.

Look: I'm not unaware of the wealth our deal cutters are creating, and I'm not unappreciative when they sign my paychecks. In the 80s, or any other time, you had the fat-walleted fuckheads trying to multiply their millions by *any means necessary*; they didn't just disregard the reality of putting their foot on nameless faces to divide and conquer, they reveled in it. It wasn't personal, it was strictly business, and it wasn't their fault they excelled at it, it isn't their fault they were *born* into this. The only responsibility they had was to ensure that all the affluence they had no part in amassing stayed safely outside the reaches of normal, taxpaying proletariat.

Let's face it: it's not as though the five or six folks who actually flip the switches and decide *who* gets *what* (after, of course, they've had theirs) ever consented to this sudden, and by all accounts inexplicable, turn of events. They certainly didn't *plan* it this way. And you can be certain they don't condone it or in any way seek to keep it around if they can help it. But that's the thing: they can't help it. They never saw it coming. I definitely didn't see it coming. I see it every time I look at Otis: who could possibly have predicted *this*? The guys that—if they were lucky—were going to be chain restaurant managers and counter-jockeys at video stores suddenly had the keys to the kingdom, because they understood how the world wide web worked.

But I'm willing to bet some of the money I'm supposedly worth that these unsettled old sons of bitches are very interested in redirecting wealth back into the hoary hands of those used to handling it. How, they must stay awake during the day worrying, can this country continue to run *right* when so many regular people start getting involved? It happened before, in the 1920s, and if they had to eliminate alcohol for a few years then maybe it's time to start confiscating computers.

Still, I can't shake the suspicion that these visionaries are doing many of us a disservice by manufacturing this much money, for making it so *easy*. Everyone loves their job these days, and it's for all the wrong reasons. It's all about the money. The money this and the money that. You lose money to make money, you make money to make money, you *take* money to make money, you make up anything—to make money. Right now, as the new century sucks in its gut for the changing of the guard, unearned money hangs heavy in the air like encouraging ozone: a tardy rain's gonna fall eventually, inevitably, and everyone will wonder why they're soaking wet and insolvent.

Reality Check (1)

You did it.

(You didn't really think you could keep up that pace, did you? Only rock stars can do that sort of stuff, and you see how rock stars look after a while, don't you?)

It doesn't take too much to know you're in trouble, and you knew it.

(The difference between those who choose to help themselves and those who don't is that it's only when you care about trouble—and the things it has waiting around the corner—that you begin to consider things. You hope it's not too late.)

You do what you have to do:

Skip the Twelve Step circuit, but imagine what you were missing—like a rehabilitated rock star touring the country. One night stands in more places than you could count, a sea of strange faces, a different crowd every time, the standard songs, a few encores, lighters lifted in the air, and the salted trail of tears.

Begin having conversations you can actually recall the next morning.

Fall in love with everyone who would listen. Leaders, followers, those enviably further down the road, those helplessly far behind, some of them unbearably attractive, some of them irresistibly appealing, most of them exquisitely ordinary. Fall in love with all of them, anyone who would listen. Listen: when the last thing you can count on is the sound of your own voice making promises you're not sure you can keep, you need to hear it, and you want to hear other people hearing it.

Get better. Then, suddenly, the weaker ones are on you in ways you wouldn't believe. This was when you knew you were better, when you saw yourself—the way you used to be—in their empty eyes, lemmings running toward the recently dried-up river bed. It's astonishing, the sorts of things an aloof man is privy to. He hears things he doesn't want to hear, which are the exact things he never heard when he needed to hear them. So he says: Don't tell me that. *And then hears more of the same.*

Settle for settling down. Contemplate having some kids, tentatively embrace adulthood. No other keys could fit your reconfigured lock, so work hard toward retirement. And finally, if you have any luck left, you'll live happily ever after.

The end.

Two

EVERYBODY KNOWS
THIS IS NOWHERE

*B*E HYPOCRITICAL, BE cautious; be not what you seem
but always what you see.
    I didn't write that.

That is intimidating, possibly inspiring. Mostly disparaging.
We're scarcely prepared to *read* these poems, in college, already
older than the authors were when they wrote them. And yet, if
there is something to be said for late bloomers, it's that they tend
to live longer. We may, in fact, have figured out how to live forever. Ask anyone. We've certainly made it easier, now that even
our most mundane correspondence is captured, each moment, in
a million miniature universes of our making; electronic black holes
of words instead of stars. Email makes us immortal. The ghosts are
in the machines, and these galaxies won't implode even if you pull
the plug.

The brave old world never had a chance, not against the
only enticement that liberty, love and especially life stand in the
shadow of: money. It's easy being green. Ask anyone. Especially

these grinning genies, let out of the (champagne) bottle, who are already worth more—on paper—than their fathers amassed in fifty years. This is America, and everyone here is dreaming. Ask anyone: they'll pinch themselves and insist that they're awake. What is life, anyway, but a day and night fight to fend off the big sleep that is waiting, under the rainbow, no matter how deluded or diversified we might be?

Listen: the ant could afford to scoff at the grasshopper. The ant had a whole colony, an entire *system*, to support him when winter finally came around. And ants are nothing if not industrious; they're admirable. They're also slaves. Ants were running the show all the way into the 1980s, but this last decade did a number on them. Exterminated, but they'll never be extinct. Ultimately, they'll still be around, working their asses off, maybe allowing themselves a sweet second or two to shake their heads and say *I told you so* to all the creatures left out in the cold. A day that has to come, someday, when the lights go out and these mansions crumble under the empty weight of unkept promises.

* * *

Now get a load of *this* guy.

My neighbor, whose name I've of course forgotten—if in fact I ever knew it in the first place—(and, being roughly my age, never objects to and always answers my irrefutably cordial salutations which include *chief, dude, bro,* and the ever appropriate and all-purpose *man*) is standing outside my door: I can see him through the peephole.

While I wonder if I should wait to see if he'll knock again, he knocks again. It's eight-thirty in the morning, what's the worst thing that could happen?

"Hey Byron," he says, embarrassed or anxious. Or both (at least he remembers my name).

"What's up my man?" I say, not missing a beat.

"Listen, sorry to bother you… you on your way to work?"

"Yeah, actually… why, is everything okay?"

"Uh, yeah, listen, do you mind if I come inside for a second?"

I back up obligingly, resigned to roll with it. What choice is there? After all, I did open the door.

He corners me in my kitchen and asks if I know anyone who might be interested in buying a condo. *His* condo, for instance.

"I'm sure there are plenty of people who would love to live here," I offer.

"Yeah, I know, but… I mean, do you know anyone who's looking to buy a place?"

"I'd be happy to ask around, you know, put the word on the street and whatnot…"

"Yeah, that'd be cool, I'd appreciate that."

He looks away and it's my turn to say something.

"Everything okay?"

"Yeah, well, I got laid off, you know? So I'm just gonna move home for a while, with my folks. You know, till I get my shit straight."

"I hear you," I say as encouragingly as possible, but it's only half true. I *do* hear him, but I also hear myself (saying *I hear you*) as well as the voice inside my head, which is processing this situation and repeating the verdict: Not good, not good, *not good.*

He is sweating, his hands—which seem puffy and pale, I've never noticed what unbelievable meat hooks he has, though admittedly, the only times I bump into him are in the hallway as he disappears into his end unit with a case of Miller Lite cans under one arm, McDonald's or some other fast food monstrosity in the other—exhibits *A* and *B*, are shaking like the lid on a boiling pot, they are very obviously not obeying their master, and before I have half a chance to put two and two together he interrupts my internal assessment and looks at me searchingly.

"Hey Byron, you got any beer?"

At eight thirty-three in the A.M., there is only one possible answer to a question like this: "Sure," I say.

I open the refrigerator and remember: I drank my last beer last month, which makes me a liar.

"Actually, I don't," I start, but sense that will not suffice, so I hold the door open and let him inspect for himself, which he does, making us both feel better—or worse—depending on how you look at it. He accepts this answer, but is clearly not satisfied with my response.

"Oh. I have plenty of liquor, if…"

"Yeah, do you care if I take a shot of something?"

Are you sure you're okay? (To myself I say this).

A pint glass is obviously inappropriate, so I grab a juice glass and put it down on the counter, sliding it over to him like a bartender from a black and white western. Eagerly, he has grabbed my neglected and indignant fifth of single-malt. I tell him to help himself.

He pours a generous, bordering on unbelievable, belt of my booze and inhales it in one febrile motion. This is strictly business (to myself I say this).

"Better?" I inquire, and actually mean it, I actually want to know.

"Uh… do you mind if I get another one?"

"Hey bro, knock yourself out," I say. Stupidly.

He doesn't notice because he's too busy securing the second round in case I try and give last call at the last second. Even the sweat on his forehead seems relieved. Although I know exactly what time it is, I can't help myself from looking up at the digits blinking on my oven: 8:34.

He looks at me and nods his head, expressing gratitude with his burning eyes. The eyes never lie. Then he snatches a tube of toothpaste out of his front pocket, puts it in his mouth and pulls the trigger.

"So, you wouldn't mind asking around, you know, just see if anyone is looking to maybe live here… I'll cut a deal…"

"No problem," I assure him.

"I'll hook you up with a finder's fee too…"

"Oh don't worry about that man, I'm happy to help."

Not good, not good, *not good.*

"Let me give you a card," he says, putting the toothpaste back and reaching into his other pocket. I'm surprised, in spite of myself, that between the shaking and the sheer size of his hands he can even fit them into his shirtsleeves.

"Fuck," he says, frazzled or furious. Or both.

"What's up?" I ask.

"I left my fucking cards in my place…"

"Well don't worry about it, let me just write your number down and…"

"No, let me run and get them, and you can hand them out and shit…"

"Okay."

I wait (too long) and go down to get them myself.

On the way, I think: Gambling debts? Drugs? Or both?

Drugs, it must be drugs.

Whatever it is, it's something I know I want no part of. It's obviously something my neighbor wants no part of either, or we wouldn't both be here right now.

I knock on the door.

It opens, quickly, and my neighbor walks out, shutting it behind him. Apparently I'm not supposed to see inside. Perhaps I don't *want* to see inside.

He follows me into the hall.

"Hey Byron, I appreciate anything you can do."

"No problem dude, I'm happy to help…"

"Listen," he leans in close. "Do you mind if I grab another shot?"

"Sure man."

I've already locked my door on the way out, so I let myself back in, tricking my dog into thinking a full day has already passed.

The bottle and glass are still on the counter, forming sticky circles of an early morning crime scene.

"Do you mind if I pour a stiff one?"

"Help yourself, chief."

You want to take the bottle with you? (To myself I say this).

He pours a shot that would give Liberty Valance pause, polishes it off, and then pulls out the toothpaste from his holster.

I ask no questions, he tells no tales.

I tell my dog to hold down the fort (again) and my dog looks confused or disappointed. Or both. I lock the door (again) and escort my soon-to-be-ex-neighbor out.

"Thanks again Byron."

"Okay man, take care of yourself."

"Give me a call if you hear anything."

"Will do."

Both of us seem to understand, as we go our separate ways, that we'll never see each other again, and we are each somewhat deflated, probably for opposite reasons.

* * *

"It is amazing what you can accomplish if you do not care who gets the credit."

I didn't say that.

The Don, again, quoting a dead president, again (Harry S. Truman for this week's meeting).

Let's be honest here; it's not as though these *consigliores* of capitalism up on F5 are thrilled with the notion that, while they are unquestionably calling all the shots, there still *are* lunatics in their asylum. Lots of them.

If there wasn't so much money being manufactured at twice the speed of greed, it's very likely that these esurient executives would stop, look around, and feel more than a little wary. Even suspicious. Even *frightened*.

Take Boyd Bender.

What does a guy like him think when he eyes a guy like *me* waltzing in and out of the corporate offices? What does *he* make of all the earring-wearing, mascara-sporting, hair-in-the-eye-having, sandal-sporting, purse-carrying freaks? And that's just the men.

I suspect he must feel a little like Colonel Kurtz, pre-disintegration: ennobled but also overwhelmed by the sheer magnitude of disciples streaking through the exposed shadows in their T-shirts, doing his bidding but unable to speak the language in which he rewrites the rules every day. That is a serious drawback of becoming a god, especially if you are the sort of deity who would prefer not to mingle with the wretched masses. Sooner or later, if you get used to looking down on the world, you'll have to expect that millions of simple faces will stare right back at you, patient and praying, angry and impatient, waiting for whatever wisdom, whatever fortune, whatever *direction* you can find it within your dark heart to bestow.

The horror... the horror (to himself he thinks this.)

* * *

Otis calls me and tells me to come to his office—it's a matter of life and death. I'm only slightly surprised when I walk in and see him kicked back in his chair, carelessly emptying a potato chip bag into his mouth.

"Life and death, huh?"

"You better believe it," he says, making sure to show me as much chewed mess as possible. "You are not going to *believe* this shit."

"What?"

"Close the door."

"Why?"

"Don't worry, it's not anything offensive as far as you know."

He points to his monitor, which has the freeze-framed image of what appears to be a praying mantis.

"I didn't take you for the Discovery Channel type," I say.

"Discovery Channel my ass… check this out, dude."

What follows is an insect cage match, a sort of prehistoric Thunderdome: two bugs enter, one bug leaves. The praying mantis tangles for a few minutes with what looks like a dung beetle (I know this because I am the Discovery Channel type): the close-up shots reveal what menacing pincers they have, angles not commonly shown on the Discovery Channel. The two circle each other, and whether or not they are interested, the cage is too small, and money is, after all, on the line. Instinct overcomes everything else: they fight. Each time the camera pans out, you can see a room full of Asian businessmen. They're buttoned up with coat and tie, but the looks on their faces indicate that this is how certain types of (obviously wealthy) jerkoffs let their hair down.

"There's no way this is real," I say.

"Ask that praying mantis if it's real."

"There's no way this is legal."

"Of course not," he says. "That's what makes it so perfect!"

I look at the bills trading hands—it is like a busy morning on Wall Street with premium cocaine and other people's money.

"There's no way this is real."

"Are you kidding me? Listen amigo, the Japs know how to get things done…"

"The Japs?"

"Or maybe they're Korean, whatever. The thing is, they understand the bigger picture…"

I don't bother to ask Otis in what way forcing insects to fight for their lives contributes to any sort of bigger picture. Also, I'm certain he has an answer, and I know I don't need to know it.

More insects are waiting to join the party: spiders, scorpions, bees, things that look like miniature black rhinos. Other things that, when the camera zooms in on them, are scarier than any horror movie I've seen, scarier than anything I've ever imagined.

"That's right," laughs Otis, speaking to the screen. "What do you say *now*, Mr. Wasp? Not so tough without your whole nest backing you up, are you?"

I wonder how Otis would feel inside that cage with the tarantula that has just made brutally efficient work of Mr. Wasp. I wonder how Otis would feel inside that cage with *Jean* coming after him.

"Oh shit! Look at this thing, whatever the fuck it is. You think it knows he's the bad-ass of the bunch? I bet this one is the heavy-weight champ!"

Maybe Otis is on to something. Maybe these insects actually enjoy this. Maybe they are from the sketchy part of town and are happy to fight their way out of poverty and obscurity. Maybe the insect world needs rock stars too; creatures who have it all and then watch it all fall apart because of booze, drugs and debauchery. Or maybe they were modest, diligent insects with families to raise and retirement to plan for. Maybe some of these insects were simply on their way to church, thinking profound thoughts about the great arachnid in the sky, only to find themselves snatched up and made reluctant recruits for a more evolved pest's idea of entertainment.

"You know what I'm thinking?" Otis asks.

I have no idea.

"*This* is the Internet, bro, *this* is what our company has tapped into. We are helping make all this possible."

I don't disagree.

"This is going to change everything we used to think we knew."

Again, I don't disagree.

"Shit, it's *already* changed, this freight train ain't slowing down!"

I still don't disagree.

"I can access this site, for free, check out these videos, for free, and save them and watch them as many times as I want, for free. And you know what the best part is?"

Otis waits for me to guess, but I'm too busy not disagreeing.

"The best part is, someone's making *money* from this!"

Yes, of course. There's always that. I'll admit, it's impossible to argue with any of it, particularly that last part. And yet, merely not disagreeing, I understand, will not be sufficient.

"Otis," I say. "I don't disagree."

* * *

It's not unusual for me to go an entire day without saying a word to anyone up on F5, what with all the closed doors, urgent meetings and power lunches. So it's usually a refreshing change of pace when Chazz comes up after hours and answers all the questions I've never bothered to ask.

"Ever think about Hell?"

"Hell?"

"Yeah. You afraid of Hell?"

"I don't believe in Hell."

"I didn't ask if you *believed* in Hell, I asked if you were afraid of it."

"How can I be afraid of it if I don't think it's real?"

"You think all *this* is real?"

"You got me there."

"Ever think that we're in Hell, right here and right now?"

"You mean *this*?"

"Well, does this seem like Heaven to you?"

He's got me there.

Sometimes I'm ready to get back to work before he's finished talking, so I'm relieved when he says he needs to get going, and surprised when he mentions a wife I've never heard him discuss before.

"You're married?"

"Of course man, what you think?"

"You don't wear a ring."

"I don't believe in 'em."

"What does your wife have to say about that?"

"She don't give a care, long as I come home every night!"

I point at him and smile, and he winks back at me, a grin that conceals as much as it reveals.

"And what about you?"

"I don't believe in rings either!"

"Yeah, well, do you believe in marriage?"

"I believe in *love*..."

"So what's the problem?"

"I'm not sure love believes in me."

"Are you afraid?"

"Yeah, sometimes."

"That's good."

"You think?"

"Yeah. The cats who aren't afraid never even know what they're missin', even when they got it. Know what I'm sayin'?"

"I'm not sure."

"You will, one day."

I hope so (I think).

* * *

No one should be happy to be on an airplane at 7 AM. No one should be happy to be *awake* at 7 AM. Unfortunately for me, it appears that the only two people happy to be awake, in the air, and alive at 7 AM are on this same flight. Sitting directly in front of me. Speaking. Loudly.

What could anyone possibly have to say, to someone else, on a plane, at 7 AM?

Like virtually all of us, they're required by work to be here. Unlike virtually all of us, they're inexplicably tickled about it. And there is only one conceivable excuse for being delighted to be on a business trip at 7 AM: money. To be fair, they don't seem to be talking about money—yet—they're talking about love. Then again, if they're actually enjoying this ritual, love is just a metaphor for money.

And then, before smug self-approval allows me (for once) to

shut my eyes in peace, there is the maddening intrusion of alternate explanations. Perhaps this exultant young man in front of me is in the unfathomable thrall of fate. Perhaps, against all possibility, and in accordance with the inviolable intricacies of cliché, this fortunate fellow has met the stranger meant to be his soul mate.

And then: perhaps if I didn't always sit here, moping and miserable, I would meet *my* soul mate one of these mornings, enabling me, finally, to make some sense out of these loathsome business excursions. After all, isn't this how it always happens?

(Dad, how did you meet Mom?

You'd never believe it, but we met on a *plane!*)

Why shouldn't that be me?

It could.

And yet. It's not likely. After all, any time I'm on a plane at 7 AM, the smart coin bets on the certainty that I'll once again opt to remain silent, in my shell, eyes ironed shut, wishing I was anywhere else in the world.

* * *

Dead man talking:

"Far better it is to dare mighty things, to win glorious triumphs, even though checkered by failure, than to take rank with those poor spirits who neither enjoy much nor suffer much, because they live in the gray twilight that knows not victory nor defeat."

In these meetings every time someone has something important to say, they have someone else say it for them. In this case, it's Theodore Roosevelt. I'm not necessarily complaining: even in death, Teddy is arguably more energetic and articulate—not to mention a great deal cheaper to procure—than any of our living ex-presidents. He is certainly a hell of a lot more enlightening than the people in charge, who've assembled us today to talk about the state of our business.

(Uh oh.

For the last several years I've been mostly surrounded by middle—and middling—managers who went from washing windows to overseeing Windows upgrades for entire departments, but who floated from promotion to promotion on the ozone of stock options. These were people I could deal with, or never feel unduly out of my depth associating with, personally or professionally. Whenever in doubt, I could usually throw a multisyllabic word, no matter how senseless, in their general direction and get away unscathed, or at least throw them off my trail.

Now, with so much restructuring and fat-cutting, I'm increasingly finding myself in rooms with people who actually understand business. People conversant in MBA-speak and comfortable inside a ceaseless series of spreadsheets, people who can converse more fluently in PowerPoint than in person. People using words I don't understand. Words I fear. Words I've never *heard* of.

I'm intimidated. I'm lost. Worst of all, I'm bored.)

"*Ubiquity* is the continued mission for the upcoming year," the man who signs my paychecks says, then smiles. "Domination is only the first battle; after you've killed the competition, then you win over the wallets of the uncommitted masses!"

More talk of money spent and money made; milestones met and media hits. Ubiquity means *branding*, someone else avows. The silver rabbit's silhouette, the sublime black *swoosh* and the golden arches are each invoked as totems of our time, cultural touchstones to be taught someday in computerized classrooms.

Heads nod and eyes sparkle in rhythmic unison; the more palpable the shared enthusiasm becomes, the closer I come to crawling out of my skin.

Any questions or comments?

Long insufferable silence.

Someone say something!

Free bird! (To myself I say this.)

Then: eventually, inevitably, the word is spoken that reveals the *real* reason for this meeting: re-org. Anyone who knows anything—myself included—understands that the *R* word is not spoken lightly, is never employed before a modicum of thought has been expended considering its rationale. The strategic implications are, as always, exhaustive and ultimately irrelevant; the practical presumption is simple: the word re-org is a not-so-secret code for the reality that a lot of people are about to lose their jobs.

* * *

There's something in the air.

You can smell the spirit of cooperation in the germ-infested environment: Since the weather is being so accommodating, everyone is feeling obligated to get sick. Invisible agents of ill communication hover overhead like lightning rods for infection.

"Otis, you look awful."

"I *feel* awful."

"I mean you really look sick…"

"I really *am* sick!"

"So go home for God's sake!"

"Are you kidding me? I stay here so I can have some *peace*. If I go home do you know what's waiting for me?"

"A bed?"

"No. Screaming babies and getting shat on… and that's just my *wife.*"

"It has to be better than being at work."

"Are you crazy? I go home and the real work begins. This place is a paradise."

"It can't be that bad…"

"You'll see."

"Come on…"

"If I get in my bed my wife will yell at me, if I get on the couch I'll have to watch that godamn purple dragon who is trying to turn our kids into sissies."

"It can't be that bad."

"Do you want to know a secret?"

"I'm not sure."

"I make it a point to complain about work, all the time."

"Why?

"So my wife doesn't realize how much easier I have it."

* * *

Holiday season.

We are having a business lunch that makes the beer bashes look like stations of the cross. And to what do we owe this pleasure? Well, our pleasure is business, apparently. That, and the fact that the person paying our tab has more liquidity than Aquaman. *The Don* is the type of diner who can put restaurants in a different tax bracket. It sometimes seems like the dot-com bubble materialized simply to illustrate that an executive like him could exist.

We have the banquet room reserved. We have sparkling water so expensive it can cure cancer, or at least cause it. We have the manager serving us, because *The Don* has flummoxed our hapless waiter with his (increasingly outlandish) questions and exhortations. We're having a difficult time keeping conversation going (everyone is too busy talking to speak) but all of us are smiling, and this seems to be a more effective form of communication. I have questions. Before I bother to ask them, I remember that the answer to all of them is *money*. The manager has questions as well.

"Did you folks care for some starters?" Starters being appetizers that taste the same but are more expensive.

"Bring us one of everything," *The Don* says.

The only thing keeping this scene from being ironic is the absence of irony. I reckon the only way you can hope to counteract irony is to co-opt it before it gets started. Even irony follows orders if you decide you can afford to *own* it.

"Who says you can't have steak for lunch?"

Jovial, our very own Santa Claus beams, willing to open the wallet wide, and more than a little bemused to see so many junior executives reduced to greedy junior high school students.

"I'm not sure what to get," someone says.

"How about one of everything?" someone else suggests, jokingly. I think.

The great man raises one eyebrow and we all have the rewarding opportunity to see him think a new thought in real time.

"Hmmm… that could work. I'll tell you what, if you can eat at least one bite of every entrée, order them all."

I'm fairly certain that *The Don* is not joking.

It occurs to me (as things invariably occur to me whenever I behold our COO in action), *The Don* is not only utterly in his element—even willing to adapt and improvise on the spot, as we just witnessed—he is unquestionably of his time. Homer, for instance, had his Greek gods to immortalize, Genghis Khan had his enemies to annihilate, Henry Ford has his machines to manufacture; *The Don* has conquests to claim, the unconquered and undiscovered. He's not unlike Napoleon, only he has the advantage of facing neither armies nor the elements, because these battlefields are electronic and the spoils are printed on paper.

The Don considers the wine list and it's not clear if he is deliberating which bottles to order or which vineyards to acquire. Either way, against all likelihood, it seems we will not only be allowed to drink today, we will be obliged to drink very expensive items from a part of the menu none of us knew existed. I'm a bit envious, obviously, but I'm getting used to the sensation.

It is, as always, instructive to watch *The Don* do the things he does so well. I'm not even unconvinced he doesn't still have a soul, albeit one with the unmistakable imprimatur of dead presidents. I'm certainly not implying that he has a dilemma because, unlike just about every other honcho on F5, he actually seems to be *happy*. And yet, I can't help but wonder: what would Ahab do when he finally killed the white whale? Would he find peace? What would Ahab do once he realized he'd *become* the white whale? That the imperative previously compelling every action, every thought, was now his recently acquired acumen? What would he do, then?

Probably what white whales do: chew the legs off their competitors and simply stay alive by ceaselessly swimming into deeper and more dangerous waters.

* * *

Sick again.

Sort of.

It's in there; it knows it can have me if it wants.

It's the same old story: it can't quite commit, can't decide if it wants to take the time, miss the opportunities out there with all the other throats, noses and heads, asleep and unaware.

It knows me, feels like it's been here before.

A few extra minutes, assisted by the snooze button and self-pity, and then an emotional send-off from my sheets as I head for the shower.

Lost in lather, I sneak up on myself, grab a handful of wrinkled flesh and say "Cough." Granted, I touch myself more often than a professional baseball player, but somehow it seems appropriate, or at least *official* to check for those telltale lumps whilst naked, wet and upright. As though any carcinogen-in-progress could be caught unaware. Then again, I wouldn't put it past cancer. Everyone knows cancer is a coward: always doing its grim work in the dark, under cover of consciousness, never man enough for a fair fight, not letting you know until it's usually too late, while it busily pits organs against each other and pays off death by living to fight another day.

We've come a long way in our effort to live forever: we have armored cars, air bags, email. We've got accountants and attorneys to keep the money dread at bay. But when the going gets tough, there's nothing quite like a good dose of denial. And yet, the old things are still out there: accidents, old age, apathy. Money, they say, can't buy you love. Even worse, despite no lack of attention and energy, we've found that money can't buy you *life*, either.

Knowing you are going to die presents problems, naturally.

For instance, life and how to live it.

Do you just go out and suck the marrow out of life? You should. Because death sure as shit is going to suck the marrow out of *you* when you die.

* * *

My hypochondria is acting up again.

It's an annual routine; giving up a lunch hour to make sure I'm not dying of some undiscovered disease, or about to have a stroke, or a heart attack, or just to be certain I'm not pregnant.

All around me in the waiting room they are waiting: good reasons why I'm still single and may never find it in me to become a father. Sniffling, contagious little kiddies, coughing and sneezing, crying and carrying on—and that's just the mothers, some of them younger than me but appearing old enough to send me to my room without supper if I don't keep my eyes on the *Sports Illustrated* in my lap.

I have, I reckon, a close to ideal arrangement with Dr. Know, my PCP, who I try to see as seldom as possible, but still end up visiting entirely too frequently (once a year being twice as often as I'd prefer). I find that I'm always honest with her, no matter what she asks—and she only asks the tough questions—not necessarily out of respect, though I do respect her, but more because I don't know what else to do. Being a doctor, she disarms me. I can't charm her, like I could my female college professors; I can't bullshit with her, like I can with my colleagues, I can't speak casually while carefully avoiding any revealing issues, like I can with all my relatives, and I don't want to sleep with her, like I'd like to do with just about every other woman. When she looks at me, she sees through me, she sees blood and bones and veins and arteries and illnesses waiting to occur, I am another breathing page out of a textbook, a number to be crunched, a prescription to be filled, a case to be filed, a sickness to be cured, and as long as she will tell me I'm going to make it, I'll endure anything she decides to ask of me or put in me.

"You can put your pants back on," she says, after she's said a lot of other things, none of which sounded too terrible—not that I was in any shape, sartorially speaking, to protest too much.

"Have you gained some weight?" she asks, as if she isn't holding my chart.

"Well…"

My doctor gives me one of her looks.

"Look, I didn't *ask* my body to act this way, I didn't even give it permission!"

"That's not the way it works," she scolds me. "Once you turn thirty, everything sort of slows down."

Tell me about it, I don't say.

"So what can I do?"

"Start eating healthier foods. And exercising."

She waits for a moment, for dramatic effect, or perhaps to allow the absurdity of this remark to settle in my system.

"And stop drinking coffee," she adds, with a casualness that betrays a black, arctic heart.

"How about breathing? Should I just go ahead and give that up too, complete the tri-fecta?"

"Oh come on, it's not so bad. Your body will love you for it."

"To hell with my body, what about my *soul?*"

"I can't help you there," she smiles.

"Okay, I'll make a deal with you: how about I give up the cigarettes once and for all, just go cold turkey, and I'll check back in six months?"

She frowns, confused. "But you told me you don't smoke?"

"I *don't*… but you gotta give me *something*, I have to grab *something* to feel good about!"

"That's cheating."

"Well, I want extra credit anyway."

"You're only cheating yourself, if you want to stay healthy, you'll take my advice."

Who said anything about staying healthy, I just want to stay *alive*... (To myself I say this).

* * *

With all the road wars, gunfights, lawsuits and thought-revoking smack-downs (and that's just the nightly news), it would seem that this rage, being all the rage, has finally sated itself. But it takes two to mangle. So what does the angry young man do when he needs to uncork some simmering hostility and there is no one there to receive it? If you can't put a fist to flesh, apparently you can still put pen to paper. How else to explain the loveless letter (***edited due to sensitive content) left on my mostly innocent windshield?

Hey F-head!
   Who the F taught you to F-ing park you F-er! You're F-ing lucky I didn't key your F-ing car you motherF-er!!!

Wow.

This one's a keeper, I'm definitely saving this, with the full understanding that I may well have happened upon a handwritten document from a future president of the United States. Or per-haps my current boss.

I need to tell somebody about this; share it with someone who might shed some light on bile of this magnitude. There is only one person up to this particular task.

"This is William."

"What's with the *this is William* shit?"

"Byron?"

"When you answer the phone, Whitey, just fucking say *hello* like a normal person!"

"Huh?"

"*This is William?* What are you, a *businessman?*"

"Actually, yes…"

"Well for Christ's sake, you don't have to *act* like one…"

"By…"

"What."

"What did you call me for?"

"Never mind, forget it. I'm disgusted with you."

Click.

"This is…oh hey Byron."

"Hey."

"What's up?"

"I have to tell you something."

"Okay…"

"A while back you sort of freaked out…"

"By…"

"You wish you hadn't, but you're cool with it."

"Hey man, look…"

"You'll get better. Most people do."

"Byron…"

Click.

* * *

Back at the office, I see the human bundle of joy, my beloved Jean, walking wanly toward me.

"Hi Jean, Otis out today?"

"Yeah, his wife is having the baby."

"Well, he's never used *that* excuse before!"

Is that supposed to be funny? (To herself she says this).

"Can I ask you a question?" I ask.

After she's finished changing the oil and checking the tire pressure, she frowns, lifts my mouse and nods, pulling a not unimpressive fur ball from its belly.

"You need to *clean* this thing regularly," she sighs. "That's why your cursor is so sluggish."

"How do *you* know my cursor is sluggish? Oh, you're talking about my computer!"

She gives me a look and I catch my breath, waiting. But the look softens and after a second, I'd swear, I see what, coming from anyone else would be a blank stare, but, for her, is the early stages of an actual smile.

"I mean, I deleted the outbox and ran a defrag and rebooted," I begin, relishing my opportunity to throw around my uninspiring arsenal of computer speak.

"So," she leans in close, confiding. "You got your résumé updated?"

"Uh…"

"You've heard the rumors, right?"

"Are they checking everyone's résumé?"

"Is that supposed to be funny?"

She actually said it this time. I'm not sure how to respond.

"Uh…"

"How often do you update it?"

"Me?"

"Once a week? Twice?"

"A *week*?"

"You should."

"Once a *week*?"

"At least."

"How often do you update yours?"

"Every day, pretty much."

"Every *day*?"

"Why not? This is the single most important document I'll ever work on, right?"

"Uh…"

"It records my forward progress, how much I'll make, what titles I'll have, it's a scorecard of all my achievements."

"But, I mean, what can you possibly update that often?"

"Are you kidding? I try to learn a new skill every day."

"Every *day*? How is that even possible?"

"You ever look inside one of these things?"

"Uh…"

"You really don't know much about computers, do you?"

"As little as possible."

Fortunately for both of us, her beeper goes off, and she has the perfect excuse to remove herself from my impractical presence.

After she's gone, I ask myself some awkward questions.

Every *day*?

Is it possible there are people out there who really *enjoy* this shit? Maybe this is what it's like for someone who actually has discernible skills. Maybe, if you have something perceptible to provide the corporate world, this is how it works. Maybe, if you allow your business cards to speak for you and a job description tells you how to think, it's necessary to act like this.

And yet.

Every *day*?

No, there's no getting past it. She's just fucking nuts.

* * *

Sleeping.

Phone ringing.

It's probably Whitey, in need of his self-administered lullaby that someone else is obliged to hear. That someone is me.

"Goodnight," he says, after he has said a lot of other things.

Talk to you tomorrow (to myself I say this).

Reality Check (2)

You are high above the ground, alone on a decayed ladder, looking unsteadily beneath you at the splintered rungs which spiral out of sight.

You are afraid to look up, but as time passes your eyes grow accustomed to a feeble light that illuminates the sudden commotion below: you can discern distant shapes climbing toward you. Instinctively, you secure your grip, unnerved by the discordant and unintelligible voices.

These shapes slowly become solid figures and eventually you can identify their shaded faces—mouths all open in a synchronous signal as they quickly cut the distance, moving with renewed vigor as they spot you. Panicking, you lose your grip and flail at the open air, but somehow you do not fall.

Then: you understand that this impossible balancing act is being facilitated by the dark heads you have been standing on. You look down and see thousands upon thousands, filling the space beneath and around you, creating the bulwark between you and the nothingness below.

You look up at the light—at the ladder, leading ever upward—and climb toward what you can claim, causing the bodies below to lurch forward. Lost in the shuffle, one face is thrust forward, a face you recognize, a familiar smile and arms outstretched in greeting, or perhaps in supplication: a face screaming for assistance, a face you suddenly thrust your foot into, securing your grip on the ladder. You stop and watch the body drop away, disappearing into the darkness.

Three

LAWS OF THE JUNGLE

"JUST ABOUT EVERY species practices, and in some cases perfects, certain forms of cannibalism."

I didn't say that. The guy on TV, that anonymous narrator with the fake American accent did. Listen:

"Do you know which creature, relative to its size, is irrefutably the most aggressive on the entire planet?"

Got me.

I'll confess, the answer was not my first, or fifth choice. Not a lion (he explained), or an elephant, or alligator, or ant or even a *gnat* (which I would have guessed, just to be ironic, because as small as gnats are, there have to be even smaller insects whose asses they can kick—otherwise there wouldn't be so many goddamn gnats).

Check this out: there is a type of frog in South America so insatiable that not only does it attack and attempt to eat anything and everything smaller than itself, it even attempts to ingest things *larger* than itself. Seriously. Not infrequently (he explained), this overkill (so to speak) leads directly to death: it's not suicide, it's even more senseless. When these little fuckers get their mouth around something—another frog, for instance—and refuse to let go, they will hang on until they choke themselves.

Awake.

I woke up the other morning imagining that a frog only slightly smaller than me had attached itself below my waist, and before I could explain that only one of us was going to make it out of this alive, it ripped off its frog mask and I saw that it was actually a person. And here's the scary part: this person happened to look a lot like me, and he seemed to smile, as if to let me know that he was indeed picking on someone his own size. And then his mouth expanded ever so slightly, working its way up and closing in on the rest of me. Eventually, inevitably, I awoke, and was aware of two things: first, I was alive; and two, one can't believe everything one sees on television. If you do, it will give you nightmares, and we get enough of those just watching the director's cut called reality all the hours we're obliged to stay awake.

* * *

"Okay, and finally, what aspects of your job do you feel you may have performed *more* effectively during the past year?"

Well…

I could have drank less, eaten better, slept more, not wasted so much money, read a few of the books drowning in dust on the bedside table, called more relatives, called fewer friends, tried harder to avoid easy excuses, made a better effort to support ill-paid musicians, dedicated fewer days to becoming a Robin Hood for the corporate world. I could have avoided attempting to do anything *other* than work, and generally wishing the worst for everyone involved at (insert name of company here).

Oh! You mean my *day* job? My job here? The job you pay me to perform?

Well…

There's always more money to be made. Right?

The problem is: I am making money for men who make money from nothing.

(To myself I say all this).

"And what do you look forward to in the coming year?"

Uh. Being employed? Continuing to do exactly what I do now. Except less.

And before I know it, it's over. Easy. Then the man who signs my paychecks and buys many of my beers tells me to sign on the dotted line.

"Cheers."

There's little not to like about this: a three minute review, few questions asked, and even fewer lies offered in response.

Question: What's not to love?

Answer: There has to be more than this.

(More money? Sure. More power? Certainly. More meaning? Maybe. More *soul*? Sorry.) See: there's plenty more where all *this* came from—at least for the fortunate ones still around after the layoffs—and I've just been told that I can have as much of it as I'm willing to work for.

Look: there are people I went to school with who'd happily sell five years off their lifespan to get in on this action; I know guys who can kowtow circles around me, pals who could pucker up and kiss asses all day if that's what it took to get their mouths in the door. I know I'm one of the lucky ones. And yet. It isn't enough, because I can't stop remembering that there's more to life than this. This job feels like a woman I have no business taking to bed. Anyone else would envy me and I may even envy *myself*, but it's all about the splash and the show, it's all about the quick kill, the miracle that only lasts a moment, the type of bliss that burns off like a candle, needing to be ignited again each morning. Days that are all like our business dinners: self-indulgent, sybaritic, swilled, savored, and then filed away in a folder that is quickly forgotten.

The kind of days that will keep me up at night, later, when, at long last, I come to ask myself: isn't there more to life than *this*?

* * *

Lying in bed, thinking about geometry.

Like: how my arm next to her ass makes a right angle. Or, how her legs in either direction form an isosceles triangle (or is it scalene?). Scaling the perimeter from her belly button to below is heaven. Or, how the distance from my rectangle to her Pi is infinity. Or: A cup plus B-cup equals See. Proof: *if* her panties come off, *then* I will be pleased. Two shapes under the sheets are congruent to each other. She turns 180 degrees. I check my work. Pass/ fail, graded on the curves. Obtuse, an open book exam, I ask for extra credit.

* * *

Just as I'm thinking I haven't heard from Whitey in a few days, the phone rings.

"What's up Whitey?"

"Just getting back from Cali."

"Oh, that's right. Orientation training for the new gig?"

"Yeah."

"Did Silicon Valley survive?"

"Yeah."

"Did *you* survive?"

"Yeah."

"How did it go?"

"Okay. I'm just jetlagged like a motherfucker."

"Come on, don't give me that crap."

"What do you mean?"

"Jetlag?"

"Hey, haven't you ever had it?"

"I don't suffer from jetlag."

"Well, you're lucky then."

"I didn't say I wasn't *susceptible*, it's just that I refuse to suffer from jetlag, on general principle."

"Have you ever taken the red eye, asshole?"

"They made you take a *red eye*?"

"Actually, only the junior sales staff took the red eye, the rest of the team stayed out west an extra day…"

"Junior sales staff?"

"Yeah, we need to make cold calls for six months before we can move up…"

"Cold calls?"

"Yeah, if we show we can bring business in off the streets, they start allowing us to handle existing accounts."

Off the streets?

"I mean, it's rough right now, but you should see the guys in the President's Club, they're making more money than we could ever spend. At least that's what they say."

President's Club?

"Trust me, these dudes are *all* about the Benjamins. That's why they stayed out there, the company expensed a night on the town, out in L.A.!"

All about the Benjamins?

"I wanted to stay out there Byron. I wanted to be out there so bad I could taste it. But it makes us look good that we came back to cover the phones while those guys were all out of the office, you know?"

Cover the phones?

"Some of those guys were saying that when they were junior sales staff they put in eighty, sometimes a *hundred* hours a week, so we shouldn't complain, you know?"

A hundred hours?

"For every hour of overtime you work, that's one dollar closer to your first BMW, that's what they kept saying…"

Your first BMW?

"I need to get some new suits. These guys kept talking about how it doesn't make a shit of difference if we're in window-less rooms making our calls, you have to *act* like everyone can see you…"

Some new suits?

"If you *look* like you're used to flying first class, people pick up on that, it carries through in your voice, you know?"

Flying first class?

"I thought of that the whole way back—that's the thing about red-eyes, it's night out but you can't sleep at all…"

The whole way back?

"I just kept thinking how badly I wanted to be up in first class, you know? I mean, those bastards get cocktails before anyone else has even boarded the plane…"

Thank God for Whitey, I don't know how I'd deal with my problems if I didn't get to hear his, which provide a backdrop, or a sort of psychological safety net. Although, for all I know, he may on to something, this time. Apparently, refinancing mort-gages is where it's at. The dot-com world is already a relic; it's back to brick and mortar mendacity these days. Suddenly, everyone's stocks aren't worth shit, but their houses are worth twice what they paid for them. So people are borrowing money against the inflated value of their property. Even I can understand that; people have been doing it forever: that's America. Somehow, people are making a great deal of money managing these transactions. People like the people Whitey is working with. He told me the water is warm, if I find myself abruptly out of work (or, if I ever want to make some *real* coin), they are hiring at his shop. Apparently they can't keep up with the volume. Even I can understand the concept of supply and demand; it's just that anytime the demand seems dispropor-tionate to the supply, I get nervous. If you tell me my condo is worth twice what I paid for it, I may believe you. But I'm not sure I'm willing to bet my bank account on it. If this type of logic pre-vailed, I'd have already retired on all the stock options I acquired in the early part of the millennium.

Whitey talked for a long time about how great this gig is, and how much money he plans to make. As always, I hope he's right. But it's what he told me at the end of our conversation that I can't get out of my mind: he confided how he'd felt some stiffness in his chest (on the right side, i.e. the *left* side) while finishing off some self-administered sexual release the other evening ("Not even that vigorous a session," he added, "it was actually kind of run of the mill."). As he identified the location of the pains (or were they palpitations?), it occurred to him: "Holy shit, what if I'm having a heart attack?" Imagine the humiliation, the irredeemable ego-blow it would entail to have paramedics transporting him, rock hard and rigor mortis, in the back of the ambulance; or someone kicking down the door three days later to find his rotting body, legs akimbo and boxers around his ankles? But then (he considered), fuck them. Enough people die in traffic—to or from work—or even worse, the poor fools who die *at* work, a myocardial infarction on the company dime. What kind of backward-ass early twenty-first century shit was that? No, when they pried the Vaseline from his cold, dead fingers, let them find a satisfied, unashamed man: his hardware in one hand, remote control in the other. A shit-eating grin, obviously, on his face.

* * *

I cooked for myself tonight.

Big mistake.

It's the thought that counts, but I ain't impressed.

I know my way around the kitchen, but the kitchen isn't impressed either.

It's never a complete wash because my dog enjoys my cooking, although I've seen what *he* eats.

You'd think I'd have learned a thing or two, some tricks of the trade, from all my years behind the bar, sneaking drinks to excitable chefs. And you'd be right. Here's what I learned: always have someone else prepare your food. Someone who *knows* always knows better than you. Cooking for oneself might be good for the checkbook, it may even be good for the soul, but it's not good for the economy. It's not good for all the sous-chefs out there sweating the late shift. What about *their* needs? How can I calmly plate my own pasta knowing there are unappreciated, sullen crumb artists working the sandwich station? What about all the inedible Chinese take-out it's my patriotic duty to support?

Fast food, if it has nothing else going for it (and it doesn't), is *fast*. Eating well is just as easy as eating badly—it's all about habit and routine. But who has the time? I'm the last person to complain about improvement, and while I celebrate the trend of fresh produce replacing canned reincarnations stacked on shelves, I can also appreciate the lack of *thought* that went into those readymade meals from the 70s. Cans, cardboard and freezer-burned foil are no place to preserve fuel for families, but they are effective. And what if you have no family? That's when the alternative of ordering in seems sensible, practical.

And if it still perturbs me to put efficiency before elegance? I can remind myself that in the U.S.A. I am doing right by these inviolable laws of commerce, I am plugged into this progress, part of a bigger picture, even though no one knows what that means. Or I can kid myself that I'm saving my enthusiasm for the future, when I'll have someone special to share these meals with, when the creativity I cook up will be enjoyed by people other than myself (or my dog), and I can regard meals at home the way I've learned to look at life: one evening at a time, each occasion an opportunity to attempt something new, or savor something I learned a long time ago, when I looked forward to the better days yet to come.

* * *

Otis lets out a low whistle as he steps into my office.

"What's up?"

"You may want to stay out of the bathroom for a few hours…"

"Oh for the love of Christ."

Otis rubs his stomach gingerly.

"That might be a double feature, but I'm pretty sure I took care of it all…"

"Did you kill it?"

"The bathroom? It was in pretty bad shape when I walked out. If I didn't kill it, I mortally wounded it."

This is what he says, but it isn't what it *sounds* like. It is practically impossible to make sense of his speech because of the chipmunk cheeks stuffed with… whatever it is he's crammed in them.

"Otis, open your mouth."

He does. There is the expected wet sock of snuff on his left side; but there is also a bird-feeder ring of sunflower seeds on his right side. And, somehow, he is working an imposing wad of bright pink bubblegum. I shake my head; he shrugs his shoulders and winks at me.

"Hey, I went out last night and bought some anti-virus protection…"

"For your dick?"

"No, dummy. For my *computer*."

"Well what in the world would you do something like that for?"

"That new virus!"

"Virus? You really worried about that baloney?"

"Better safe than sorry, right?"

"Well what do you have that's so valuable on your home computer?"

"Are you joking?"

"Uh…"

"Dude… my *porn!*"

"You're married and you still need porn?"

"Are you kidding me? I need it more than ever."

"You kill me."

"What, are you trying to say, you're not worried about *your* porn stash?"

"What porn stash?"

"Don't bullshit a bullshitter."

"Okay."

"Come on. Are you kidding me? *You* don't have porn?"

"It doesn't really do it for me."

"Do it? It doesn't have to *do* anything, it just has to be there; it just needs to exist."

"I have no problems with it existing; I'm just bored with it."

"Well then you're not normal."

"Okay."

"And you're definitely not *American.*"

"Uh…"

"And worst of all, you're quite possibly queer."

"Anyway… can you do a virus scan on my computer while I'm gone?"

"Where the hell are you going?"

"The Big Apple."

"Ah… another trip to the *real* HQ, eh?"

"Well, I'll be in the city, but this meeting is in some fancy hotel."

"A little pre-layoff pep rally?"

"That's what I'm afraid of."

"Well, *we* don't have anything to worry about."

"You don't think?"

"Nah, I'm not too concerned."

"Really?"

"I mean, I'm not gonna *let* myself be worried, there's tons of places out there dude. Everyone's hiring."

"I guess. But it wouldn't suck to keep the jobs we have, would it?"

"If not here, somewhere else."

"You're really not concerned? Even with another bambino to buy diapers for?"

"Not me. The rules have changed pal; it's the gold rush all over again."

And then, as always and as if on cue, his beeper goes off, signaling that someone important needs him and ensuring that, as of this moment, there is still enough work for him to do. These days, it seems, that's all any of us can ask for. In any event, no matter what anyone else says, until ESOs actually count as legal tender and I can get food and drink and pay rent with it, I'm going to remain skeptical that all these theoretical fortunes are going to theoretically last forever.

* * *

It's freezing and that's unfortunate.

It's snowing and that lends itself to isolation.

It's cold but that can be cured with company.

All the more reason to join the happy crowd, headed for happy hour.

Standing paralyzed at my car, I know what I've got and what I can have.

I've been here before. Recently.

There's nothing anyone can give me tonight that I can't get myself.

I haven't had a drink in… months. Centuries.

I could get the hang of this, I think.

I've been through it before, of course. The only problem is, the second I start feeling better, I find it's tough to toast one's health without a drink. But in this hot and bothered brain freeze, I'm capable of all kinds of crazy thoughts.

Just toss it all out, an unsolicited voice in my brain (somewhere on the lonely side, I figure) offers up, predictably. Just get up and throw all those bottles and cans in the trash, the teetotaler behind my cold shoulder says. Get rid of it, all of those chemically-enhanced excuses, and then when you want them—when you *need* them—you won't have to worry about it; they'll be gone.

No, I say to myself. That's a cop-out, isn't it? That's a sissified solution, a plea for strength born in a moment of weakness. That's not reality.

Reality?

What's that?

* * *

When I first took this job I got in the habit of referring to the time—admittedly too long—spent in the service industry as the *bad old days*. It wasn't because I had no fun (I did) or that I thought there was any future in it (I didn't). It wasn't that I felt joining the corporate world (grad students and waiters refer to it as the real world) was any type of instant ticket to peace or fulfillment. But it did remove one from the front lines of a scene with too many lives on the fast track to nowhere. Most people there fail to understand where they are, and where they're not going.

And when I think of the place some people never find a way to leave, it makes me remember one person in particular. More than the implicit slights suffered or the stalled potential each day I strapped on an apron, when I think about what I could never afford to lose, I think of Izzy. That, of course, was not his real name, but it was what everyone called him. When he and I first met I would have sworn he was in his mid-forties, but in fact he had only recently turned thirty-six. Not old in the nine-to-five arena but ancient in the restaurant business. A lifer who had never been promoted to general manager, he was a satellite drifting through the soiled orbit of a franchised business. He was never handed his own place to run, and he seemed entirely satisfied with that arrangement. In fact, as I came to see for myself, he counted on being an assistant behind the scenes, the hardened soldier who could close up shop and count the checks. We were often the last two left, hours after the final customer had called a cab or taken the DWI dare. After a shift that started at 4 PM Izzy would set up camp in the sweltering office in the back of the kitchen, going about the unexciting but excuses-free business of closing up.

When Izzy showed up for his shift the following afternoon he always looked like someone had scraped him off the bottom of a greasy skillet. Red eyes blurred, his neck shrieking in silent agony from the burn of a blunt razor, the cigarettes and coffee escaping in slothful waves from every inch of his sagging skin. Head bowed not in deference but disdain of the daylight; he could scarcely formulate the words being signaled from bruised brain to long-suffering lips. He would step up to the bar, shake his head and ask me to call him an ambulance. Then he'd disappear into the men's room for a minute or two, emerging like a televangelist with a badly ironed shirt. He could barely tie his shoe, but after his magic act in the crapper he'd be ready to plate a thousand entrees and run laps around the building in his wingtips (managers who wear comfortable shoes are never taken seriously, but they don't realize until it's too late that it's not because of the shoes).

For the next eight-to-ten hours, in between return trips to the powder room (occasionally he may have even used the toilet), Izzy was constant, awkward motion. All the waiters were in awe of him and all the waitresses were repulsed by him (especially the ones he'd slept with). Izzy could sweat out more alcohol in a single shift than most of us could drink in an entire weekend, and he never missed a day of work during the two years I knew him. Even if you didn't catch him ducking into the bathroom you always knew he had recently refueled because he would suck his teeth like someone trying to extract snake venom. The lip smacking and teeth licking were, to me, the black and blue collar stage of development between rock star and burnout, the line so many in the service industry straddle before they get out or go under.

None of this fazed me, which is not to say it wasn't unsettling, but grunts in the trench don't offer advice to their sergeants, so I mainly focused on my own unsavory habits. But I could never figure out how Izzy, when he retreated to the office each night to match receipts, guest checks and time sheets, was able to polish off an entire bottle of peppermint schnapps, or why—or how—that swill became his weapon of choice. When he finally went home, closer to sunrise than midnight, that bottle he took back with him would always be empty. At first I figured he was trying to impress or even intimidate me (full success on both fronts), but after months of the same scenario, I had no choice but to acknowledge that his appetites and obsessions had, at some point, evolved from unhealthy to superhuman. That bottle was not something he wanted, and was no longer something he needed; it was simply something that he *required*, along with the bathroom breaks and the air his lungs inhaled. I worked dozens of shifts where I didn't see him eat a scrap of food, but he never went into that office without his bottle of schnapps. And at least once a week he'd arrive at work with fresh bottles he kept to stock the bar. I could never fathom the physics, or biology (or algebra) that enabled a man to drain a fifth each evening and still function, but I also learned the hard way in high school that some subjects would, for me, remain forever mysterious.

By the time he took his transfer to the next location (never a demotion but never an advancement) he looked like he could collect social security. How long can that lifestyle sustain itself? I asked myself, then, and ponder it now. Where is Izzy today? Is he in an assisted living facility somewhere, or at the bottom of a river? Will I find him patrolling an intersection one night, not embarrassed to ask for tips after all these years? Or did he take the hard way out and start a family; his bad habits replaced by diapers bought in bulk, baby bottles, and manicured lawns? Has he subscribed to an altogether different sort of salvation, whacked out of his skull with sobriety?

* * *

I'm listening to the old woman again.

The fast food fiasco in its bag has already gone cold, but this time I don't care. This time I don't mind putting in the time; this time I'd do anything to be of some use to someone who obviously has no one who can console her when she cries.

She is crying, now, in the hallway and I'm not sure if I should hold her, if just hearing her will suffice, or if there is simply nothing, at a moment like this, that a child like me can conjure up in the way of commiseration that a woman like her has not already heard and seen through in her not inconsiderable life experience and the unfair share of hurt and harm this world is all too eager to hand out to all of us, over time.

"Why?" she asks, again, and I can't answer for at least two reasons: I don't know (the answer, or what she's asking about), and it's obviously not *me* who she is really asking anyway.

I may not know what she's talking about, but she is still holding the letter, a scene that makes me remember that all those melodramatic moments in badly made movies have their roots in reality. I don't know what the letter says, or who it's from, and perhaps I'm not supposed to know; it's not important that I know, only that I'm here, at this particular moment, to provide a brief, human buffer against the knowledge that in the end, all of us, whoever we are, will be alone.

"Why?" she asks, again, and again I have nothing I can hope to say.

It's a long time before I realize she has left and I've been standing out here, alone, still unable to find anything useful to say. To her. For myself.

Reality Check (3)

You didn't know what had given you the idea to conduct the experiment, but your curiosity had been sparked after learning about data *and* hypothesis *in school.*

You imagined yourself an eleven-year-old biologist as you captured the crickets and collected them in a glass jar. When you put the lid down—which you had methodically punctured with holes—you weren't sure what to expect. Would they fight? Suffocate? Multiply? It was exactly this hopeful uncertainty that provided your hypothesis.

With great anticipation you checked the crickets' progress the following day, and were disappointed by the lack of any remarkable drama: they were crowded together, stepping on top of one another, jockeying for space and position. When you put your face up close to the glass there seemed to be one fluid mass of black, rather than ten separate insects. Then you noticed that one of the smaller crickets was limping; somehow it had lost one of its legs. Or had it been torn off?

It was then that you felt a premonition of the horror you had constructed, and a voice you had never heard before admonished you to turn the jar upside down and let the crickets free. But curiosity and expectation overruled your aversion, and you deflected the possibility that this experiment was cruel by recalling what you had learned in school: it was survival of the fittest. The strongest would thrive and the weak ones would perish, that was all. That was science, *and it was the way the world was.*

It was your contentment, perhaps, that caused you to forget about the experiment for several days. You raced home from school the afternoon you remembered, eager to examine what had occurred.

Breathlessly you had crept into the basement and held the jar up to the light in order to better inspect your data. The first thing you noticed was the smell. The jar reeked of whatever had transpired during your three-day absence. You put the jar down quickly and the crickets began jumping, agitated by the commotion you had caused. You peered inside and your stomach tightened at what you beheld:

half of the crickets were moving—they scurried and bounced over the other half, whose lifeless bodies lay in pieces in the middle of the jar. As you looked more closely you were overtaken by a combination of disgust and fear: a primordial response to the unalterable laws of life and death. The weaker crickets had not merely died—they had been killed, and eaten. You comprehended what cannibalism was, but even as an eleven-year-old you were cognizant of the fact that crickets did not naturally subsist upon one another. You understood as you looked down that they were only acting out of the desperate will to survive because of the environment in which they had been placed. And the idea that the crickets were slaughtering each other as they struggled in a pile of their own waste and limbs induced a self-loathing doubt. Again you were overwhelmed by a desperate urge to take the jar out-side and smash it on the ground so that the remaining crickets could escape, and live.

But you resisted the impulse, this time not because of curiosity, or scientific detachment, but fear. You were afraid to touch the jar because you suddenly sensed that the crickets were aware of your pres-ence and were staring at you, hating you, and you were momentarily subjected to the vision of being inside the jar with the crickets, fending for your life with nothing but brute instinct to defend yourself. The unendurable stench filled your nostrils, gagging you, and you turned and ran out of the basement, scared and ashamed.

Four

UNDERTOW

IF THIS IS Paradise, why does everyone seem lost?

I don't understand how it's possible, in such a tightly managed environment, where we are paid to pay lip service to the company line, where we remain *on message* like a political campaign, that word of layoffs could leak out. Everyone I talk to lately is looking at me as if I know anything, and I don't. I don't understand how people who've never been up on F5 have heard about plans that may or may not have been concocted up here at their expense.

Unless. Unless it's intentional. Maybe *that* is how they do it: let it leak out to a few important folks who can then disseminate it accordingly amongst the louder mouths on their staffs. Or, more likely, see that it gets whispered in the ears of a few nobodies, like Otis, or me for that matter, who won't have any compunction about spreading the secret as far as they can. Then, like an airborne illness, it infects everyone it comes close to, and sooner or later it's all everyone is talking about. And, in the grand scheming of things, this is good, because by the time *everyone* thinks they might get let go, the ones left standing after the massacre will feel relieved, even lucky. And loyal.

I'm worried about myself, I'm worried about Otis, I'm worried about anyone about to get caught in the crosshairs. But most of all I'm worried about Chazz. It sort of sickens me to even think about such things, but the fact remains that the mailroom is so... *90s*. Maybe in the 80s—in any era other than now—he actually would have had access to the type of information he hopes (or, I hope, not what he erroneously believes) he has.

Take Otis: everything that used to incriminate higher-ups in a paper trail is now intangible and electronic, so if a decision-maker's eyes need to see it, it won't originate or end up anywhere near the mailroom. Funny how it always plays out like this: the people who don't particularly care either way are the ones with access to incrimination. This may not even be unintentional, as all our fates seem so obviously random. Thus, while Otis may or may not have almost unimaginable opportunities to read between the lies, the mighty men of F5 are not idiots—they invented the Internet (just ask them); they aren't just going to leave the emperor's clothes they decide not to wear in dirty laundered files for any overpaid imbecile to sort through.

"Welcome! You've got *jail*..."

"What's the good word, Chazz?" I call out over my cubicle.

He pokes his head around the corner and winks at me. "*Ain't nuthin going on but the rent*, brutha B-boy."

Against my better judgment, and at least in part because I sense he expects me to, I ask if he's heard the latest rumors circulating like an unchecked rash.

"I hear *everything*," he smiles. "But that doesn't mean I *know* anything, dig?"

I pause and consider how ingeniously he avoided revealing whether he was aware of incipient bad news.

"Well, the word on the street's that the company is dropping the pretty-big one: at least five hundred people are getting laid off later this week."

He whistles gravely, but doesn't say anything for several seconds, and then he looks at me carefully.

"I guess *you* got nuthin to be afraid of," he says coolly. It was the first time I'd ever detected a trace of enmity in his voice, at least directed my way. "Otherwise you wouldn't know anything about it."

He is, of course, correct. I contemplate it, and find that I can't think of anything particularly useful to say, on behalf of the people in charge, or myself. So I say nothing.

* * *

Something *has* changed.

Up here on F5, everything happens first, everything happens fast. Something unfortunate is hanging in the air, as though someone forgot to flush the toilet. Yes, it stinks up here all of a sudden, and the stench is spreading quickly through the building. You can read it on the faces; you can see it in the eyes. The eyes never lie.

Look: Boyd Bender, a man who would let wild dogs maul a toddler if he could clear a profit, reluctant to make eye contact. And this is a man who *lives* for making eye contact. He looks away from no man; it's your job to avert your eyes from *him*. Everything about him screams this unspoken rule: from his shark fin shirt creases to the golden weight of the world in his watch, from his unrepentant Italian ties to his fifty-dollar silk socks. And there he goes, appearing almost self-conscious as he slinks toward another *mano a mano* with *The Don*, discussing whatever it is they need to decide behind ominously open doors. All of them are in there, the four polo players of the apocalypse, debating who will live and who will cry.

Listen: you have to strain to overhear what they aren't saying, these brazen billionaires who can overtake an entire country club (maybe even an entire country) if they feel unruly enough. Of course, these are men allergic to indoor voices, their intractability so obviously rooted in arrogance—real, authentic, *earned* arrogance—that it's all right, it's oddly refreshing. Here are the generals you'd gladly follow into battle; they are leading the pack, they are driving the tank, they'll deliver us from evil. Except something has changed.

See: beneath the smug shell and the unflappable game face something else has allowed itself inside—however reluctantly, however much it may have been resisted—something has snuck into the equation. It's not deliberation (you can see that on display in the meetings); not quite concern (you can see that expressed when they open their car doors); not exactly awareness (anyone can see the ways their wallets eradicate that temptation); it's something much more subtle, more insidious: it's the unforeseen specter of accountability.

Secrets: the sold shares, the cooked books, the dirty deeds, the dodgy deals, the erstwhile economy, the wrath of gods greater than themselves, the fifth act of an unwitting tragedy, the unknowable answers of what might ultimately await them—after the layoffs, in the new org chart. Or perhaps this awkward new energy originated somewhere else, somewhere outside their offices. Maybe it's an uncoordinated yet collective epiphany: that despite the brazen new world they've created, the irritating, obsolete *old* order still clamors on occasion, still has some things to say, still needs to be accounted for, however uncomfortable the timing.

Questions: Once wealthy, what do you work for? What are you moving toward? How do you get your fix when the blue blood turns black? What can you acquire if everyone else has been killed? How can you make the money promise to preserve you, that it won't give its heart to the next influx of hungry heroes? Is it necessary to start burning some of this Internet oil, to build flaming battlements of deferred hedge funds, to cut and run with the 401(k), to cash it all in at cost if and when that ugly day ever comes? Why not get out now? Walk away smiling, untouchable, gliding directly out the back door, no lawyers or accountants or cops marching alongside eventually, inevitably?

Conclusions: Because. In the end, there are forces even more malevolent than money urging them on: posterity, pride, and mostly the inescapable understanding that even *they* might die someday. And, after all, they have an empire to defend, legacies to establish, a future to foment, electronic souls to enshrine. There's a lot of work left to do.

* * *

Business dinner.

Celebration? Sort of. It's the end of the calendar year, end of the fiscal year, end of the *world*. Layoffs? I'm not sure, and they're not saying.

They are drinking. Everyone is drinking, or beyond drunk and drinking water, or coffee, or anything to pacify the poison already bicycling through their bloodstreams.

I'm much more sober than I have any reason being, more than I would have thought possible, considering the two-paycheck priced bottles of vino splayed out before me like so many vestal virgins.

"Red or white?" someone asks.

"I have to be on a plane before sunrise," I reply.

In the bad old days this would not have been an undue deterrent, but I'm a new man now and I've got the BAC to prove it. I'm headed to the corporate office in NYC, slated to sit through a series of meetings: doing that with a hangover was self-immolation spread out over eight or nine unbearable hours; how am I possibly going to manage it *sober?*

So. Why am I even here, and what purpose could I possibly be serving, an antelope amongst these lions? As usual I'm just along for the ride, innocent by association: I am ghostwriter-in-residence, contributing columnist of the policies and prevarications that enable the visionaries on F5 to justify and explain (to paying customers, to a prurient public, but never to themselves) their strategy for squeezing more blood from this stone called capitalism.

As I belly up with my bottled water, I must begrudgingly acknowledge the platitudes of my old English teachers who always said: if you can write, someone will always want you to write for them. If you are willing to write what other people are willing to pay you for, you might even find yourself making a living. If you are lucky enough to find yourself surrounded by wealthy and prideful people, you can climb higher than you ever imagined. Anyone worth a damn enjoys having someone they can employ to do their light work for them, someone who will dot the I's of their investments and cross the T's of their triumphs, liberating them to do the noble deeds they were put on this earth to accomplish.

Listen: I *am* lucky to have this job, and there is no shortage of people who'd gladly go a few hours sans alcohol to sit amongst these armed robbery barons. I just don't happen to be one of them; my problem is, I *need* to be more than a little drunk to pass less than a little time not making small talk and impersonating human fly paper for all the boasts, burps and bullshit sticking to everyone. Still, I didn't deserve this gig any more than anyone else. I was just in the right place at the right time. If it turns out I'm the wrong person, that's between my empty wine glass and me.

The Don is drunk.

Holding court, holding his drink, holding all the cards, as always. Holding a lit cigar even though this is a non-smoking section. He speaks, he laughs, he stands, he is the king of all he sees. He follows me into the big boy's room and I watch him dizzily shift his considerable weight—the weight he throws around—from one foot to the other. I am unconcerned: even if he falls, his money will protect him.

This is not the part of the fantasy sequence where the great man pulls me aside and slurringly assures me that I'm his guy, that the future opens ahead of me like the checkbook as big as the Ritz, that as long as I stay on the train, the tracks go on forever. This is not the moment when I sell my soul for the smart money, the security of shares that will put my unborn sons and daughters through law school and med school, respectively.

This is also not the night when Boyd Bender, appeased by his second bottle of Barolo, winks at me and promises to disclose the secrets hidden behind his perpetual poker face; that he really *does* have an alter ego after hours, that he does not actually sustain himself on the blood of lesser businessmen. All of this is impossible. For starters, Boyd does not get drunk. Why? Drinking brings pleasure, and Boyd Bender has neither the time nor the interest for such unproductive emotions. Boyd on a bender? Not in this lifetime. Not on his watch. Not until all the money is gone.

* * *

Dreaming.

It's ugly out there, at work, in the frog-eat-frog world, where the fat ones eat as much as they can, getting bigger so nothing smaller can swallow them. Mostly, for the rest of us, it helps to stay out of the way, stay alive by remaining uninvolved, survive by keeping silent, feigning indifference while still aware that we are in their sights at all times. And it's always the big ones we are so scared of, the spiders and the snakes, but they are judicious, models of efficient evolution at work. There are no underachievers alive at the end of the day in the jungle. But eventually, inevitably, we learn that it's the little fuckers, as always, who pack the biggest punch. And, as always, everything is relative. Look at one of those miniature monsters under a microscope: ever seen a dust mite? Hollywood has nothing on nature; it's *almost* enough to make you believe in God.

It's ugly in here, asleep, in the after-midnight arena of dreams and enigmas, where parts of the brain we don't even know how to use while awake are punching the clock, putting together the pieces of all the things we see but can't understand.

A flashback:

"How would you like a little more responsibility in the coming year?"

"I'd love it," he lies.

"We'd like you to take a trip to HQ."

"New York City?" he replies.

"Affirmative."

"What's on the agenda?" he asks.

"A seminar we want some folks to attend. It's mostly sales-oriented. But you can pick up a lot of good stuff."

"Who's presenting, one of the executives?" he wonders.

"No, it's a consultant from a group we've used in the past."

"Oh yeah, I've heard of them," he nods.

Oh I've heard of this *group* all right, he says—to himself—and immediately prepares himself for the worst.

* * *

Phone ringing.

Fuck.

Finally:

"Yeah…"

"By?"

"Yeah."

"It's me."

It's Whitey.

"What time is it?"

"I don't know… it's late, I mean, it's *early*."

"Okay."

"Can I talk to you for a minute?"

"Sure."

"Thanks man. I'm sorry to call you, I just needed, you know, I really need to talk…"

"All right, I'm here, it's okay."

"Okay, I just want to talk…"

"Talk to me."

"Well, like I said, you know, you remember…"

"Yup."

"I kind of flipped out…"

"Right."

"And, it kind of fucked me up, you know?"

"Yes, but you are better now."

"Thanks Byron," Whitey says, after he has gone on to say a great many other things, most of which neither of us are likely to remember in the morning. In a few hours.

"It helps to talk," he says.

"I know."

"And I'm glad we… I'm glad I can talk to you."

"Me too, bro."

"It's just good to talk sometimes."

"Keep talking."

Here's the thing I want to tell Whitey, (I think): You're going to be okay. Really. Sure, you're in the advanced stages of a mid-life crisis now (proving what an overachiever you are, knocking that item off the list before turning *forty*), but once your feet start sinking into the existential ooze, you'll have two options—keep sinking or come up for air.

My money is on Whitey; it'll never be as bad as he thinks it is and it will never get as bad as he doesn't know it can be. Inexorably, the fortress of family and mortgage and mortality will engulf him and he'll work his way toward an *authentic*, appropriate and well-earned mid-life crisis. When he's in his mid-forties. The way it's supposed to be.

Whitey, I want to say, I'm not saying I'd want to *be* you, but I'd be lying if I didn't say I envied you. A little bit, anyway.

Reality Check (4)

So we're in the 2000s already. So what? What did the much-hyped millennium offer us that we had not already paid to see? Fin de siècle? *Everything is already dead, or dying. Or else, as always, people are too preoccupied with life to actually be living. And yet, (you think) when one considers the alternatives, it is, as always, as good a time as any to not be alive.*

The farther out we go, the more powerful the pull, the appeal of those pretty-good old days, that apparently easier-to-understand era. People are strange. People are predictable. Nostalgia for the 90s, already? People are still nostalgic for the 50s. This should not be surprising, actually, as history reminds us that people in the 50s were nostalgic for the 50s. A past, perhaps, that we have not yet caught up with. Which might explain the inexpressible charm—the longing—for old things we still do not understand.

The future rarely delivers the devastation so direly predicted by poets or pundits, all of whom are much too wise for their own good. Then again, those that foresee the future seldom stick around to see the disasters they describe. They are too busy drowning in the debris, the horrors of the here-and-now.

The present tense will pull you down before the future ever gets a chance. Unless you happen to be amongst the lucky ones, in which case you are already downstream, swept away in the undertow.

That, in any event, seems to be the story.

Can you stick to it?

Five

IF YOU LIKE THE SHOW, GIVE UP THE DOUGH

I'D MAYBE *WANTED* a decent night's sleep a few times in the past, but I can't recall a time when I'd needed it more desperately. Therefore, I knew, of course, that I'd get nothing of the sort.

You'd think I'd get used to it after a while. But no: every morning is a new opportunity for fresh pain: each second of stolen sleep an eternity, either eye opening its own agony, any alarm clock an ordeal.

The airport, even at this cheerless hour, is teeming with cranky commuters, lots of suits and surly attitudes, entirely too many people traveling this close to Christmas. Not yet time to return home; much too late to be going anywhere on business. In other words, a lot of self-pitying suckers just like me.

Up in the air, alive, the sun shows off all it can see, up here where *to be or not to be* gets decided every single second. I look around at befuddled businessmen, suppressing panic attacks because they can't use their cell phones. The woman next to me, hunched over her laptop, keeps snatching suspicious glances in my general direction. I am, of course, reading what's on her screen, but what does she expect? The guy on the other side of me is playing solitaire, only metaphorically. The stewardess stares me down sweetly, daring me to accept a cup of coffee that was most likely brewed last week, reheated this morning, and spent the last several hours roiling around in an airtight cask, asphyxiating on its own fumes. Politely, I decline.

Just as I'm drifting off into a cantankerous catnap, the pilot interrupts the silence to announce that air traffic control has not given us the go-ahead for landing, whatever *that* means. Even up here you can't catch a break, even the unfriendly skies are backed up, impeding forward progress, inviting exasperation. Even up here the clouds won't part until the big money has cleared customs and changed hands.

Touchdown. Everyone leaps to their feet, elbowing each other for the honor of not getting off the plane first. I pretend to be patient and enjoy making the woman next to me, who can hardly stand not having her portable computer opened and available, wait her turn. After a few near rumbles, shouting matches and rugby scrums in the aisle, I stoically join the clustered masses on the concourse, reluctant but ready to throw myself on the mercy of a Big Apple that will chew me up and spit me out before I even know what hit me.

Welcome to LaGuardia, the man moving past me does not say. I'm in too much of a hurry to stop (like always, like anyone else), but there is something so familiar about him I'm compelled, despite everything I've learned, to pause and look back: he's still there, off to the side, shabbily clad, immediately recognizable by his contrast to everyone around him; he wants to approach one of these businessmen, but all of them are walking too fast, too deliberately, too purposefully.

Automatically, the doors move aside and frigid air earnestly greets everyone headed its way. It takes about five seconds (as always) to feel the cold and then the money dread: if it weren't for the money, it wouldn't take much—in a strange city, lost, alone. Cold. Broke. That's how shit like starvation and sleeping on grates gets started. Quiet in the corners, huddled under bridges, working the frenzied crowd for a friendly face, hoping for the handout that never comes.

* * *

Of *course* the line for taxis is indefensible, even for New York City. One look at this mess and it seems safe to wager it will take longer to get a cab than it just took to fly a few hundred miles. And then there's always the morning traffic to argue with. If I wasn't inclined to look on the bright side so often, I don't know how I'd suffer through these disagreeable occasions.

The cab and its driver are both clean and smell inoffensive, even nice, even—dare I say it?—*enticing*. And yes, it's an odious (smelling) stereotype, but until we cease to be surprised by a painless experience in a pleasantly-scented cab, we'll continue to appreciate them as the exception and not the rule.

I don't wear the seat belt in cabs, since cabs never crash. Besides, why attract attention? Why give potential tragedy the time of day?

Moving fast—too fast for any circumstance other than getting me where I needed to be, and I'm not even in a *hurry*—each person he passes and each grunt of approval I offer signify the following, mutually understood assurance: every car in the rear view is another ten cents tacked on to the twenty percent tip he's already got working.

We each appreciate the rules: if I was in the car beside us— if I was anywhere on Earth except his backseat—we'd be mortal enemies, but as it stands, we're on the same team, this is our war and we'll endure much and stoically make it to the promised land, one man together.

True, some cab drivers don't want to talk; (some don't speak your language, some may not even speak) but some *want* to talk, some want to talk very much indeed, and will initiate the action and then wait, like de-fanged cobras, ready to pounce, aggressive yet harmless, for any opportunity. In fact, with some folks you get the vibe that they're so starved for conversation, solidarity, or just that elusive human touch, that they would not only waive your fare, but pay *you* if you'd let them pull over and shoot the shit; or even better, slide into some bar and order a round of anything on the rocks, or best, take you to their modest but clean and adequate abode, where their plain but polite wife would whip up some of the best home-cooking you could never pronounce or even describe other than to say it was as impossible as the entire incident. In sum, it's unlikely.

And yet, some of them are out there all the same, waiting.

* * *

Walking into the hotel, there's no turning back now. I see the sign that says (insert name of company here) and I walk cautiously toward whatever it is that awaits me.

Good feeling: this is nothing to worry about, what are the chances they'd fly me up there just to *fire* me? Bad feeling: there are worse things than getting laid off. Like keeping a job, for instance.

"So," Chazz had asked, echoing what everyone else has been asking me. "You headed up to the *real* HQ?"

"Well, this meeting is in some hotel in NYC..."

He had looked at me skeptically (like everyone else who'd asked me).

"So, you have *no* idea what to expect?"

"I don't know man, they just said it's a full day of meetings."

I see how you are, his eyes had said, (looking at me like everyone else had).

But the truth is, I really don't know. Other than how idiotic it seems to send a bunch of us up to another city, just before

Christmas, to sit around and talk about the decisions to be made in a year that hasn't started yet. Unless. Unless there are things I'll be finding out; things I don't necessarily want to know about.

This is probably an opportune time to make a confession: I am, truth be told, not very good at my job. Don't get me wrong, I'm terribly *competent*; take a look at my recent review.

The problem lies with my attitude. It's *my* problem, because to this point I haven't been stupid enough to tell anyone how I actually feel. It's not just that I'd prefer not to be here (I would); it's not that I haven't drank the Kompany Kool-Aid (I haven't); it's not that I take all these good things for granted (I do). It's that, unlike everyone else up on F5, I keep asking myself questions that money can't answer. All the executives whose shadows I sulk beneath are understandably ecstatic—which is not to accuse any of them of actually being *content*. They've put in the time necessary to understand that time truly is money, and the more time they spend, the more money they'll make.

It would be (and often has been) easy to disregard these hollow men giving all the orders as money-grubbing remoras, riding shark-finned stock options all the way to immortality. And yet, even I will not deny them their due. They actually *enjoy* this shit; they truly love what they do, and nothing would please them more than continuing to do it, without interruption, for the rest of their lives.

So? So how long can I afford to remain in the company of so many powerful people who seem certain they're doing exactly what the gods men like them created put them on this earth to achieve?

It is difficult to get a man to understand something when his salary depends on him not understanding it.

I did not say that.

Even worse, I did not think it, until just now.

* * *

I almost don't recognize her—she looks that different, that much better—and it isn't until she begins speaking that I know for sure. Someone's voice, even if they've obviously undergone rigorous training and practice to cultivate a polished, professional manner, is always a foolproof indication of the person disguised behind the lost weight, shortened hair, business attire and implacable demeanor. The voice gives her away: this is the woman who once asked me to marry her.

As only one of thirty faces, I have the advantage of seeing her first, so I know that she *knows* it's me when we finally make eye contact. After all, I haven't really changed that much. She blinks and a quick expression of surprise supplants the amiable nice-to-meet-you greeting she'd had plastered on her face as she approached the front of the room. She recovers so quickly I cannot determine if it's embarrassment, or pleasure—or neither—that she'd revealed before reverting to that impenetrable mask.

I know how *I* feel. Although I give her a controlled and confident *we'll talk later* wink, I am immediately aware of the diametric positions compelling our participation in this ordeal. She is here, and getting paid, to be in charge; I look around at all the sales weasels surrounding me, new babes who couldn't quite get their mouth comfortably around the teat of e-commerce, three or more months of not hitting their quotas having downgraded their status from *still finding his way* to *get with the program or get gone,* and this was their last chance to learn how to feast on the flesh of straight commission before the carcass rotted. And then, this: she probably thinks I'm one of *them.* Ouch. One thing, the only important thing, is obvious: we're all the same in her eyes as she stands, sovereign before us, sorcerer to her apprentices. Nothing to do but settle in, sit back and suck it up.

* * *

I attempt to concentrate and stay tuned to the introductory remarks (yes, these people take themselves so seriously that it's actually deemed necessary to send out a cheerleader to prepare the crowd, not unlike an opening act at a rock concert), but I cannot help thinking that this fancy banquet room would be infinitely more appropriate, and better served, facilitating a wedding reception, or some similarly festive function complete with drinks, dance and tacky music.

But here I am, partaking in a real 90s experience—even though it's a new millennium—a genuine power-to-the-people, five hundred dollar per person motivational presentation. The topic—which one would presume had reached its apotheosis several years back, but was clearly still enticing enough to fill up hotel conference rooms throughout the country—is printed on the packets each of us received upon arriving: *Sales Strategies For The Industry Expert.* The brilliance of this intentionally oblique title was its hypothetical applicability to just about any enterprise, be it telemarketing, hawking cleaning supplies to large corporations, or creating one's own business. Of course, it was billed as an opportunity to enhance administrative skills, to crystallize convictions and absorb the open exchange of ideas and opinions. A brainwashing session, in short.

* * *

Generous applause.

It's no use, my mind begins racing: what is she thinking?

Had seeing me (and there was no way she didn't recognize me, it hasn't been *that* long) brought on an irrepressible surge of memories? Or was she enough of a pro to block out all obstructions and focus on the task at hand? Speaking slowly, but purposefully, her eyes work the crowd, seeking to infuse us with excitement, to find some solidarity in her message.

This was not new to her, as she, like myself, has had plenty of experience acting. Anyone who has spent more than a casual college summer in the service industry, waiting on tables, understands what a veteran performer on stage for the sixtieth show in a row surely perceives. Knowing the part so intimately you could recite it without thought; you could even imagine yourself elsewhere while your mouth spoke the speech. It is the only way to avoid slipping up and letting out a string of profanities, or conveying how you *really* felt about your customers. I know; I've been there. To have heard my recommendations from the wine list, you'd have thought I cultivated the grapes in my own vineyard, or that I prepared the desserts from scratch in my kitchen, or that I personally hauled in the fresh catch, keeping only those fish worthy of being served in such a superior establishment.

So when she starts talking about how P.R.I.D.E! stands for *perseverance* (period), *resourcefulness* (period), *individuality* (period), *direction* (period), and *excellence* (exclamation point!), I recall the time we screwed standing up in the meat locker, freezing our asses off, just for kicks on a slow night. Or how she used to sweet-talk me into topping off her endless cups of black coffee with Irish whiskey, and how I never could refuse because before I became a bartender I'd been the one who convinced her that you made better tips with a nice, steady buzz. I had told her how, after a while, you could get it down to an art form: knowing just the right amount (too much was as bad as none at all, you were worthless in either extreme) to get that glorious numbing of the senses that made such demeaning work tolerable. And then you were able to pretend you gave a rat's ass if one of the obnoxious yuppies was a strict vegetarian, or which Chardonnay best accompanied chicken with pasta, and so on.

And then as I hear her saying something about how she hasn't been sick, or caught so much as a common cold in over two years, call it confidence or the power of positive thinking, but she just *never* got sick anymore, I recall the times when we'd start drinking, *really* drinking, after last call, not going home until the sun was up. It was not unusual for us to drive past people on their way to work, freshly showered in their corporate costumes. Then, finally, crashing until the sun set again, like lazy vampires, ready to do it again. Endless nights, the same night.

I was in a pretty sad state for a while, back then. She was worse. I didn't need drugs, I'd say, I was busy enough trying to soothe myself simply, with alcohol (sound familiar?). But I was lucky in that I had the ability to try something, anything, and then let it go. Some people, like her, can't do that, they're into it all the way, whatever it was. In her case it was a lot of things. Your body can operate on cruise control for a while until it finally has enough and starts to pay you back. And the deeper we went, the more I began to contemplate alternate options. A change of environment, for starters (sound familiar?). But she still talked about driving down to Mexico, or hitting Las Vegas: get married and gamble as much as we had, make or break it, alone, together. She didn't take it well when I finally announced that I was busting out of the business, with or without her. She eventually did leave town, but I had no idea where she ended up, and I never heard from her again.

* * *

Laughter.

I look up at the projection screen: there he is in livid color, the former next president of the United States, eagerly taking credit for the reason all of us—directly or indirectly—are sitting here right now.

More laughter.

"Of *course* Al Gore didn't invent the Internet," she asserts. "We know that. *He,*" she says the name of the man I carefully avoid every day at work, "invented the Internet!"

I look around the room: just about all of them are tuned in, attentive, smiling, laughing appropriately at her jokes. It's all part of the script—this is, after all, a *feel good* seminar. And I've heard about the other type, thanks to Whitey, where you're shuffled in Bataan Death March-style, then some slick-ass hotshot in his perfectly pressed suit steps up and starts screeching like a Pentecostal preacher. And everyone sits there, exerting their best effort to be properly intimidated and awestruck as he struts up and down the aisles talking about how it was their *privilege* to work for this company, how they'd already *made* their name and the staff was just along for the ride, and how *his* only interest was ensuring the dead weight got deep-sixed, *et cetera*.

So I'm well aware that three separate sets of ears are listening to my cocktail waitress-turned-corporate-prodigy's sales pitch: hers, ours, and the important ones who had made all this possible. They aren't in the room, of course, but their presence is palpable. Each ghostwritten word she spoke validated their reality, those once-cynical carpetbaggers who happened upon the epiphany (the geniuses!) that they could take this sermon—the same malarkey you could hear for *free* at an AA meeting, or any church for that matter—and, like everything else in America, bundle it up in a neat, presentable package and trumpet it as The Truth. The brilliance lay not in their commodification of it, but the recognition that there would never be a scarcity of people in desperate need of affirmation. Then their guidance, that voice of experience and authority, would penetrate the chaos and guide anyone interested—and willing to pay, literally, figuratively—down the righteous road toward self-actualization as they reinvented themselves. This was once every citizen's prerogative, now it was their obligation. And like any other nickel and dime self-help methodology, the proof was in the proverbial pudding, *they* did it, so can you!

"...Sometimes it's good to slow down, to kind of step back and assess things," she is saying. "For instance, earlier this year I was laid up for a couple of days, I don't know why, I must have caught something or other..."

"But it couldn't have been a cold!" I blurt out, cheerful and cocksure, not even aware I'd spoken out loud until all the faces turn toward me, most of them amused at my audacity. And quickly, before their eyes refocus to the front, once again I catch a flicker of discomfort, a sliver of self-consciousness slide across her excessively made-up face. Then, once again, like the specialist she's become, she reins it in and reclaims the grinning guise, able to laugh with the others at the prankster's joke at her expense.

* * *

When it's finally over, I don't linger behind with the handful of well-wishers and overly impressed brown-nosers who have crowded around for some final dispensation of wisdom.

I rush outside for a whiff of fresh air, and reality. Even the congealed fusion of gasoline, urine, smoke and stress smells uncompromised, even serene after the last several hours. I stand for a while, watching the sullen cars and surly cabs go through the motions of being forever in motion. I stretch my legs for a spell, looking for myself or at least a friendly stranger in the low tide of leering faces. After a half hour without success or succor, I deliberate upon the next logical course of action.

Take a guy.

Someone who looks a lot like me, for instance, walking into a swanky hotel bar.

The waitress sees him, but seems in no particular hurry to do anything about it, which is fine because he isn't drinking anyway. In fact, this is the first time he's set foot in a bar since he decided to dry out, and he feels like an alien, being neither behind the counter nor beside a crowd. It's difficult for him to suppress a surly tinge of bitterness at the sight of fellow working stiffs who don't seem to have a care in the world. Casually, he looks around and notices several things. She's there, as he knew she would be, but she's not alone. He hadn't prepared for this possibility, so he finds a table toward the back, as far away from the action as possible. She's still talking fast and furious, and she's holding a glass of white wine. Damn her, he thinks. She can still hack it. Clearly the center of discussion, and the others' attention, she hasn't lost a trace of her transformative glow, and her voice soars above the recycled air and competing conversation in the room.

"So, you've seen what *I* do," she is addressing three faces he recognizes from the seminar, one man and two women, all of whom had, coincidentally or not, been sitting right up front. "What is it exactly that you all do?"

"Sales," the man replies, shrugging, as if there were no other possible option.

"Sales!" she echoes, smiling. "You know, for the longest time I thought that was a dirty word, but one thing I came to realize— we're *all* in sales."

Even those of us who aren't any good at it, he thinks.

The waitress finally finds her way over to him and nods expectantly when he asks for a club soda with lime. Maybe it will look like a vodka tonic, he thinks.

"Even those who don't realize it," she continues, all teeth as she smiles, still fully in character. Perhaps she was never *not* in character these days.

"Teachers? They're trying to sell knowledge to indifferent students. Lawyers? They're hoping to sell their dubious legal services…"

"Even waiters and bartenders," one of the women interjects, an apt and eager pupil.

"*Especially* waiters and bartenders," she exclaims, unfazed. "Although those are the easiest type of sales around, aren't they? People don't come in unless they've already decided to eat or drink!"

Dutiful laughter all around.

"How about you, did you ever wait on tables?" the other woman inquires.

"No, I never did," she replies, cool as a catfish. "But I wish I'd had the opportunity, so many interesting people I'm sure…"

Finally, she looks over and sees him seeing her.

-So, you really bought into this, huh? he asks with his eyes.

-So, how's the corporate ladder working out for you? she responds with hers.

Touché.

And the conversation continues. In his mind.

-Looks like you finally became what you always said you were so scared of...

-Looks like you never went for the PhD, like you always talked about doing...

-I figured you'd be dead by now.

-And I figured you'd be teaching or something, not attending seminars...

-It's all part of the plan.

-What plan?

-Well, it's complicated.

I see, she says, looking away. The spell—or whatever it might have been—broken almost before they had a chance to feel it. And that's that; she's obviously more interested in her own conversation. He can't blame her.

"Actually, I should be grateful," he continues, quietly addressing his harmless beverage. "I know guys—guys we used to work with—who got DWIs and *had* to attend some sessions. The people at those meetings are like religious freaks; they've simply substituted one addiction for another. In the meetings they train you to get drunk on abstinence."

The waitress approaches.

"Can I get you anything else?"

"How about another life," he suggests. Tactfully, the waitress walks away, pretending she didn't hear him.

He looks back across the room, waiting for another glance, hoping for another clue. He can't even overhear their discussion anymore. Is it his imagination of has she almost imperceptibly hushed her voice, as though fearful somebody might be listening? Somebody like him, for instance. He listens but aside from the white noise of other overtures he's not interested in, there is nothing.

He really has no right to begrudge her for cleaning up her act, he knows.

And a damn impressive act it was, too. He certainly never saw that type of potential back in the bad old days. The bad old days that don't seem so bad after all, huh? Then again, a previous job is not unlike a previous relationship: hindsight is obscured by the ego's insistence on reshaping lost time. It is easier for us to like ourselves if we are able to believe that where we came from, or where we are going, is on the up and up. Which isn't to say he actually *enjoyed* kissing ass for tips. But he had to admit, those customers were smarter than he gave them credit for being: they weren't pretending he had any interest in them so long as he kept their drinks refilled. So what? He was king of a tiny universe, that's all. A big drunken fish in a smoky pond.

He drains his drink and spits an ice cube back into the glass.

"You can't go home again, right?"

Again, no response. Nothing.

The thing is, he thinks, you shouldn't *want* to.

So he doesn't.

He leaves an unnecessarily generous tip on the table and stands up. He has to call upon every ounce of will to keep his eyes straight ahead as he moves past them, away from the chatter and the laughter. And as he takes the last long steps toward the door, he realizes he had been wrong. If he'd heard that voice without seeing her face, he would have had no idea who she was.

* * *

Walking.

New York is an extraordinarily self-contained city: the sheen from the collective smiles and sneers in these crowds belies an unremarkable lack of substance. Everyone, it seems, is striving to be something else, something they're not. Something better, it would seem, is there for the taking. And everybody is anxious to secure their share of what they assume is waiting for them, evanescent, just out of reach. Each individual, mostly the residents drawn here from less desirable places, and even the visitors and tourists, all are actors. Everyone unwittingly involved; co-conspirators in this discordant symmetry.

The street musicians, however, seem removed—at once apart from and a part of the never-ending hustle. It's not like the old times, when just about every corner was staked out, and the quality, with the possible exception of New Orleans, was by far the finest you'd encounter in this country. These days, it's even difficult to determine which ones are homeless and which are playing the part. It's like trying to decide which bar to stop and drink in: five hundred thousand of one, half million of the other. And what difference did it make? Maybe some, maybe *most* of them were the real deal, authentic, legitimate professionals, who couldn't make it, or didn't want any part of the industry.

Take this guy.

The one in front of me, with a silver guitar plucked by long, filthy fingernails, could not have sprung from anything other than unhurried experience. The gravelly voice attainable only after a lifetime of cigarettes, stale air and sour times; hair greased back, perpetually resistant to the fickle fads of fashion; the prototypical pompadour, coarse cheekbones you could strike a match or sharpen a knife on, the gaps between his chipped teeth perfectly spaced, like rows of cultivated corn. Was this bottle of ill-spirits in human form here by choice or circumstance? Fortune or fate? Was he temporarily stalled, accidentally anchored on this concrete stage, or was he happy to be here, sopping up the indifference that surrounded him? Would he be better off in a recording studio, more authentic in a standing-room only auditorium, a spotlight instead of a traffic signal staring back at him?

I look around and see several dozen mirror images of myself, well-bred city slickers and pretty-faced posers, lumped together like a shallow sea of apathy, drifting back and forth. Maybe stopping for a song or two, and then moving on. The story of our lives.

"I went down to the crossroads, tried to flag a ride,
Nobody seemed to know me, everybody passed me by…"

Scattered applause.

"Thanks for taking the time to pause for the cause y'all and remember folks, if you like the show give up the dough!"

Sold. My wallet is in my hand and I'm fingering the bundled bills, lifting out a well-worn hundred that looked like it could have been on top of every bar in the world, maybe even mine, way back when. I step up and toss it into the hat, turning away quickly before he notices. If I see his reaction it would ruin everything.

Suddenly I feel full of life and recall how, as a bartender, I used to get the occasional hundred-dollar handshake. Not the ones at holidays or from the regular customers, but the special ones: the random gifts that served as statements as much as gestures of generosity. And how I used to tell myself someday *I* would be that guy, the one on the other side of the bar.

And then, this: What type of statement were they making?

Something a lot like my life flashes before my eyes.

All at once the good vibe is complicated by a single, important question: was it possible that those sanguine stuffed-shirts—with their monkey suits and gold money clips—had also needed a reason, and were merely dropping that bloodless money on the bar, in the hopes of displacing their own nagging feelings of doubt and distraction?

* * *

You can't go home again. But return flights operate on more literal levels.

Up and away in a matter of moments, back to where we came from. Soon we'll be flying over the city, reliving the day in reverse, a dissipating view of winter wonderland: festive lights on top of familiar lights, hope over fear, fantasy over factory, the genius of children over the idiocy of adults, the decorated landscape disguising the frantic mothers and fathers—all out to put in their time for the uncommon cause.

Takeoff. I look out my window: the hurried horizon, no longer keeping up, then retreating in mist beneath the tops of the trees.

I look down, far below, where miniature people inside miniature cars sit in miniature rows, stoically and slowly moving forward in the directions of their miniature houses and the miniature respites that may or may not await them. The sky continues to sag, ensnaring everything around it in an ancient embrace. The people, and then the cars, and then the earth all slip away, leaving only lights that shine like our money tells them to. I look down at the waning waves of lights, and these lights do not look like a thousand sets of eyes, they do not make the darkness more discernible, they do not appear as poetry. They are exactly what they are: they are progress, they are pain, they are power. They are the calm crucible of machines that control the lives of the men who made them.

Transaction completed, the flight attendant hands me my drink. What can I get for you, she had asked. Scotch on the rocks, I had said—either out of habit or because I really wanted one and was more than a little convinced I *needed* one. I tilt the miniature bottle and the ice underneath sighs in agony or ecstasy, or both, and begins to do its job. The art of the in-flight cocktail, which I endorsed back in the days when I used to drink: take it slow and savor it. Stop and breathe, get in close and take a good look. Get your nose in there and smell it. Slow and sweet.

(*The sky is dark, like my thoughts*…

No.)

Shake it softly, let the ice insinuate its way around the alcohol. Eventually you can tease it a little with your tongue; it is as much about the experience as it is the gratification. You won't need to remind yourself to take it slow: only amateurs or the immature want to rush things.

(*The clouds hang heavy, like my heart*…

No.)

It is always a minor (or, if it has been too long, a major) revelation how amazing it can be. As long as you respect it, can control your passion and indulgence, it always tastes like the first time. Inevitably, it will all be over before it even started.

(*The air outside is thin, like my patience...*

No.)

This is not necessarily something to regret so much as resignedly acknowledge: these are the unalterable rules of engagement. The moisture builds, and it will work toward easing that slight burn in the back of your throat. When you finally put it to your lips, it offers total return on investment.

(*The cabin is cold, like my memories...*

No.)

It is a practice one has to understand in order to properly appreciate. It becomes a matter of commitment. Let the ice mellow that alcohol for a long time, as long as you can stand it. Maybe you close your eyes and think it over a while longer. If you allow the feelings to flow, it might take longer than you expect. You might even forget who you are or what you wanted.

(*This trip's almost finished, like my faith.*

Okay.)

"Can I get that for you?"

The flight attendant, otherwise occupied or indifferent, doesn't seem to notice when I dump my unsipped, perfectly beaded plastic highball into her overstuffed bag.

Reality Check (5)

A recurring vision:
    Maybe bad luck; maybe a blessing.
    Now what?
    To yourself you say this.
    Of course, you could see it coming. You feared it, you obsessed about it and, when you allowed yourself to be honest, you looked forward to it. You knew it was coming, and the day it finally went down you put your belongings in the clichéd cardboard box and practically floated out to your car. Kind of like a dream. Is this your reality? What is reality.
    What did the future hold?
    Who knew. (You knew, now, what it didn't *hold.)*
    Maybe poverty, maybe luck. Maybe a new house, maybe a life in the streets. Maybe there would be love; maybe a miracle. Or maybe you would live happily ever after.

So…what happened?
    The decision had made itself, actually.
    Laid off. *You found yourself able to welcome it, eventually, when you (finally) understood that you were just human agency interfering with the inevitable. Once that first card falls—or is deceitfully drawn—from the royal house of polished paper, it's easier to make those not-so-difficult decisions.*
    Or, you had awoken each morning for entirely too long in a cramped aquarium, always moving even when you weren't thinking, afraid even when you were unaware of yourself. One day you looked through the glass with your fishy eyes, and saw yourself, somehow. Standing alone. Free.
    Or, after waking up at the end of each day for too many years, one time you made the sensible mistake of staying asleep and having a dream. In this dream you were the only insane person in a building full of functioning (or, sane) people. And you got it: this is so much

easier to accept than forcing oneself to swim backward against the tides, struggling to force truth to flout reality.

Or. Everyone gets laid off. If you work at a place that is very obviously existing on borrowed time—not to mention venture capital—you are not unwise to get out while the getting is pretty good: severance, vacation time rolled up, a little COBRA action. Better than begging or backstabbing, only to buy a few more months, only to show up that last day to locked doors and no paychecks, no recourse. Or else: you finally forgot about your wallet and considered the status of your soul, and you ran away without looking back, laughing all the way to whatever the future was holding hostage.

Or perhaps it was your inability to blame anyone—including yourself—for the fact that you had never become a teacher, a veterinarian, an actor, an astronaut, a poet, or even a police officer.

Whatever it was, it was time to face reality. Whatever that was.

This could be your story, if only you could bring yourself to stick to it.

Six

THE END OF THE WORLD
AS WE KNOW IT

APREDICTION:
The world as we know it will come to an end,
eventually, inevitably—whether we like it or not—
and nothing will change—whether we like it or not. Things will
change, of course, things are always changing, but not the types of
things that certain folks are forecasting, the same folks who happen to be buying or selling the causes or effects of our sickness and
redemption. It's nothing we haven't lived through already.

1984, for instance, was supposed to be a bitch. Remember?
And while I was old enough—then—to see that there was some
real f'ed up s. going down, the bad guys didn't make us all goose-
stepping slaves (because, through a lucky break we never banked
on, it turned out that *we* were the bad guys. Good for us).

So, no Big Brother smack-downs, no subterranean shelters, no
star wars. The only winter we saw featured the sort of snow sent
by God, not mad men acting in His name. What didn't kill us
made us stranger, *et cetera*. So: when conflict did not come, people

had no choice but to get back on the script, doing to one another what they'd prefer to have done to someone else. Even the millennium came and went, remember? Then those planes flew into our buildings—two years too late for the opportunistic end-of-time Internet prophets—and yet we find ourselves borne ceaselessly into the future, whether we like it or not.

* * *

It's ugly, as though a virus has infiltrated the building, spreading from the top down: suddenly, the fear of God is palpable in just about every face. Loyalty, dedication, conviction, all given way to consternation and the abject state of anticipation.

Working where—and with whom—I do has finally made me privy to the type of information that, at times like this, everyone desperately craves. I see the papers, the documents that pass from the desk of our COO, signed off by the cool-blooded Boyd Bender himself, handed down to the calculating claws of the HR Director, who then disseminates them accordingly. It's a decidedly mixed blessing: I can be reasonably certain of my own secure status (although experience had served to ingrain the understanding that *no one* could afford to be entirely aloof to the greedy lull of layoffs); I also am saddled with this mostly undesired knowledge. I know, like an eavesdropping angel, which individuals are about to be jettisoned for the greater good—casualties of the impersonal adjudications of the executives, who proceeded in all things with one hand on the stock-market spreadsheet and the other hand vigilantly covering their brass balls.

Strictly business: the compulsory attrition of a floundering corporation.

Against my better judgment, I agree to accompany a large group meeting for drinks across the street. Not surprisingly, there are—as I should have anticipated—a handful of faces in the crowd whose heads, if asked, I could confirm were on the chopping block.

Nothing personal: I do my best to get drunk on tonic &

tonics, safeguarding myself from any direct, or meaningful conversation about *the situation*. Everyone is on their best behavior, solidarity in the trenches or awareness that some of us may need good references.

Check Jean out: plastered, acting friendly for once and proving that alcohol is okay, even necessary for people allergic to anything approximating intimacy. Like Jean. I've gotten rather used to seeing people act the way they truly feel and blame it on booze. Personally, I was always honest even when I was plastered, only more so.

Enough. Time to make a break. If only I could find my keys. Go figure, this never happened when I drank. Maybe I'm too sober to drive?

After sabotaging the plan for an easy exit by asking everyone if they've seen my keys, I realize I must have left them in the office.

I take the atypically empty elevator up to the top floor, wondering if this is one of the last times I'll have the pleasure.

When I walk around the corner, I'm surprised to see Chazz seated at my desk, holding a piece of paper under the light.

"Burning the midnight oil?"

He didn't hear me coming, and spins around quickly, face flushed, the cat in the act of being caught by the mouse.

"Hey Byron, my man… hey bro, I wasn't trying to snoop around your desk man, I actually just wrote a little note… look, here you go…"

He hands me the message he'd meant for me to see when I returned to work. In big block letters he had scrawled the following words: IT'S THE SAME THING HERE AS EVERYWHERE ELSE: *MAKE ME WANNA HOLLER!*

"You know something, Chazz?"

"What's that, my brother?"

"You're a pretty sharp dude."

"Oh I'm sharp all right, like a switchblade!"

"That's what I'm saying."

"Just make sure you tell *them* that."

"Them?"

"You know, *they*."

"Who's *they*?"

"*They*, you know, the ones who don't like it when people like *me* tell them what they need to hear. I tell it like it is, and nobody digs anyone doin' that, especially *black* people, know what I mean?"

"I hear you."

"Yeah, I guess I know a few things," he says, after a while. "But I ain't like *you*, dig?"

"How do you figure?"

"Well, it's like this: I know what I know, right? But I don't got them *book* smarts like you do, know what I'm sayin'?"

"Trust me, my friend, it ain't all it's cracked up to be."

I hope Chazz knows I'm telling the truth. Or appreciates that if I was bullshitting him it would be easier for both of us.

"No, see, they *do*," he says, shaking his head. "They mean *everything*…"

Before I can interject, he holds up his hand.

"You're different, you ain't like most of the fools in here, dig? But what you just said… no one else around here would ever say no shit like that. No one else would even *think* it."

I have nowhere to turn at this point but the trusted crutch called cliché, and I lean on it heavily, shamefully. All of a sudden I hear myself saying things like keep the faith and hang tough and it's all going to work out. Things a lot like what I was paid to write: solid, comfortable, predictable and ultimately worthless.

"Yo, Brother B-ball," Chazz calls out as I walked toward the elevator.

"*Every Day I have the Blues!*"

I know this one, I think: "B.B. King?"

"Nope, Pinetop Sparks."

Damn.

I put a floating holiday to good use by switching off between the bed and the couch. I hate to waste a sick day actually being sick. The thought of what's going on at work makes me ill enough: A pack of grim-faced lackeys from the HR department walking around, delivering pink slips to each lucky individual, one at a time.

I try hard, but can't conceive of a more awful or inappropriate way of handling such unsavory business. Why not instead bring them into a large room, or have their supervisors tell them privately, or even call them on the fucking phone? *Anything* other than sending a group of officious minions to butcher such a delicate affair, like so many little grim reapers.

What do they say after they tap you on the shoulder? "Time's up?" Something better? Something worse?

Maybe I'll have a chance to find out.

Be hypocritical, be cautious; be not what you seem but always what you see.

What he said.

If you had lived in the 50s, you would have taken a real job right out of college, or you may not have gone to college. You would have had to start earning a living to support your family: married at twenty-two, a father within the year. That's just the way it would have been.

Maybe you'd like your job; maybe you'd be content. Maybe you'd consume so many steaks and cigarettes and whiskey sours that nothing could touch you. You would be obese, an impenetrable fortress of flesh, and no pain could get past you.

Or maybe you'd work and eat and smoke yourself into a muddled mess and punch the clock prematurely—another casualty of the Cold War. Maybe you'd be smart enough to have left your family something, and maybe your wife would remarry and live off the fat of your labor and you wouldn't begrudge her because you were in a better place, drinking Bloody Marys on the great golf course in the sky.

Or maybe your wife, being of her time and unwilling to start over, would instead focus her energies on the grandchildren and church functions and the increasingly mundane exigencies of old age. Maybe she'd wish to meet another man but understand her prospects were poor—after all, she was once married to a big slob whom she somehow stayed devoted to and still mourned. Plus, there were always the kids to contend with. Used goods are used goods, whether you're talking cars, real estate or relationships.

Maybe she'd solider on, alone, oblivious to the insanity of the 60s and 70s, indifferent to the surreal psychoses of the 80s and 90s, and grow into her shrinking body the way a spider's web settles into a windowsill.

Maybe she would eventually understand that the family home— the house in which she lost her virginity, raised her children, cleaned a thousand rooms, cooked a million meals—had outlasted her, and embrace the inevitable.

Maybe, in the end, she would be a lot like the woman across the hall. She's had a good life (please allow her to have been happy: in your mind if not in actual fact). She, at least, once had a husband, and maybe a son and daughter whom she dotes on and who love her dearly, but they live so far away and are so busy with work and kids and life and time just slips away and so it goes…

Or maybe it's even worse than that: maybe she was never married, never found exactly what she was looking for, or the right ones over-looked her until it was too late. Maybe she was cursed with the burden of being always apart, in all the important ways, from the utterly average, anonymous faces she came into contact with day in and day out, and like almost no one else she knew, she was unaware of it.

Maybe that woman across the hall is a lot like you are. The way you will be.

You want to walk out your door, but you can't.

And this time, for once, it's not because you don't want to, it's because you're desperately certain that she won't be outside waiting for you.

Seven

SEND IN THE CLOWNS

PHONE RINGING.

I actually think about answering it, and then figure I may as well stay in character.

Someone's knocking at the door.

My dog does what he does best: running in circles, howling and hollering, and mostly acting as though he's never seen another person before.

"Whitey, what are you doing here?"

"Were you expecting Santa Claus?"

"Was that you that just called?"

"I've been calling you all day."

"Funny, I've been ignoring calls all day."

"Anyway, I've come bearing gifts."

"SpaghettiOs?"

"Obviously."

All smiles, he unloads his bag of goodies on the counter. Something about him is different.

"How are you doing?" I do ask.

"I'm good," he says. He sounds like he means it. "How are *you* doing?"

"I'm alive."

"Well, that's a start. I called you last night too, are you sick or something?"

"What's it look like?"

"So what's the latest word on the layoff of the century?"

"It's all going down as we speak. A lot of lucky people are getting an early Christmas present."

"Damn. Well, those chickens had to come home to roost sooner or later."

"I guess that's about right."

"Anyway, if you end up getting axed I can probably hook you up."

"I'm not a salesman, Whitey."

"Neither am I. Well, I don't even call what I do sales anymore. Not when people are paying to give you money."

"Sounds too good to be true."

"Nope, it's the new reality. I'm onboard the mortgages gravy train."

"Mortgages?"

"Dude, they're *printing* money. Do you know how many people are refinancing right now?"

"A lot?"

"Let's put it this way: the market is so unreal right now, anyone who gets in on this will be able to *retire* by the end of the decade."

"Sounds too good to be true."

"You'll see."

I'll drink to that.

(To myself I say this.)

***

A new day; same story. Back to work, back to the future.

As I navigate the familiar route, I almost drive off the road when I see a building I've never noticed before, waving to me from the side of the road. It wants me to notice, as if I'm not going to notice. Office buildings, especially ten-story monstrosities, do not just pop up overnight, do they? Even these days, where anything is possible, this can't be happening. But there it is: people, who had presumably been up and at 'em since before the sun came up, streaming in from the five story parking garage, putting in their time before they'll enjoy a well-earned rest: dinner, maybe a *digestif* and several hours of somnambulant sit-coms before the nightly newscasters lulled them to sleep.

Sleep. Somehow while I'd been asleep, the splendid imprimatur of industry had struck again. Overnight, a miracle of the modern age had occurred: clandestine plans had been approved, blueprints implemented, construction commenced. Trees had been felled, brick and mortar meticulously amassed, offers had been made, salaries negotiated, moving vans hired, new houses occupied, paychecks deposited, kids sent to imprudently priced daycare, new dentists and family doctors consulted, second children conceived, extramarital affairs instigated, divorce papers served, summer softball leagues formed, cutbacks announced, departments laid off, stock options doled out and quickly cashed, inestimable hours and dollars spent on alcohol, cigarettes, dangerous as well as non-addictive drugs, pornography—always the pornography—and unused health club memberships.

Industry and big money are all about initiative; they don't sleep until the job is done. And the job, of course, is never done.

***

As I walk out of the elevator, I am not entirely surprised to see empty desks and silence embellishing the already austere façade of F5. I *am* surprised, as I turn the corner, to see *The Don*, standing imperially—as always—and then speaking the words I never thought I'd hear:

"Step into my office."

Oh well. Fear fights with surprise and gives way to relief. Suspense is overrated anyway. Let's get this over with.

"The bad news: Your job no longer exists."

There is an uneasy moment while each of us allows this information to register.

"The good news: You've been promoted, reporting directly to me, effective immediately."

What happened?

Apparently, in addition to all the other wonders routinely performed on this floor, they now can control eternity: an employee died and was brought back from the dead without even knowing it.

I guess that makes me a zombie. Or a vampire. Or something.

Then *The Don* speaks in a strange language for several minutes, saying words such as *merger, acquisition, accelerated options, new branding strategy, re-org, emerging markets,* and then, ultimately, the spell is broken by a word even undead employees can acknowledge: *money.*

***

When I walk back to my soon-to-be-former cubicle, more oddity awaits me. I'm not certain what's more perplexing: the fact that both Otis and Jean are still around, or the fact that they're standing next to each other, smiling.

"What's up, guys?"

"Just happy to still be standing," Otis says.

"I know what you mean."

"I was telling him about Friday," Jean says.

"The layoffs?" I ask.

"No, the *arrest!*"

"What arrest?"

"Oh, that's right! You weren't here on Friday either..."

"Well, what happened?"

"I'll give him this much, at least he went out with a bang and not a whimper."

"Who?"

"Chazz!"

"I had a feeling he was getting laid off," I say.

"No, he didn't get laid off, he got *fired*."

"What are you talking about?"

"He practically started a riot in the cafeteria."

Excited, I quickly imagine the altercation: Chazz, standing before a handful of executives who'd had the gall to show their faces amongst the employees that day, sounding out on behalf of all the abruptly discharged workers. Finally, a cause for him to rally around.

"Did anyone see what went down?"

"Well, I didn't see it, but I heard all about it…"

"So what's the story?"

"He just… *exploded*. He had this complete tirade…"

In spite of myself, I can't believe my intuition had been correct.

"What did he do?"

"He went ballistic, he practically assaulted the cashier in the lunch room. A whole group of people had to pull him away…"

"The cashier? I don't understand…"

"He just snapped, he said she overcharged him for his sandwich or something. He started screaming and cursing at her…"

"Overcharged him for his *sandwich?*" This is all I can think to say as I try, unsuccessfully, to envision Chazz making a scene over something so senseless.

"Well, apparently he's had all kinds of problems over the years."

"Problems? Like what?"

"Supposedly he'd spent time in and out of rehab at some point, when the security officers escorted him out he kept yelling that he was a veteran…"

"Yeah, I know," I say softly, a disquieting image unwrapping in my mind. "He told me he would get migraines, some sort of Post-Traumatic Stress Disorder, from combat I guess."

"Well, I talked to someone in HR, and she said he was never *in* Vietnam. They pulled his records. He's been in jail, and the nuthouse, but he definitely was never in any war."

"Nuthouse?"

"Yeah, you didn't know that?"

"No."

"Well, I guess he fooled you. He fooled everyone."

A moment of discordant silence while they both stand there, still smiling. Solidarity and survival go hand in hand, they seem to have finally figured out.

I need to get away from them. Immediately.

But I know Otis expects me to say something.

I don't say anything.

There's nothing to say.

What *could* be said?

Send in the motherfucking clowns.

***

I head for the relative serenity of the men's room. I can't discern which is stronger: my disappointment at the prospect Chazz had conned me, or my culpability at putting so much stock in his stories. Or maybe it was something else altogether.

Okay, I think.

If what they're saying is true, then almost everything Chazz told me was a lie.

Okay.

Then, this: practically everything I told *him* was a lie.

And so. What did it change?

It changed everything.

It changed nothing.

When I return to my desk I look down and notice the piece of paper staring up at me, like a confession. Or an indictment:

MY BROTHER: I DON'T KNOW ABOUT YOU, BUT I'VE DECIDED THAT AFTER TODAY I AIN'T FATTENING NO MORE FROGS FOR SNAKES!

It was, of course, signed by Chazz. Apparently, after our conversation, he'd felt obliged to leave me another message. I can suddenly see him, sitting alone after I'd left, possibly—and understandably—looking through the mess of my paperwork, searching for a clue as to whether or not one of those pink slips had his name on it. Alone in our big building, which was as preposterous a place for him as any of the other institutions in which he'd purportedly been detained. After a while I pick up the paper and turn it over. In the same large scrawl he had written: BY: SONNY BOY WILLIAMSON.

Ain't Fattening No More Frogs For Snakes.

Yeah, what he said. What *they* said.

I close my eyes and see myself repeating it, loud and proud, watching the expressions on their faces as I stroll out of this office, my head up, content with the certainty of my convictions. Leaving this charade—leaving *them*, all of them—behind.

The way I'd like to believe Chazz had done.

For what shall it profit a man, if he shall gain the whole world, and lose his own soul?

You didn't say that.

But, as you walk through the office, trying not to make eye contact with anyone, you're thinking it. And then something strange happens: you look up, preparing to force yourself to smile, and notice no one is there.

The office is dead. There's nothing there: no desks, no chairs, no people, nothing. All the computers: gone.

It's inexplicable; it's a miracle.

An entirely new type of American Dream?

For the first time in as long as you care to remember, you'd readied yourself to make a decision on your own, one you wanted to make, one you were unwilling to make. And here you are, not quite able to believe the decision had already been made for you.

(Some of it happened, some of it was going *to happen. Reality? What was that, and what did it matter? This was your reality now, and your reality was not* their *reality. You understood that, now. Reality? What was that.)*

The office was dead. And as you look around, you can't remember ever feeling more alive.

This is your story. All you have to do is write it.

Epilogue:
MAYBE A MIRACLE

R UNNING OUT OF gas.

My car needs fuel too. As I pull into the station, sure enough my man is out there, like the sun setting in the west. Out there, always, in the heat and the rain and mostly in the ceaseless, crushing boredom. Out there every day, very likely taking away a lot less than some street-corner wino stuck in any second-rate American city.

While I pump manifest destiny into my machine I can feel him behind me, screaming his same silent song. And then, finally: enough is enough. I turn around, but he's not looking at me. He's sitting on his milk crate, studying the traffic, reluctant to make eye contact even with the cars. He says nothing, sees nothing, but surely he hears everything. How can he not, when it's all there, right in front of his defeated face? And it occurs to me, I've never once seen a single person give him money or even acknowledge his existence.

What can you do?

"Hey man, I'll take one of those flowers; I'll take all of them…"

The stranger looks at me suspiciously and shakes his head. He hasn't understood a word I've spoken.

"Listen, I'll buy all of them…"

I pull out my wallet and start speaking the language everyone understands.

I keep giving and he keeps taking. I don't count and he doesn't complain.

Finally, I've done all I can do, and he smiles. He says a lot of things, silently, with those grateful eyes. I need to leave before he tells me any other things I probably should hear.

I almost make it to my car. Suddenly, before I can stop myself, I turn around to tell him a thing or two with my own eyes.

But, somehow, he's no longer there.

He's gone: the man, the milk crate, even the flowers I was just holding in my hands.

A mirage? Maybe a miracle.

Now it's only me and an endless stream of traffic, blowing by in both directions.

"Have a nice day," I call out, to whoever might be listening.

Not to mention a nice life.

To myself, I say this.

Acknowledgments

TO BECOME A writer, one needs time, patience, practice, a vision, and resolve that's equal parts unreasonable and unyielding. But first and above all, a support system is essential. If bad families have inspired some extraordinary material, a good family enables a writer to focus on the fiction, not needing to settle scores or engage in psychoanalysis disguised as literature.

As such, I am greatly indebted for the love, encouragement and consideration my family has provided. To my father, Jack Murphy, I once again offer thanks for ensuring I had every opportunity, and no excuses. I remain grateful that you instilled in me a work ethic, an appreciation for honest effort (and honesty, period), an understanding that integrity supersedes material gains and superficial gratification, and above all, an appetite for experience that can never be satiated. "When will I stop being curious?" I asked you once when I was a kid. "Never," you said. It remains the most useful and inspiring reassurance I've ever received.

Aside from my parents, my first—and biggest—fan is my sister. Janine, thank you for always wanting to read what I write, and for being proud and protective as only a big sister can. Thank you, too, for demonstrating that wonderful moms run in our family.

Scott, thank you for being a big brother, an unwavering husband to Janine, and extraordinary role model for my niece and nephew, Madeleine and Anthony, who have become two of my favorite people. Special gratitude to Andrea: thank you for being a perfect partner in crime for my father, and adding comfort, love and class to the Murphy clan. Humble appreciation to my grandfather, Martin Mastandrea: I certainly inherited your hairline but I hope every day that I can emulate a fraction of your tenacity and endurance. To both sides of my extended family: all my love and appreciation for being, in no particular order, companions, role models, and fellow travelers, bound by blood.

It's been my pleasure and great fortune to work with the amazing Jane Friedman. I consider Jane every writer's best friend for her indefatigable promotion of literature, and I'm only one of countless authors who have benefited from her generosity and wisdom. Being able to work closely with you on this project is a genuine blessing and I'm elated to consider you a friend as well as a colleague.

To Caitlin and Rick at Caitlin Hamilton Marketing & Publicity, my deepest gratitude for having faith in this project and providing an invaluable business acumen and savvy I otherwise would be sorely lacking. In addition to being complete professionals in the best sense, I thank you for your optimism, assistance and for being very affirmative and exceptional human beings.

I offer ceaseless praise and admiration for Beth J. Bates and Mandi Perry at Web Strategies. The idea of building a "brand" (however modest) is something a writer dreams about but usually has no idea how to execute. How fortunate I am to have such rock stars looking out for me. It's a pleasure to work with you, and while I have nothing but high praise for your expertise, I'm even happier to have you as pals.

My oldest friend Mark Seferian always gets the first and most enthusiastic shout-out: I've correctly called you my ideal reader, but you are of course much more than that. My love for you has no bounds, and I continue to be humbled that you see in me things

I don't understand or imagine; we bring out the best in each other and my life would be profoundly inadequate without you. Did I mention your remarkable and adorable wife Laurel? Or your little angel, Elliotte? I can't wait for many more exploits with all of you!

Unbreakable affection and gratitude to Beth Wolfe, my little sister, unofficial business manager and benevolent yenta. Thank you for your unflagging allegiance and dedication; this journey would be different without you and not for the better.

My band of brethren is both larger and more loyal than anyone has the right to conceive. Let me acknowledge a special quartet with whom I share all good fortune just as they have borne me up and guaranteed I'm never alone in times of need. The electronic ink, cocktails and conversations I've exchanged with Mike Shields, Rob Simms, Jamey Barlow and Matt Canada might have produced one hundred novels, but none of them would have come close to approximating the real-life adventure, comedy, camaraderie, consolation, joy and sustenance that this special friendship continues to provide. Counting you amigos amongst my inner circle is the gift that keeps giving.

Next, the trio of old school scalawags: Matt Gravett, Marc Cascio and Jerry Erickson. I couldn't—and wouldn't—want to try and calculate the adventures (and misadventures), the good times, the great times and instances where you've illustrated what genuine friendship means. It remains refreshing, and restorative, to count on a select cadre of companions to keep me honest, amused and fortified as we fumble our way into adulthood.

A special shout-out to my brother A.J. Hernandez: not only have you always been a vocal advocate of my work, you were perhaps most excited about this particular project and why it needed to be realized. Your interest and faith helped entice me to return, once again, to a novel that, I now realize, simply needed time to marinate and a few (hundred) more edits. Let's fire up some celebratory stogies!

Drew Floyd, Tom Hoyler, Scott Hughes and Ben Mayrides:

I've learned—and gained—more from you four than you've ever gotten from me.

Mark Hanlon and Kirk Munson: there is old school and then there is ancient school. And then there's something even older and more inexpressible. You don't get to choose your family but you do have a say in the brothers you go into battle with, and I treasure you both for having my back and keeping me (mostly) out of harm's way.

To my colleagues at The Weeklings, I'm honored to be associated with such a remarkable group of writers and people. Singular adoration and acknowledgment to brothers Sean Beaudoin and Greg Olear: I can sincerely attest that you've made me a better writer and more, you've made me want to be a better writer. That's something I'll always hold a special place in my heart for, and I look forward to many years trying to repay and prove worthy of your advocacy.

Only the luckiest students stumble into the classrooms of teachers whose lessons last a lifetime: Devon Hodges, Steve Goodwin, Don Gallehr, Chuck Cascio and John Taliaferro, I am one of innumerable apprentices to whom you bestowed your skills and wisdom. My work, at its best, is a testament to your selfless instruction, patience and example.

A list of friends who I'm happily obliged to imitate as best I can: Dave Greenspan, Norm Happ, Chris (and Kelly) Holland, Jason (and Karen) Herskowitz, Tony James, Dan Webb, Steve Flavin, Richard Sapio, Jim Boyer, Dave Ferguson, Cindy Boyd, Karen Valanzano, Steve Koenig, Shawn DuBravac, Angela Titone, Christine Franca, Alex Davis, Tom O'Donoghue, Greg, Linda, Bethanie, Jeremy and Melissa from the Neuner clan, Jane Baniewicz (Tanbark Strong!), Father Mark Mealey, John and Jennifer Sample, Vickie Batsedis, Sheri and Cindy Wassenaar (the Wonder Twins), Pamela Humphreys, Kira Mayrides, Laura Hoyler, Melissa Hughes, Deanna Floyd, David Carrier, Kim Drinkwine, Tom and Karen Carter, Lee Slivka, Jamie Casello, Cerphe Colwell, April Eberhardt, Lydia Bird, Scott Carter, Jack and Maureen

McGurk, Ted and Virginia Putnam, Jenna Blum, Julie Kearney, Larry and Christine Ponzi, Amy Casbon, Mason and Kimber Miller, Katherine Rutkowski, Rick Kowalski, Holly Chichester, Jon Phillips and a cast of characters that hopefully knows how much I cherish and value them.

Julene and Randy Slusher: thank you for being two of the most loyal, generous, hilarious and *real* people I've ever met.

John and Lisa Santoro: as if bringing Riley and Logan into our world wasn't enough to earn my eternal gratitude, my entire being glows with light and joy every time I see or even think of you. And that goes for Bob and Myra, Sue-Sue, and Kelly and Terry.

To all the executives and fellow foot soldiers at the various companies I've worked, thanks for the memories, material, solidarity and, at times, sanity you've provided.

For my friends who do with musical instruments what I try to do with pen and paper, I'm hopeful we'll spend the rest of our lives solidifying the bonds of improvisation and our mutual admiration society. In particular, Jon Madof, Aram Bajakian, Jamie Saft, Yoshie Fruchter and Mathias Kunzli, our world (mine in particular) would be a hell of a lot less satisfying and soulful without your extraordinary gifts.

It's my pleasure and honor to have spent two indescribable weeks at the Noepe Center for Literary Arts. To Justen Ahren and Jack Sonni, I hoped to meet brothers in arms and discovered kindred spirits; I hope I provide you with a portion of the passion and purposeful fervor you instill in me.

Finally, when a writer is at a loss for words, something special is happening. Heather Sherard, I knew what I was looking for all my life; thank you for giving me more than I ever dreamed of. You've shown me a type of love, support, care, commitment, and kindness that transcends any attempt to articulate or adequately acknowledge. I'm the lucky one and you are The One.

As ever, it ends the way it began, with my mother Linda Murphy. Every good thing I do is because of you—and attributable to your influence. I'll never stop trying and I'll always have faith because your love provides an inextinguishable light. If I'm able in small part to prove myself worthy of the sacrifices you made and guidance you provided, I'll consider this life a dutiful homage to your beloved memory.

SEAN MURPHY HAS been publishing fiction, reviews (music, movie, book, food), and essays on the technology industry for more than twenty years. He has appeared on NPR's "All Things Considered" and been quoted in *USA Today*, *The New York Times*, *Forbes* and *AdAge*. In addition, he is an associate editor at *The Weeklings*, where he contributes a monthly column. He writes regularly for *PopMatters*, and his work has also appeared in *The Village Voice*, *The Good Men Project*, *All About Jazz*, *AlterNet*, *Web Del Sol*, *Empty Mirror*, *Elephant Journal* and *Northern Virginia Magazine*. He is the recipient of a Noepe Center for Literary Arts Writer Residency. His best-selling memoir *Please Talk about Me When I'm Gone* was released in 2013. Visit him online at seanmurphy.net.

Made in the USA
Middletown, DE
08 June 2015